The President's Wife

A Novel

Hannah Stevens

Verde Press
Phoenix, Arizona

Best Wishes,
Hannah Stevens

Printed in the United States of America

First Edition

The text of this book is composed in Caslon Old Face BT

Book Design by Bold Impressions

ISBN 0-9759303-0-3

Verde Press, Phoenix, Arizona

For Alan

Honesty is the first chapter in the book of wisdom.

– Thomas Jefferson

The President's Wife

Air Force One

President James K. Walters paused for a moment in the doorway of Air Force One, waving to the press with one hand while holding his black cocker spaniel, Harry, under his other arm. He slowly descended the stairs of the airplane, waving and smiling, taking every opportunity for this photo op. Every time I walk down this ramp, he thought, I get more votes. He had just returned from his August working vacation at his ranch just outside Fort Collins, Colorado.

He saluted the Special Forces guards standing near the aircraft and walked across the tarmac to the waiting helicopter that would take him to the landing pad at the White House.

His press secretary, Stanley Thompson, greeted him, "Welcome back, Mr. President. I trust your vacation was restful. We have a lot of work to do in the coming weeks, and we will have to stay on top of everything. We have a meeting planned with the secretary of defense and the vice president this afternoon to go over the war plans."

The president acknowledged this information with a nod and climbed into the waiting helicopter. He walked to the back of the aircraft to a special area where he seated himself in the large, oversized, tan leather chair provided for the leader of the most powerful nation in the world. He lowered Harry to the floor beside him. The ride to the White House would only take a few minutes, but James hated this part of the trip.

He had been afraid of helicopters ever since Marine One almost crashed over twelve years ago when he and his father, then President James Walters, Sr., were landing at Edwards Air Force Base in a thunderstorm. The helicopter tilted to one side and nearly broke off one of the rotors, and it scared the hell out of him. And he hated the way they took off. Instead of nose up, the nose stayed low as the rear of the machine led to pick up the elevation. It seemed unnatural to him.

No one spoke during the fifteen-minute flight. Upon landing, the circus began again. Reporters lined the path from the helipad on the south lawn of the White House. As soon as the rotors were still, James emerged from the aircraft, again with Harry under his arm. Only this time, as soon as he walked down the steps, he released the little dog and Harry scurried up the path ahead of him with the reporters snapping photos. It is important for the president to have a dog, James thought. It's good public relations. Millions of people own dogs in this country and they are all potential voters.

James saluted again and waved and smiled as more people gathered around the president. He continued walking up the path to the White House.

James had been in office for three and a half years, winning the election by a narrow vote. His roots were from a prominent ranching and land-baron family in Colorado. James' paternal uncle, Robert Walters, had been a U.S. senator in the fifties, and James' brother, George, was currently governor of Colorado. His mother, Claudine, from Corsicana, Texas, was from an old moneyed oil family that had started the Texaco Corporation and, with the merger of the Walters and Warner families, perpetuated a powerful dynasty.

James, a graduate of Harvard University with a degree in political science and then Harvard Law School, was destined for a career in politics with the dream of being president of the United States of America one day. And with hard work he had achieved his goal, but was it worth it? His normally dark-brown hair had turned almost all white in the first two years, and his amiable smiles turned to frowns, drawing deep lines of wisdom on his forehead above his dark, bushy eyebrows. But he was fit. At six feet plus, he was trim with very little body fat. He made sure that he worked out for at least one hour every day. His routine consisted of thirty minutes of weight training with his personal trainer, a brisk 45-minute jog, and he sometimes finished this off with a twenty-minute swim in the White House swimming pool. Another daily ritual was the afternoon nap. Although he worked hard from eight in the morning to five at night, he always took a break for a nap around two in the afternoon.

"Refreshes the soul," he would tell his staff members. It did prepare him for the evenings of dinners, parties and fund-raisers he attended almost nightly. In this election year, James had been working extremely hard to raise enough money for the upcoming election and to counteract the assault of the Democratic party. James was the first president to be elected on the Patriots ticket. The Patriots formed from the Republican party after James' father lost the election to William Roberts in a landslide almost twelve years ago. Their hawkish vision of America was very different from mainstream Republicans, embracing military buildup, a pre-emptive strategy in dealing with enemy countries or those perceived to be, an increase in the Pentagon and government agencies to support the military and a monstrous budget to fund it all. The differences were so great that the moderate Republicans, who supported smaller government and conservative spending, split, leaving this radical wing of the party hanging with seemingly nowhere to go. But they rallied quickly, gathering more of their kind from former right-wing Republican administrations, and created the Patriots party. James had been honored when the Patriots party made him their presidential nominee four plus years ago. And when he won the election, he was ecstatic, even though it was indeed a narrow victory, winning with a slim number of electoral votes. His opponent, Harrison Baker, vice president to Adam Johnson, captured the popular vote by half a million votes. This of course rankled the Democrats, many of whom cried foul saying that James had stolen the election with fraudulent voting practices in two states, Ohio and Michigan.

This meant that James had to work twice as hard now, and his vacation had consisted of a series of fund-raisers across the country from California, speaking at a Patriots dinner in Fresno designed to target Hispanic constituents, to a large affair in Detroit to reach the working-class members of the autoworkers. James was by far the most successful fund-raiser in the history of politics, but his party would need every dollar they could get, as the state of the nation did not look good. Unemployment was at an all-time high of seven percent, and the leading indicators were driving down an already unsteady stock market.

The war in Iraq that he had started one and a half years ago was not going well, with body bags coming home every day now, and the Democrats and many others who had opposed the war were questioning the validity of attacking a small, sovereign nation even though Iraq's President Saddam Hussein was a tyrant. The Patriots had won five seats in the Senate and three in the House of Representatives in the mid-term elections, but the Republicans still maintained the majority in the House and the Senate. His ratings in the polls were plunging from the high of sixty percent after they had started the war to fifty-two percent today—still quite high but the trend was alarming.

James walked up the stairs to the family's private quarters with the Secret Service following close behind, as is standard operating procedure. He opened one of the French doors leading into the private apartment and walked down the hallway to the West Sitting Hall, which served as the family living room in the White House with its large Palladian window overlooking the Rose Garden. Marta, the second floor maid, had just finished dusting the Queen Anne tables as he walked in. Marta was one of some ninety staff members behind the scenes, working many times six days a week to help make the White House home for the First Family and host to a million and a half visitors and dignitaries each year. Before James and Carol, the First Lady, had come to the White House, many of the maids and staff would become invisible as they entered a room, much like they did in the early 1900s. But Carol treated them more like family and as equals than merely servants, much to James' chagrin.

"Hello, Marta. Everything shipshape, I hope."

"Mr. President. It is so good to see you. We have everything ready for you and the missus. We've been working all morning to make things nice for when you came back. Did you have a nice vacation?"

"Yes, Marta. I worked too hard but it was wonderful being back on the ranch again."

"Where is the missus? She is not with you?"

"No, Marta. She's still back in Colorado. She had some business to take care of, but she'll be joining us in a week or two."

"She be away that long, huh? She's kind of your rock, you know what I mean. You will miss her, huh?"

"Yes, I will miss her. Is there food in the refrigerator for lunch?"

"Yes, sir. There's cold sliced ham and cheese and lots of fruit. We bought everything this morning so it should be nice and fresh for you and the missus."

James rolled his eyes, "Thank you, Marta. That's all for now. I won't be needing you for anything the rest of the day."

"Yes, sir," and Marta quickly left the room.

Back at the Ranch

Carol Walters sat at her desk in her office on the east side of the house going over her appointment book to see what she would have to cancel for the next couple of weeks. The morning sun filtered through the Victorian lace curtains, creating ephemeral patterns on the desktop as she flipped through the pages of the days in her life. A luncheon with the wives of the cabinet members on Thursday, lunch with the vice president's wife on Friday and the following week two luncheons, one with the League of Women Voters and another with the volunteers for the Red Cross. There was nothing that she couldn't cancel or postpone.

She had just finished emailing her son, Andrew, and her mother to let them know she had not gone back to Washington with James. She'd thought about calling each of them but didn't want to alarm them, and emailing avoided questions. This was business as usual. She was staying behind to clear up some problems on the ranch with a disagreement between the ranch manager and one of the wranglers. When James suggested that she take care of this, she was happy to oblige.

James and Carol had spent most of their married life working and living at Mountain Sky Ranch. The land, two hundred acres, had been a wedding gift from James' father, and soon after Andrew had been born, they built the first small ranch house, bought a hundred head of Black Angus cattle and started working the ranch after James had lost his bid for a second term in the state senate. James hired a couple of wranglers but did most of the work himself in those early days while Carol managed the books. It was a hard life in the beginning with many disappointments, losing cattle to disease and a couple of winters where severe weather nearly starved half the herd. Carol remembered the winter of '85 when they had to haul hay out on the range in a raging blizzard, with snow hitting them sideways, just to keep the herd alive. But eventually the herd grew to three hundred head and they started making a profit. They built the new big ranch house where Carol and James now lived when they weren't at the White House and hired Tom Flanders to be ranch manager. The small house they had lived in during the early days was now being rented by their housekeeper, Nancy Johnson, and her husband Jack, head wrangler and mechanic for the ranch.

Carol thought back to those early days and how life had been much simpler. Even though they had obstacles to overcome, they had been happy working together for the common goals of raising Andrew and making the ranch profitable. James was an attentive father, spending time with Andrew hiking, skiing, mountain biking and occasionally taking a day for trout fishing at one of the nearby mountain streams. He taught Andrew everything he knew about the outdoors—how to start a fire without matches, foraging for food, how to build a shelter if you were stranded in a storm without your tent. He also taught him about taking care of the environment and our planet earth. "You carry it in, you carry it out," James used to tell Andrew on backpacking trips. And they would even pick up debris and trash that other people had left behind.

Yes, those were the good days and then James was asked to run for president. Carol had been one hundred percent behind James because she knew he would make a wonderful president. She believed in him. And at first it was exciting, always surrounded by adoring crowds, attending dinners and fund-raisers and the media attention. She would watch the evening news and see herself with the president-elect and she thought then that, yes, this was a good thing. They could make a difference in the United States, and they could make a difference in the world. Carol had always wanted to champion the cause of quality education for everyone in the U.S., regardless of economic circumstances. She was of the mind that education was the key to having a working democracy. Knowledge is power.

Carol recalled the day James was sworn into office—January 20, 2001. The day was bright and clear but bitter cold after a nor'easter had dumped a foot of snow on Washington the day before. Bushes and trees bent over with the weight of sparkly white powder like too much frosting on a cake. Fortunately Carol had selected a warm royal-blue cashmere coatdress with a stylish cloche hat to match for the occasion. They stood on the large stage constructed for that special day, surrounded by past presidents, past vice presidents and dignitaries, Speakers of the House and Senate, and of course family members—Carol's and James' parents and Andrew who was beaming from ear to ear. Looking out over the throngs of people crowded into the west front of the U.S. Capitol, James stepped forward, looking very dapper in his navy blue pinstriped suit with a black wool overcoat. He put his hand on the Bible held by Chief Justice Ronald Warrington and repeated the words of the oath of office for the president of the United States of America.

"I do solemnly swear that I will faithfully execute the office of the president of the United States, and will, to the best of my ability, preserve, protect and defend the Constitution of the United States."

James then turned and shook the hand of the former president, William Jay Roberts, and then the hand of the former vice president and finally turned to Carol. Searching deep into his eyes she could see the yearning enveloping him as a tear trickled down one cheek. He put his arms around her, kissed her lightly on the mouth and then on her cold cheek, and whispered into her ear, "Sweetheart, we have arrived. I have finally fulfilled my deepest desire." Carol held him, knowing in her heart at that moment that she was going to lose her husband to the world. They broke apart and she turned to the cheering crowd, waving and smiling, but her heart was breaking.

That evening as a light snow began to fall again, James and

Carol reluctantly attended the inaugural balls. James despised formal affairs and Carol wasn't that keen about them either. But duty called and James, stiffly wearing an Armani tuxedo, and Carol in her ivory gown embroidered with Austrian crystals by Oscar de la Renta, her first designer gown, feeling very far from the ranch in Colorado, attended fourteen balls, spending not more than fifteen minutes at each in order to get them all in. Being the guests of honor, they were shepherded into each of the galas and escaped the cheek-to-jowl dance floors and hors d'oeuvres that tasted like cardboard. Leaving the last ball in the early hours of the morning, she felt like Cinderella in a monumental way and hoped that the limousine wouldn't turn into a pumpkin, as they had stayed well past the midnight hour.

The very next day they moved into the White House with a flourish. In the beginning, life was grand living among history with the ghosts of past first families, and every day was more exciting than the one before. At night, Carol and James would steal away to their bedroom and read together and talk about the day's happenings, the politics and posturing of the Speaker of the House or some prominent cabinet member. James listened and they discussed, and then James would share his ideas, his feelings, and they would curl up together, two people as one like they had been on the ranch in the early days of their marriage. Carol felt that James needed her. But when the Iraq invasion began two years into their presidency—Carol called it *their* presidency because it was hers as well as James—the distance between them began to grow. Their evening talks became shorter, and when she tried to talk about the war, James would cut her off and say that they were handling it and she shouldn't get involved. In other words, don't worry your pretty little head.

At first Carol was worried that James might have met someone; there were many attractive young women working in the West Wing in advisory positions, as staff members, secretaries or interns. She confronted him one night and asked him if he was having an affair, and he just looked at her like she was out of her mind, so she thought that couldn't be it. And then she started to get on the Internet and read about what this war was all about and again confronted James. He blew up and said he would not discuss it with her again and to stay out of public affairs. It was his job and his alone. The silence continued and the gap widened until Carol began to sleep in the guest bedroom almost every night and James didn't ask why.

Coming back to reality, Carol recalled how James had instructed her to stay at the ranch to resolve the wrangler problem.

"Carol," James bellowed with authority, "you need to find a solution. This guy is causing Tom too many problems and yet he won't fire him. Tom is just too soft. You know how he is, always wanting to give the ranch hands a second chance."

"I know, James, I know. But most of wranglers have been given that chance. They're a different sort of guy. They're not like you. They chase cows all day and at night all they want is a few beers, a thick steak and, well, maybe a lady friend."

"Lady friend? You're too polite. This guy has been running down to Denver, hanging around with prostitutes, drinking and then he gets arrested for getting into a brawl in a bar. What if the press gets a hold of this story? We have an image to keep up," James yelled. "We just can't have this stuff happening on our ranch, the ranch belonging to the president of the United States of America."

"Image? Is that all you think about? What about Jerry? What if he can't find another job? What will happen to him?"

"Carol, you can't worry about that. If he's going to pull these kinds of stunts, then he has to go. And if Tom isn't tough enough to deal with it, maybe Tom has to go."

"But Tom's been with us for 15 years."

"I don't want to talk about this anymore. Just take care of it."

He was the president of the United States and he seldom let her forget that. James stormed out the door to be joined by the ever-present Secret Service men, his shadows day and night.

Carol dialed Anne Hutchins' number in the East Wing of the White House. Anne, her social secretary, was part of a team of fourteen men and women selected and assigned to assist Carol in the many official and unofficial responsibilities that came with being the wife of the president, including making appointments, writing speeches, public relations and assisting Carol with her special projects. Of course they were all paid staff members and Carol was . . . what was she? A volunteer?

Anne answered after several rings. "Office of First Lady, Carol Walters, Anne speaking."

"Anne, this is Carol. How are you? Is everything going okay?"

"Yes, fine. We are all fine. When are you coming back? We are planning the Symposium on Education and we need you here to give us some direction."

"I won't be back for a couple of weeks, Anne. We've had some problems at the ranch and James asked me to stay behind and clear them up."

"This symposium is coming up next month and there are still a lot of loose ends," Anne said.

"I think we had better postpone it for now. There's just too much happening with the election coming up. Let's shoot for early spring of next year."

"That's assuming we're still here."

"That's the chance we have to take, Anne. Also I need you to cancel my appointments for the next couple of weeks. Oh, and I'll call Diane myself."

"Sure. Is there anything else I can do for you, Mrs. Walters?"

"Yes, you can call me Carol. You keep forgetting that. I am just another human being, no better than any other human being in this world," Carol said with humility. "Thank you, Anne, you are a great help to me. I'll be in touch."

As she hung up the phone, she thought about her last statement and how she had had many advantages in her life because she had married into wealth and how most people never have the opportunities that she has had. And now she was wondering how she could use her station in life to help others who were not as advantaged as she.

Carol dialed Diane Martin's number, the vice president's wife, thinking about how, since James had become president, he was impossible to live with.

The phone rang five times until finally someone answered.

"Diane Martin's residence, this is Sheryl speaking."

"Hello, Sheryl, this is Carol Walters calling. Is Diane in today?"

"Oh, Mrs. Walters," Sheryl said in a somewhat surprised tone. "No, she's not here at the moment. Can I give her a message?"

Carol hesitated. Should she just leave a message or say she would call back? She would leave a message. She really disliked Diane and only attended functions with her because it was her obligation to do so. Diane was a social snob who had never known what it was like to work for a living. But this was true of many people in Washington. Most of them were the wealthy elite and had never cleaned a toilet or even been to the grocery store, unlike Carol who came from a middleclass family of modest means.

"Yes. Tell her that I will be unable to have lunch with her on Friday. I've had to stay behind at the ranch to take care of some business here."

I don't have to explain, she thought to herself. She was always too nice.

"I'll tell her, Mrs. Walters. Hope it's nothing serious. Will you be back in Washington soon?"

None of her business, Carol thought.

"Soon, I hope. Thanks, Sheryl, I will ring her when I get back."

Growing up in Boulder, Colorado, Carol was the youngest child of Jonathon and Ellen Stuart, although, she felt more like an only child, as her brother Rodney was eight years older than she. Needless to say, they did not have a close relationship. Rodney adored his little sister but at the same time thought her to be a pest when she tried to tag along with him and his buddies. And so Carol, who was extremely feminine, was also a tomboy. She played football and softball with the boys. She climbed trees, sometimes climbing to the very top of the tree, swinging back and forth on the wind, daring her friends to follow. Boulder was a small town in those days, and Carol rode her bicycle everywhere, exploring canyons and arroyos of the southwestern landscape. Children of the fifties had much more freedom than they do now. You seldom heard of them being abducted or harassed or bullied, and it would have been unheard of for a child to even think of bringing a gun to school in small-town, rural America. It was definitely a better time to raise a family.

Rodney was the studious one and had a 4.0 average in high school, while Carol, although extremely intelligent, was more social and spent her spare time with friends, going to movies, sock hops, football games; studying was not high on her agenda and she scraped by with mostly Cs. She also was a bit of a rebel, smoking cigarettes and drinking beer, likely trying to rid herself of the conservative image of her family. Her dad an engineer who had worked for Coors for 20 years, was even and steady, but an absentee father working many hours in the week, and when he came home he spent most of his time in his office drawing up plans for his many inventions, attempting to build that super new something that would make the Stuarts millionaires. Her mother, like most mothers of that time, was a housewife, taking care of the children, cleaning the house, cooking, washing and ironing the clothes, the many thankless tasks to be done for a family of four. Carol's parents had since divorced and her mother remarried.

After graduating from high school, Carol had attended the University of Colorado where her grades improved tremendously. She had always thought teaching the noblest of careers, having the opportunity to shape children's lives by giving them the tools to go forth in the world and make a difference. "Children are the future," Carol would often say. "They will take the baton and carry on with making our society better."

Upon graduation from college, Carol immediately applied for a teaching job with the Denver School District and was accepted. So she took the summer off and went to Europe with two of her college friends, Hillary and Sophie, for three months, backpacking, hitching rides, sleeping in youth hostiles or with newfound friends in the south of France. It was the trip of her life and opened her mind to other cultures and how other people lived in the world. In August of that year she came back to teaching eighth grade in the Mountain Heights Middle School in south Denver, a lower income area with many Hispanic children. She knew in that first year that this was indeed her calling. She loved the children, and they in turn loved her and responded to her in a positive way. It was at this school where she met James several years later.

Carol thought back to that day, twenty-four years and some months ago. James was speaking on the role of state government in education at the Wednesday student assembly. The minute she saw him on that stage, she knew she would marry him. He was so self-assured; he was a man who knew what he wanted and how to get it. And he was very handsome. His dark-brown hair was neatly trimmed in an executive cut, his face had that masculine, chiseled look, long and lean and tall, and his body was trim with small hips and wide shoulders.

Carol, a petite 5′4″, dark brown hair cut in a bob and brown eyes, approached the stage after the presentation to talk to him. There were dozens of people surrounding him, and she had pushed her way through the crowd and finally found herself standing in front of him.

Looking down at her, James said, "Did you have a question for me?"

Her mind went blank. "I uh . . . I had a question, but I've forgotten what it was," Carol said embarrassingly.

His eyes looked into hers and the connection was there.

"Well, maybe if you give me your phone number, I can call you and by then you will have remembered what you wanted to ask me," James smiled warmly.

She thought, give him my phone number; she had never given her phone number to a strange man before. But this man was not a stranger. Most everyone in the state knew him, she rationalized.

"Yes, it's 956-4354."

"And your name is. . . ."

"Oh, . . . uh, Carol Stuart," she managed to say.

"I'll call you soon." His large, cobalt blue eyes never left hers.

Two evenings later, the phone rang. She had been so busy grading exams that she had almost forgotten about the meeting at school. When she answered and heard his voice, her heart started to pound and the palms of her hands were moist and clammy.

"Is this Carol Stork?" he asked.

"It's Stuart. Yes, this is Carol."

No apology for not getting her name right, "This is James Walters. Do you remember talking to me a couple of days ago at the Mountain Heights Middle School?"

"I do," Carol said.

"You had a question for me but you seemed to have forgotten what the question was. I know it must have been important. I am calling you back so that you can ask it. Do you remember what it was?"

Carol stammered, "Uh, yes, I do."

Carol thought for a minute. What was she going to ask him? It really didn't matter. Any relevant question would do. "I wanted to know how the legislature makes decisions on spending for school districts?"

"Most of the large budgetary spending for schools is decided by the voters."

And he went on to explain what that covered and how the measures came through the state Senate and how the bills became referendums. They talked for an hour or more, and then he asked her to dinner the following Friday night and she accepted.

James picked her up at her apartment promptly at 6:30 that Friday evening and drove her into central Denver where they had a reservation at Darios, a very romantic Italian restaurant. As they approached the *maitre de,* James whispered something to him and they were immediately led to a table in an alcove, secluded from the rest of the patrons. James ordered the best Chianti and moments later the waiter returned with the wine, poured some for James to preview and then poured a glass for Carol, and they both sipped wine until the waiter came back for their order. They ate and they drank and talked about everything from politics to sports. James agreed with Carol that education was key in a free society and that public schools were the cornerstone for education in a democracy. In fact they agreed on most everything. It was a magical evening, and when James walked her to her apartment door, he asked when he could see her again, and Carol said that next weekend would be fine.

The weekend dates turned into Tuesday and Wednesday dates; James and Carol could not get enough of each other. It had been two months since they had started dating when Carol decided it was time for him to meet her parents. James came to her apartment early on that second Saturday in May and carried her bag to the car, opened the car door for her and then walked around to the driver's side of his Ford Bronco. He sat for a while just looking at Carol.

"What are you thinking about," Carol asked.

"That I love you very much and I want you to be my partner and my wife forever," James said. And he pulled a small box from his pocket and took out the solitaire diamond ring.

"Will you be my wife?" James asked as he slipped the ring on the third finger of her left hand.

Tears ran down Carol's cheeks.

"You are unhappy? I don't want to make you cry."

"No. I'm so happy. Yes, I want to be your wife forever and ever. We will have a wonderful life together, I just know we will."

They were married two months later in the small chapel of the Boulder Valley Christian Church. Seventy-five of Carol's and James' closest friends and family attended, and after the ceremony, a wedding lunch was served at Carol's family home in the backyard garden, decorated with white ribbons, satin bells and sprays of flowers everywhere. It was a small, simple wedding and Carol wore an off-white, waltz-length satin dress with a lace bodice and gardenias in her hair, and James was dressed in a dark navy blue suit with a white shirt and light-blue tie. The day after the wedding, they flew to Acapulco, Mexico, for their honeymoon.

Upon returning, Carol moved into James' house and continued teaching until she became pregnant with their first child, Andrew.

Andrew

"You are talented."

"Oh, in what way?" Alison looked at Andrew suspiciously.

Andrew lay beside Alison, the latest lady in his life.

"Oh, very special ways."

"Tell me, you tease," Alison started to tickle Andrew.

"You are the best lover in Colorado."

"Only Colorado? How about the best in the USA? Or best in the world?" Alison said jokingly. She caressed the hair on Andrew's chest and then moved her hand to his belly and then to his manhood, willing him to come alive again.

"Okay, best in the world. All I know is that I love making love to you."

"All I know is you love to make love."

"Ah, Ali, you know my innermost secrets."

Alison, her svelte body gleaming with perspiration, long straight blond hair streaming down her back, rose from the bed and walked to the bathroom while Andrew continued in his reverie. Alison had just had sex with Andrew James Walters, son of the president of the United States of America. She had no delusions of grandeur, but this was unique. She also knew there was no future for her with Andrew. He was experimenting. He had dated and bedded five women in the last year. He could have most any woman he wanted.

Twenty-one years old, electrical engineering student at CU, Colorado University, he was at the top of his class. Standing six feet tall with shoulder-length, curly, dark-brown hair like his mother's, steel-blue eyes under bushy eyebrows like his father's, Andy, as everyone called him, was strikingly good looking in a wholesome kind of way. He was a marathoner, a downhill skier, and a mountain climber. His narrow hips, wide shoulders and muscular body were evidence of this. Columbian coffee was his drug of choice, and although he drank his share of the keg at frat parties, he loved the outdoors and nature. And he loved the ladies.

"What do you hear from your parents these days?" Ali asked as she walked back into the bedroom and sat down on the bed beside him. Her hair, wet from the shower, clung to her tanned and supple back and a few droplets of water glistened like gems from between her breasts. She put on her tee shirt and pulled on a well-worn pair of jeans.

"Not much. Dad is back in Washington and I guess Mom stayed behind at the ranch to handle some staffing issues. I had an email from her yesterday and she said she would join Dad at the White House in a couple of weeks. Why do you ask?"

"Just wondering. You don't talk about them very much," Ali paused for a couple of minutes seemingly wondering if she wanted to get into this. "People are concerned about the war in Iraq. Soldiers are dying and there's a lot of trouble over there. I think the people want the soldiers to come home. And it looks like your father and his advisors aren't going to allow that. Do you agree with this?"

"No, I don't, but I try not to get into it with him."

"And your mother? Does she support your dad on all of this?"

"My mother isn't like my dad. Her thinking is very different from his. But she usually supports him in whatever he does. He wouldn't be where he is today if she hadn't. But, um . . . Ali, I'd rather not talk about this."

"Precisely. It is the woman behind the man, the wife behind the husband, to keep him centered and on track. If it weren't for women, this world would be in chaos. Well, I take that back. The world is still in chaos. As long as we have men in charge, that's the way it will be."

"A feminist, are you?" He pulled her down beside him and reached up underneath her tee shirt to fondle her breasts.

Alison giggled and pulled away from him. "Andy, you aren't taking me seriously. Is this the way the Walters men handle their women?"

"You have the most beautiful breasts and I love to touch them."

"Changing the subject again. Anyway, I have to go to my bartending job. Some of us have parents with money to pay the tuition, and some of us have to work to pay for school."

"But I don't disagree with you," Andrew said. "Men are quick to go to war. But there's more to this than just going over to Iraq and beating the shit out Saddam."

Alison cupped Andrew's face in her hands and looked into his eyes, then kissed him and pulled herself away. "I'd like to stay all day, but I have to go to work. See you tomorrow?"

"I'll call you. Maybe we can go for pizza or something," Andy said as he looked at her longingly. And Ali walked out the door, leaving Andrew to ponder questions about war and his father.

Stealth Government

The seven men picked their way carefully down the narrow, dimly lit concrete staircase into the depths of the bunker built some fifty years before in another age of paranoia and fear. Walking solemnly, single file in unison step, the head Secret Service man named Jeffrey led the way, followed by James, Jason Martin, the vice president, and Charles Robertson, the secretary of defense. Josh Dean, the secretary of state and two more Secret Service men brought up the rear. It was cool and damp, although there was surprisingly an absence of odor; a dark, antiseptic space where nothing could grow. This facility, little known to but a few FBI personnel in Washington, hadn't seen human life in quite some time . . . until recently.

They marched quietly. Upon reaching the bottom of the stairs, a long, narrow corridor opened up before them, and though it was brightly lit, the end disappeared into a void of blackness. They continued on into the hallway about twenty feet until they came to a windowless, steel gray, metal door on the right. It was unidentifiable with the exception of a rectangular gray pad attached to the wall at about shoulder height on the left side of the door. Above the pad was a panel of three colored lights of red, yellow and green, and beside the panel of lights was a keypad with numbers on it. A video camera hung over the door, ominously scanning the hallway like a hawk searching for prey. The red light was on.

Stepping in front of Jeffery, James laid his hand on the pad until the yellow light was lit and a monotone, computer-generated voice said, "Good afternoon, Mr. President. How many people do you have with you today?"

James punched the number six on the keypad and waited while the video camera performed another scan of the perimeter, and the voice said, "Thank you, Mr. President. You may enter now."

The green light came on, the lock clicked, and the door swung open. Leading the way, the Secret Service entered the room followed by the president and the rest of the group.

"That is one smart computer, " James exclaimed. "Technology has come a long way. Before long that thing will be able to recognize my face."

Jason looked quizzically at the president. "They have computers now that do that."

"Computers were never my long suit," James explained sheepishly.

The very long, narrow room looked and felt like something right out of a World War II movie with whitewashed brick walls, unadorned with the exception of a white board on one side, a huge projection screen filling the wall on one end, and a large schoolhouse clock, a holdover from another era, hanging over the entrance. A green metal-shaded lamp cast long shadows over the oblong-shaped metal table in the center of the room, and two large halogen floor lamps at either end were the only other pieces of furniture. James, Jason, Charles and Josh seated themselves on metal chairs at one end of the table closest to the door, while the Secret Service men stepped out into the hallway for reasons of security.

"Why are we meeting here?" James inquired.

"Because it's safe," said Jason.

The second hand made one and a half trips around the schoolhouse clock as the four men, with grim expressions on their faces, eyed one another.

Jason broke the silence, "There is concern about the mood in the country right now in regard to the number of military personnel and others being killed on a daily basis in Iraq. You must all realize that this could have severe implications on the election in November."

"It could be time to pull our troops out of Iraq," Josh said. Josh, an African-American, had been a four-star general in the Army before joining the Walters team. With slightly graying hair and an ever-present earnest expression on his face, he was the dove of the group. Having experienced war firsthand and seeing young men and women injured and dieing, Josh was of the opinion that war seldom solved anything and the war to end all wars eventually led to more war.

Charles gave Josh an icy stare, "Pull out? We can't do that. Not now. I agree Iraq is in disarray, but that's precisely why we have to stay. We have to get the security in place and then work on stabilizing the government." Charles had been around a long time. He had served as secretary of state under James' father when he was in office nine years ago. Everyone called him Chucky, and the name was fitting for the aging, portly man with prominent front teeth. He oftentimes said, "I can get my teeth into anything and make it happen. You just watch me." It was true; he was one of the most tenacious people in the administration and that was why he had been chosen for this job.

"How long is it going to take. It's been almost eighteen months and the insurgents are still sniping and killing our guys. And girls, I might add. We need to start rebuilding the infrastructure and we can't because it's just too damn dangerous. Nobody wants to go in and work there. We just got the water system working reliably last month and electricity is still unstable thanks to months of sabotage," James said.

James recalled a meeting they had had in this very room with the same players over two years ago before the war had begun. He had spoken first. "You all know why we are here; to plan for the war with Iraq." James walked to the screen at the end of the room, pointing to the country of Iraq nestled in between Turkey, Syria,

Iran and Kuwait in the Persian Gulf. "Iraq is strategically located in the Middle East and if we control it, we can gain control of the whole region. It is a stepping-stone that will allow us to dictate our policy to the other Arab nations in the area and also manage the largest oil fields in the Middle East." James paused and looked around the room for the reaction of the other members.

"If we gain control of this country and the oil," he continued, "we are assured of remaining the superpower into the twenty-first century. He who owns the oil owns the world. The U.S. and other industrialized nations depend on oil. If we control it, we control the world, it's as simple as that," James said.

"In addition there is money to be made there. After the bombing is over, we will have to rebuild and that is worth billions in contracts for U.S. companies, and I say U.S. because this is going to be our war. There is too much money involved here and we don't want to give it away to Russia and France," Jason said.

Everyone around the table nodded their heads in agreement like bobble-head dolls at a baseball game.

James continued, "It should be a relatively easy conquest. Iraq is very weak right now due to the sanctions that the U.N. has imposed on them for the past ten years. We'll just go in there and topple Saddam, replace him with a leader of our choice and then take command."

"The country is weak, but there are other considerations," Josh chimed in. "Even though many of his people hate him, they would fight to their death to keep control of their country and the oil. The oil is all they have and they're not going to give it up easily. I don't think it's going to be a cakewalk by any means. And when those body bags start coming back, people in this country will not be happy."

"If we sell this right, the people won't care. If U.S. citizens think they are going to be attacked, they will do anything to prevent it," James said. "Look we've had one attack in this country already. If we tie that into Iraq and Saddam. . . . Look, he's already gassed his own people. He's had biological weapons in the past, nuclear weapons, too. He could attack this country at any moment."

"We have to get our allies with us," Josh said emphatically. "We can't go this one alone. To do so would further alienate the world against us and that wouldn't be helpful. I suggest that we take this to the United Nations and then get a referendum from Congress. This will help to rally public opinion in favor of the war. Like you keep saying, nobody likes Saddam Hussein. Everyone would just as soon see him go."

"Going to the U.N. would take more time than we have. We have a window here to get in there and win this war before the next presidential election. We don't want to be in the heat of battle during that time. Although I agree it might be beneficial to have the Congress approve the measure. I don't have to remind you all that it is September and the midterms are coming up in November. That's two months away! The stock market is in a slump and there are millions of people out of work. Just having the debate on a little war in Iraq will divert attention away from the economy," James said.

Josh looked at James and shook his head, "A little war in Iraq. There is no little war. They're all big. And this one would be no exception. You forget about the Kurds in the north and the Shiites in the south. The Shiites make up sixty percent of the population. Do you think they will just roll over for this takeover you are proposing? And there are other factions in the Muslim world. The worst-case scenario would be for the Arab world to unite against us, and that could happen. They may not have the war machine that we do, but they have other means of wreaking havoc. And if we start to see suicide bombers in our pizza parlors and shopping centers, the psychological effect could be devastating. People might not go out to eat anymore and they could stop shopping altogether. What would that do to the economic recovery?"

"Josh, you're far too cynical," Jason had interjected. "We just need a solid war plan. Go in there and squash them before they know what hit them. Get control and take over the government and we're home free."

"I agree with Jason," James had said enthusiastically.

"Ok," Josh continued, "let's say we could pull it off. What about the American people? How are you proposing to sell this to the public? I don't think they will want to kill American boys and girls for oil."

Charles had looked around the table. "Oil? Who's talking about oil here? Do not even bring oil into it. Don't talk about oil. Although Americans want oil for their SUV lifestyle, you are right, they wouldn't want to sacrifice American lives for it. This has to be about Saddam Hussein, how dangerous he is and how he mistreats his people. He is a monster and we are going to liberate the people of Iraq from his hideous tactics. It's also about the threat to the U.S. If it can be perceived that he has nuclear capabilities and could possibly attack the United States, people would be on board. If the American people thought he had biological weapons that could be used on them, they would be eager to take him out."

"The inspectors are in there now. They haven't found anything yet. I say give them until the first of the year and then throw them out and we send in our bombs," Jason said. "We'll have press conferences to reinforce the fact that the inspectors are inefficient and not getting the job done. This will also keep the focus off the economy. We want the debate to be about the war in Iraq."

"And, James, I disagree with you," Jason added. "We need to take this to the United Nations. Josh, I want you to prepare for the meetings with the U.N. Even if the U.N. doesn't agree, nobody can say we didn't try. We have the Brits on our side; I say we don't need anyone else. And then getting Congress to pass a resolution will legitimize the plan and get the people with us."

And the strategy had worked. They were able to flood the news with the talk of war, burying news of the failing economy, the layoffs, the stock market tanking. And they were victorious in the midterm elections. The war was scheduled to begin in early spring; 150,000 troops were moved to the region bordering Iraq, Kuwait and Turkey, beginning flyovers and practicing military maneuvers. Then at the end of March, the president declared to the world that the weapons inspectors were not doing an adequate job and the United States was in imminent danger. The U.S. was going to attack. They gave the inspectors and any other Americans two weeks to leave Iraq. And on April 20, the bombing began. Every night on TV network news the American people watched as the bombs lit up Baghdad like fireworks on the fourth of July. They bombed Iraqi airfields, bridges over the Tigris and their communications facilities. They then attacked Saddam's palace and other places where he was known to hang out. Thousands of Iraqi soldiers were killed along with thousands more civilians caught in the war zone. Within a month, it was over. Saddam had slipped away in the night and was gone and his Republican guard had surrendered. The U.S. declared victory. But the victory was short lived as the fighting continued and U.S. soldiers were being killed, about one each day.

"We have to find a way to crush these insurgents," James looked at each one around the table.

"We're doing all we can do at this time," Jason said.

"We need to do more. We have to get the organizers, the leaders. Saddam is still alive. Is he running this show? If we offer a reward, then someone can bring him to us," James said. "Offer ten million, twenty million, I don't care how much. We need to get Saddam."

They arose from the table in unison like soldiers marching to cadence and walked out of the secure area and up the stairs into the daylight once again.

Duty Calls

Carol's phone rang about ten times before she rushed into her office. "Hello, this is Carol," she said as she picked up the receiver.

"Carol, James here. How are things going up there?"

"Everything's fine. I talked with Tom and he gave Steve a warning that if this happens again, he's out of a job. I think he'll straighten up. There aren't that many wrangler jobs available these days, and Steve doesn't know anything else."

"Good, good. Can you get back here in a couple of days? I need you to be here. Things are heating up and everybody is asking about you. They're wondering why you didn't come back with me. This just doesn't look good for us."

"Appearances. You're always concerned about how things look."

"You know how rumors spread in Washington. If the opposition suspects that there is trouble between us, they would make a big deal of it and it could hurt my chances in the November election."

Carol didn't want to comment on James' last statement. "I need to see Andrew this weekend. I'll try and come after that."

"How am I going to explain this? I tell you, Carol, people are asking."

"You'll find a way. You always do," she said in an exasperated tone. "And let them ask. It's none of their dammed business."

"We're on a stage and the whole world is looking at us. Do you understand that?"

"Yes, but we also have a right to some privacy in our lives. I'm sick and tired of the press following us wherever we go, prying into our personal lives. I want my life back."

"You'll have your life back in four and a half years and we can retire to the ranch or wherever we want to be, in luxury."

There was a pause on the other end and then, "I'll call you on Sunday and we can make arrangements then. You'll be back here on Monday, or I will have to personally escort you back," James barked over the phone. "You do realize that the convention is coming up on September 5."

"Goodbye, James," Carol hung up the phone and collapsed into the large burgundy executive chair in front of her desk. Now he's issuing ultimatums. She needed more time. She needed to talk with Andrew and make some decisions. Maybe he could help her work through this.

The drive from Mountain Sky Ranch north of Fort Collins to Boulder takes about an hour and a half to two hours, depending on how fast you drive. Carol insisted on driving their Jeep Wrangler herself, with the Secret Service following in a portentous-looking black Lincoln Navigator, bristling with antennas. They were always there, lurking, making her feel like a prisoner. At least today she could be alone in her car for a few hours during the trip. Carol treasured her privacy and alone time and she had so little of it lately.

Fall was beginning to show her face on the Colorado University campus. The leaves of the ash and maple trees had tinges of crimson, gold and yellow in contrast to the dark verdant green of the many pine trees lining the streets. Carol loved the fall season. She remembered back to her freshman year and the excitement of moving away from home and living in a dormitory. The dormitory rooms normally had two women to a room, but because the freshman class was so large that year, they added bunk beds and put three women in most rooms. It was a tight squeeze. The closets weren't large enough and she, like most young women, had lots of clothes. There was very little space for desks and it was difficult studying because someone was always talking. But they coped and they had a good time. She remained friends with her two roommates, Karen Johnson and Sheryl King. Karen had gone on to law school and became a labor relation's lawyer with a small firm in Denver, and Sheryl married a doctor, had three children and lived in Lakewood, a suburb east of Denver. Carol communicated with them often by email, and usually once or twice a year the three of them would get together for a girls' night out for dinner or lunch and or a day of shopping. Although, since Carol had become First Lady, she had not had the time for such frivolousness in the past four years. She was either campaigning or performing some other official duty for the White House.

Carol drove into the driveway of Andrew's house and the Secret Service parked in front at the curb. Carol and James had purchased the Tudor-style, beige stucco house with green trim when Andrew was a sophomore so that he could have adequate housing while he was a student at CU. He shared the house with one other student, Sean Majors, who was also a senior. The forties-vintage, two-bedroom house was not luxurious but quite comfortable, furnished with some of Carol's old cast-off furniture from the ranch and hand-me-downs from Andrew's grandparents. Another benefit of the house was the guest cottage in the rear that was used for the Secret Service. All members of the family of the president were required to have at least one agent on duty seven by twenty-four.

"Hey, Mom, why didn't you tell me you were coming?" Andrew flew out the front door and ran up to his mother and gave her a big hug.

"I didn't think I'd have to make an appointment to see my favorite son."

"No, of course not. I'm always glad to see you. It's just that I have class in a couple of hours and I want to spend some time with you."

"Not a problem. It's noon now. Let's grab some lunch. Get in the car, I'll drive."

"Let me put on a clean shirt first. I don't want to wear this ratty sweatshirt to McDonalds," teased Andrew as he went into the house.

Carol followed him in and looked around at the usual messy living room with newspapers and half-empty beer and soda cans on the coffee table. Dirty socks and other pieces of clothing adorned the couch with a pair of dirty running shoes parked permanently on the floor nearby. The dining room table was piled high with papers and a couple of paper plates with half-eaten pizza. "Andy, don't you ever clean up around here?" Carol called him Andy, whereas his father always called him Andrew. James was very proper, and when Carol first met him, she tried calling him Jim and he corrected her immediately, telling her that he hated nicknames. "I didn't think we'd go to McDonalds. I had something else in mind, like the Chalet over on Pine Street."

"Hey, I was just kidding." Andrew disregarded her reference to the messy house. "There's nothing wrong, is there, Mom? I got your email. Why didn't you go back to Washington with Dad?"

"I had some ranch business to take care of so I stayed behind. We were having some problems with Steve, and Tom just wasn't dealing with it effectively. I had a talk with Tom, and I think he'll do the right thing. Steve is a good wrangler, but he had gotten into some trouble and your Dad was worried about the publicity."

Andrew walked out of the bedroom wearing a light-blue, long-sleeved dress shirt unbuttoned at the neck with khaki Dockers.

"Dad's always worried about the publicity."

"I know. Let's go to lunch."

The ride to the restaurant took fifteen minutes. With Andrew's directions, the entourage wound it's way through the back streets of the campus, finally driving onto Pine Street and parking in the lot beside the Chalet. The restaurant, true to its name, was designed to look like a cabin in the mountains and Carol loved the rustic feeling of the log structure. They walked inside and waited to be seated by the hostess.

"Hi, did you have a reservation?" A young woman, with long brown hair pulled back into a ponytail appeared.

"No. How long is the wait?" Andrew asked.

The hostess looked at him carefully and then her eyes became very large. "Oh, aren't you Andrew Walters, the president's son?"

"No, I'm not," he said curtly. "How long?" Andrew got very tired of special treatment when people recognized him as part of the first family. He just wanted to be an ordinary citizen.

"Just the two of you? You look like him, I just thought you might be him," she rattled on. "Smoking or nonsmoking?"

"Nonsmoking."

"It'll be about ten minutes." The hostess kept scrutinizing him and looking at Carol.

They settled into a large leather couch in the foyer, and Carol looked through the dining area at the huge stone fireplace on the far side of the room. The furniture was made of smaller pine logs, and there were horse blankets draped over the railing beside the fireplace. A large Remington sculpture of a cowboy riding a bronco adorned the table next to them and oil paintings of more cowboys herding cattle in the winter and branding calves hung on the walls.

"Your table's ready." The hostess led them into the dining room to a small table at the far end next to a picture window looking out on a small garden in the back.

"How's school going?" Carol inquired as they were being seated.

"It's going well. I'm taking advanced calculus and I should be getting a B at least. But I'm also taking a drafting course and I love it. I love to draw things and I never knew that about myself."

"Are you still dating Alison?"

"Yes, I'm still seeing her."

"I hate to meddle, but I wish you would settle down with one girlfriend and maybe even think about getting married."

"You are meddling. Look, Mom, marriage is not for me right now. But we're not here to talk about me. Tell me what's going on with you."

"I'm leaving your dad."

Andrew had just taken a drink of water and started coughing.

A short, almost pudgy waitress appeared dressed in khaki shorts and a pink polo shirt. "Can I take your order?"

Andrew composed himself and turned to her, "I don't think we're ready yet. Give us a few minutes."

The waitress left and Andrew looked at his mother in disbelief. "Look, I know that you and dad have had your differences, but why this?"

"We've grown apart and I don't believe in what he stands for anymore. Something has happened to him since he took office. He used to be such an idealist, wanting to do the right thing for the people and the country, but he's changed. He's gotten involved in something even he cannot control and I can't go along with it."

"Is this the right time? It could ruin Dad. The election is coming up. Wait it out until the first of the year. Better yet wait until he's out of office."

"Now, you're thinking like your dad. I know that it could potentially hurt him in the election, but I can't be a party to this anymore. This is not who I am, never was and never will be."

"What are you talking about?"

"I'm talking about going to war with Iraq. I'm talking about killing people, and soldiers dying. I'm talking about the environment; your dad just weakened emission standards for power plants around the country through what he calls the Clean Skies Act. And how will that affect people? There will be more cancer, more asthma, and more people will die. And I am talking about women's rights. If the Republicans and Patriots control both Houses, they will appoint judges who could overturn Roe v. Wade. And when that happens, women will no longer have the right to choose. The government chooses for her. Oh, but that will not apply to everyone. The wealthy will always be able to go to another country for a spa treatment."

"Oh, Mother, you've been surfing the Web too much." Andrew always called her "Mother" when he wanted to make a point.

"Yes, I have been surfing the Web and I am learning more than I probably want to know."

"You don't believe all that stuff, do you?"

"I think I'm smart enough to know the truth when I see it. There are some kooks posting some weird stuff, but many of them are speaking truth based on facts that can be backed up. When I see the same material from several different sources, I tend to believe it. Andrew, don't minimize this."

"I'm not. But then why did you marry him in the first place? He came from a political family and you knew he was going to be in politics. And politics is dirty sometimes, you knew that."

"I did, but he had different values when we first married. He always wanted to fix the world. He believed in capitalism, but he was also for the common guy. He's not like that anymore. He's sold his soul. And if I stay with him I will be selling mine too."

There was silence between them.

"Another factor here. The war in Iraq is not the last one. They are planning more wars and in the Middle East."

Andrew shifted in his seat and took another drink of his water, thinking all of this through for several minutes.

"So you're going to change the course of the election, the path of history, by divorcing the president of the United States of America. Awesome! I love it."

"You do?" Carol looked at Andrew incredulously. "I thought you'd be angry with me. I thought you would be against this. I know how you love your dad."

"I do, Mom, but I love you, too, and I've seen how unhappy you've become in the last couple of years. To tell you the truth, I was expecting something like this, but I didn't think you'd have the guts to do it. Wow!"

"Are you ready to order now?" the waitress was back.

"Yes, I'll have the filet of trout, with a dinner salad," Carol spoke first.

"Blue cheese or Thousand Isle dressing?"

"Blue cheese, on the side, please. And ice tea to drink."

"And you, sir. By the way aren't you. . . ."

"No, I'm not," Andrew broke in. "I'll have the half-pound hamburger with fries. And ice tea is fine for me, too."

The waitress picked up the menus and left.

"So what's the plan? Does Dad know yet?"

"No, he doesn't. I've been trying to delay telling him, but I guess I'm going to have to do that soon. The shit is going to hit the fan when I do."

Andrew chided her, "This is the First Lady talking?"

"I'm a human being like everyone else."

"Can't take a joke?"

"This is not a joking matter. I am hiring a lawyer tomorrow. You remember Marshal Dale? He's an old friend of Grandma's family."

"Blockbuster case for him. National recognition."

"I wish you'd stop talking like that."

"I can't help it. This is so big. And, Mom, I have to give you credit for standing up for what you believe. I don't think there are many women who would do what you are doing."

"Yeah, you're right. Not too many women willing to commit an act tantamount to suicide."

The food arrived. Andrew was hungry and he dived into his hamburger while Carol picked at her trout. She was thinking about her last words. Would this be suicide for her?

"I'm with you, Mom. I don't know if this is right for you or not, but I'm in your corner. And I admire you for being the strong woman that you are," Andrew finally spoke as they were driving back to his house.

"As I said earlier, this might be my downfall."

They drove into the driveway. Andrew looked carefully at his mother and then put his arms around her, "I am here for you."

"I'll walk you to the door and then I have to get back." And as they were walking up the curved walkway to the front door, Carol said, "We have to be careful. I don't know if there are listening devices in the car. When you call on the phone, we will have to watch what we say. Just a precaution."

"Don't you think you're being paranoid?" Andrew said to her.

"You wouldn't believe the surveillance going on in Washington. They say that many of the senate offices are bugged. I'm just not going to take chances."

"This is getting weird. But, I think you're right. I've got to go to class. I love you, Mom. Be careful."

"I love you, too." And they embraced again, a mother-son embrace.

Carol got into the Jeep and backed out of the driveway. She turned onto the street and headed for the freeway with the black Lincoln Navigator following a few car lengths behind.

The sun was setting as Carol drove through the gate of Mountain Sky Ranch and proceeded up the mile-and-a-half road to the ranch house. There had not been a cloud in the sky all day long; the perfect fall day and now the horizon in the east was turning shades of azure to amethyst to a deep sapphire blue. Looking west where the palette was of reds and pink, the silhouette of the sole oak tree near the corral painted a picture of western serenity.

Carol waved and smiled as the Secret Service drove past her and on toward their small adobe house beyond the horse barn that had been built for them when James had first become president. She had two agents assigned to her—Karl Perkins and Paul Bartello. They were nice enough guys, but she was just tired of being followed day and night. At least they didn't sit outside her bedroom door as they usually did when she was at the White House.

Buffy, their golden Labrador retriever, and Opal, an Australian shepherd, ran down the path to greet Carol as she wearily stepped out of the Jeep Cherokee.

"Hi, guys. I'm glad to see you, too." Buffy put his wet brown nose into her hand and Opal ran round and round trying to get her attention. "You're my best friends. Let's go into house. I need some supper. Have you eaten yet?"

Buffy wagged his tail and followed, as did Opal. They'd probably eaten, but they were always up for more food. These were working dogs and they often helped with the cattle and the few sheep on the ranch. But they were also family pets and slept in the big house at night, sometimes on Carol's bed when she was there.

Carol dropped her purse in her office and headed for the kitchen to find a bite to eat. Nancy, her housekeeper, had retired to her small house located near the big house, which she and her husband Jack rented. Jack also worked for Carol and James as a mechanic. He was responsible for the trucks and tractors on the ranch and served as a part-time handyman. Carol and James treated their employees well, rewarding them with bonuses, and most of them stayed with them for a long time.

Carol opened the stainless-steel door of the institutional-sized refrigerator and perused the contents for a possible evening snack. She still wasn't very hungry, but she thought she had to keep her strength up for the battle ahead. There was leftover chicken and some broccoli. With French bread and a glass of cold milk, she could make a meal of this.

She was just sitting down at the large farmers-style kitchen table to eat when the phone rang. Somehow, Carol knew this would be James calling again. Should she tell him now?

"Hello." Her voice revealed her weariness.

"Carol. James, here," James' voice boomed into the receiver. "I've been campaigning all day. We took the Big Bird out to Iowa and Wisconsin and talked to all of those dairy farmers. I am so tired."

He often called Air Force One "Big Bird". James was in awe when he had first boarded the aircraft. "This is just for me?" he had exclaimed. "Boy, I must be somebody important." His staff looked at one another and started to snicker, but soon straightened their faces. James was a plainspoken man and he often vocalized what he was thinking. At times this created problems diplomatically, but there was a benefit; you knew where the president stood on issues. But this was the reason they didn't let him have very many press conferences. His press secretary, Stanley Thompson, most often spoke to the media and held press conferences for him.

"It must have been a grueling day. I wish I'd been there," she lied.

"When're you coming? I really miss you and I need you to help with the campaigning."

"I'm not, James."

There was a long pregnant minute of silence. "Did I hear you right? You said you weren't coming?"

"Yes, James you heard right. I'm not coming back. I am leaving you. I want a divorce."

"A divorce. You want a divorce? You can't divorce me! You can't do this to me."

"I can and I will."

"Why? I haven't done anything wrong. I thought you were really happy with our life. How many women in this country, in this world, have the opportunity to become First Lady? I've worked so hard for this. You can't do this to me. It'll ruin my chances for reelection. It'll ruin the party."

"Is that all you can think about is ruining the party?"

James stammered, "No, no it isn't. I'm thinking about our dreams. I thought we had the same dreams. You wanted this as much as I did. At least I thought you did."

"I'm not happy, James. I don't know if you've noticed or not, but I haven't been happy for quite some time now. You've been so wrapped up in your campaigning and presidential affairs that you haven't noticed."

"There must be something else . . . or someone else. Carol, are you having an affair?"

"No, James, I've been forever faithful. Not that I haven't had opportunities."

"I just don't understand."

And there was a long silence. Neither of them spoke.

"Carol, you need to rethink this. You just can't do this. Especially not now. I'm going to call you back in the morning and you'll have changed your mind. How is Andrew? Did you go to see him?"

"I did and he's fine." Carol didn't want to argue anymore. "I'll talk to you tomorrow, but I won't change my mind and that is final."

"I'm going to be on the road campaigning for the next couple of days. We're visiting three states in three days. It's going to be crazy. I'll call you when I can. But Carol, think this through carefully. This is all for us."

Carol hung up the phone and went back to her meager meal. She wasn't hungry, but she forced herself to eat and she went back to the refrigerator and got some more milk and, pouring it into the large glass, drank it all. Her stomach was aching and she thought this might calm it. She then took Opal and Buffy out for a last run before bedtime. The air was cool with the promise of fall and there was a half crescent moon hanging low in the ink-blue sky. The fresh air invigorated her.

It was 9:30 by the time Carol pulled back the covers on their king-sized bed. She grabbed a book, *Earth First,* about saving ecosystems, and sank into her pillows with her dogs nestled beside her. She hoped she would sleep tonight.

Power Brokers

James rose early on this August morning. He pulled on his sweatpants and a tee shirt, put on his running shoes and walked down the hallway and down the stairs for a six-mile run along the Potomac. His Secret Service men were right there with him, encircling him, ensuring his safety. The 53-year-old president was in excellent condition and could run an 8½-minute mile, and of course the Secret Service had to keep up with him. It became a competition every morning to see who would finish first and who would lag behind. The Secret Service were young men compared to the president; in their mid to late thirties, and to qualify for this very special job they had to be in the best of physical condition.

President Walters, James Kerr Walters, had always been rich. He had lived in oversized houses, we would call them estates, and had servants to take care of his daily tasks. He was used to it. James' father, a Colorado land baron, had been governor of Colorado before winning the White House. James maternal great-grandfather, John Kerr, immigrated to New York from Scotland in the early part of the nineteenth century and, with the help of a cousin, got a job as a clerk on Wall Street at the newly formed New York Stock Exchange. He'd left his homeland, selling the business he'd inherited from his father, a grain and feed store that was failing, with a quest for religious freedom and a longing to own land. Unless one belonged to aristocracy in Scotland, the average Scot would never own land. The majority of the land, of which only a small portion was arable, Scotland being the Island of Granite, belonged to the wealthy and was passed down through generations. If John had wanted to work the land, he would have had to become a tenet farmer.

A tenacious young man, he hob knobbed with the powerbrokers of the time, even though he was only a lowly clerk, and learned about the railroads being built to settle western territories. Hard working, penny pinching and adventurous, John longed to move west and he was finally rewarded when, through his Wall Street contacts, he was able to land an agent's job with the Kansas Pacific Railroad, which was later bought out by the Santa Fe. Railroading wasn't his calling but buying land was, and John took advantage of the times, buying several thousand acres of land for just pennies when it was offered by the Santa Fe Railroad. Now John, newly married with two children, never became wealthy from these real estate purchases, but John's son, James Kerr, was able to capitalize on it by leasing it back to the railroad and selling some of it for a profit.

James, Jr., born in 1951, was the eldest son of James and Eleanor Walters, and having two younger sisters, he was spoiled. He relentlessly teased his younger sisters, Shirley and Marcia, and was seldom reprimanded. He was the "prince" of the household and everyone knew it; whatever James wanted he got, including an Arabian horse, a new Ferrari and trips to Europe. But in spite of his parents doting, James was a humanitarian. When he traveled through Europe after graduating from Harvard *summa cum laude,* he camped and stayed in youth hostiles and he talked with people, learning about European cultures. He traveled to South Africa, seeing apartheid first hand and the suffering of the blacks living in abject poverty. This was the man that Carol fell in love with.

The trail along the river was wet from an early morning rain and the air was pungent with the smells of the earth and decaying leaves. A squirrel scurried across the path ahead, running up the nearest tree to avoid the human invasion of its territory so early in the morning.

The Secret Service kept vigilant, looking everywhere for a possible sniper. The area was always "swept" prior to the morning run to remove any person or thing that didn't belong there. This was true of all events in which the president participated, and it created a logistical nightmare for those who were responsible for his safety. Each event had to be planned down to the last minute detail; the timing, the location and position of those surrounding the president were all critical to ensure that no one could possibly harm the president. There had been mistakes in the past. Everyone remembers the 1962 assassination of President Kennedy in Dallas. After that tragic event, presidents no longer rode in open convertibles in motorcades. The 1981 assignation attempt on President Reagan by John Hinckley was a wake up call to the Secret Service; bullets were flying everywhere, wounding not only the President but also James Brady, Reagan's press secretary, leaving him paralyzed for life. Special care was taken to protect the president, even if it meant sacrificing their own lives.

James continued his run back to the White House grounds. He entered the White House and went back up to the second floor family apartment to shower and prepare for the day of meetings and briefings. He flicked on CNN news and watched and listened while he dressed. "New polls out today show that President Walters has a 65% approval rating for his handling of the war on terrorism." If the polls continue like this, the November elections would go well. They had to downplay the faltering economy, people losing jobs and soldiers dying in Iraq at a rate of one or more per day. The Patriots were gaining in the House and the Senate and with the few Republicans voting with them on most issues, they had the majority. If they maintained the seats they currently held and picked up five more seats in the Senate, they would have a clear majority. James licked his lips thinking about it. When we add even more Patriots this fall, he thought, and I win the election, I will be the most powerful president in history of this country. With the help of those Republicans who voted with the Patriots, we will have another four years of Patriot majority control of the House of Representatives and the Senate, with control of the executive branch and a majority on the Supreme Court.

After dressing in dark-brown slacks, an ecru shirt with a Gucci silk tie and brown tweed sport jacket, James left the family quarters to go to his office, the Oval Office in the West Wing of the White House.

His first order of the day was to read the briefings coming in to him from the special wire services.

Israelis once more moving tanks into the West Bank town of Jenin in retaliation for a bus bomb killing thirty people in Jerusalem in a resurgence of violence in the Palestinian uprising for statehood. The Israelis destroyed the homes of two militants suspected in the bombing.

Another warning from the al-Qaeda terror network. The next attack would target power plants across the United States.

The Indonesians found video recordings of Osama bin Laden and other extremist Islamic propaganda at two houses once rented by the alleged instigators of the attack on the nightclub in Bali that killed 200 people.

This strengthened suspicions that the al-Qaeda network was still intact and could possibly carry out other terrorist attacks, James thought. His attention went back to the world news in the newspaper lying on his desk.

The drought in the West continues, there was massive flooding in the Southeast where a hurricane, downgraded to a tropical storm, nevertheless dropped ten inches of rain on the South Carolina, Georgia and Florida coast in the past five hours and was heading up the eastern seaboard.

A 42-year-old man was shot to death as he filled his gas tank at a filling station in Alexandria outside of Washington, DC, and another similar shooting death three hours later at a Home Depot in Rockville, Maryland, of a 30-year-old woman walking out of the store.

The Dow was up 53 points to 10,543.30 and the NASDAQ down 2.84 to 1970.06.

James was concerned about the sniper shootings. This was

happening too close to home, and were the two shootings related, he wondered? Sometimes he thought it would be better if he didn't read the newspaper. The news was never good and it depressed him. And the briefings were oftentimes filled with dire warnings of imminent attacks from al-Qaeda or other countries with nuclear weapons that he didn't think he could really do anything about. But this is what he was paid to do.

He picked up the phone to call Dick Hobart, the Senate minority leader. The bill for the new Homeland Security Agency was being debated in the Senate and being held up by the Democrats.

"Dick, James here. How are we coming on Homeland Security? I expect you to get that passed this week."

"That's not going to happen. I would like to accommodate you, but I don't like the idea of these new federal workers not having the benefit of civil service. Every other government agency has this."

"Look, Dick, if we can't fire these people, then we have no control. And I might point something else out to you. If you hold up this one, your constituents will view you as being an obstructionist and you can't afford that right now. Elections are coming up. The people want this."

"Yes, they do. But they want job protection, too. Are you out to break the unions of this country?"

"No, no I would never want to do that. Look, the firemen and policemen of this country are my friends. They voted for me."

Dick made no comment on that statement. "Look Mr. President, we need to compromise on this bill. There's all kinds of fat here. Eight billion dollars to the airline industry, another five billion to the auto industry. What's that all about?"

"The airlines are in trouble right now and if they go under, fewer people will be traveling and that will have a ripple effect on other business in the country. The same goes for the auto industry."

"What does it have to do with Homeland Security? I don't see the connection here. We're giving away the people's tax money."

"Just get it done, Dick. I'm counting on you." James was exasperated with what he heard, but he knew that he had the upper hand. Ever since the terrorist attacks on New York City and the Pentagon, he could get almost anything he wanted. People were frightened and they looked to their government to protect them. What did it matter if, in exchange for this protection, they had lost many of their Fourth Amendment constitutional rights? And if he could slip in a few favors to his largest contributors, all the better.

He hung up the phone. He had a staff meeting in ten minutes and he wanted to review the agenda. They would be discussing the strategies of the campaign in the next few weeks. He would be taking Big Bird to twelve cities next week. The convention would be held in New York City the following week. Would he have the stamina to do this? He didn't like to travel. He didn't like being away from home, away from familiar surroundings, his own bed.

Stanley Thompson, his press secretary, knocked on the door and entered.

"We're ready to meet, Mr. President. Should we meet in here or in the Rosewood conference room?"

"Have everyone come in here."

Stanley went out to call everyone into the meeting and, one by one, they filed into the Oval Office and took seats on the couches and occasional chairs spread throughout the large office. Although rain was in the forecast, the sun filtered through the large windows.

Stanley looked around the room as he began. "We will be visiting ten states in the next two weeks. You should have in your hands the list of those states. These are the critical states where the races are very close, and if we go in there and barnstorm, we can infuse some money into these candidates and help get the voters out there to vote for us. Let's go over the schedule and the security measures. Al, do we have law enforcement ready in these cities?"

Tom Wiley, the security advisor to the president answered. "We do. And we will have a clearance of a ten-mile radius. No demonstrators will be allowed into these areas."

"How about the press? Have they been notified? We need full newspaper, TV and radio coverage."

"We will have the media standing ready. And we will be boosting the number of ads before and after each visit to reinforce the impact."

"Janice, can you check on the guest lists and make sure these people have been invited to the speeches and the dinners?" James asked. Janice, a stout woman with graying short hair, was an assistant to the press secretary.

"Yes, Mr. President, I will do that immediately," Janice replied.

"Well, it appears that everything is in place. I don't want any mess-ups. One mistake and everything goes down the drain. We have the advantage and we are going to win in November." James gave his pep talk. "I don't think we will need to meet again unless something unforeseen happens. So let's go out there and get this job done. I am counting on each and every one of you."

Everyone left the room except Stanley.

"How is Mrs. Walters these days, Mr. President?"

"She's fine. Why do you ask?"

"When is she coming back to Washington? She should accompany you on these trips. Let me put it another way; you need to have her with you. The people need to see that your wife is with you a hundred percent."

"I know this. You don't have to tell me."

"People are asking, wondering, why she isn't back here with you. And if they don't see her campaigning with you, the whole country, the world, will be asking. Do you see what I'm getting at?"

"She'll be back by the end of the week. Like I've been telling everyone, she had some ranch business to take care of. I couldn't stay behind and do it, so I asked her to. And then she wanted to go to Boulder and visit our son Andrew."

"You need to get her back here. You can't do this campaigning without her. You don't want the public asking questions, do you?"

"No, I don't. She'll be back."

Carol looked at the digital alarm clock beside her bed—5 A.M. Sleep was not going to come to her this night. She got out of bed, pulled on some sweats over her large tee shirt and went into her office. She started up her computer and went straight to the news section of Yahoo and then to politics. The headline read, "Patriots in Tight Race" and another read "Walters Greatest Fundraiser in History". She scrolled down the page to "Pentagon to Ask for More Troops for Iraq." She started reading. *With the Iraq insurgency increasing and the deaths of American soldiers rising, the Pentagon is proposing to send even more troops to Iraq to try to stem the almost daily attacks against the Americans. It is thought that these attacks are coming from Saddam's Baathist loyalists, and if and when he is found, it is believed that increasing the presence of more troops will help to bring law and order and a halt to these attacks.*

She read on and thought of how politics shaped the world and people's lives. Thousands of people had died in Iraq, men, women and children all to remove a "dangerous dictator". Billions of U.S. taxpayer dollars would be spent to pay for it, while millions in the U.S. went without jobs, and poor families, families with children, were starving in this country. What a mixed-up world this was, and her husband was responsible for much of it.

She checked the messages on the answering machine. They were all from James. She did not want to talk to him just now. It was time to call her parents to let them in on her plans. She dialed her mother's number. Her mother, Ellen Banks, had remarried after divorcing her father ten years ago and had moved to Sacramento where she worked as an accountant for the state of California.

The phone rang about three times before her mother answered.

"Hi, Mother. I'm sorry to call you so early, but I wanted to catch you before you went to work."

"No, I was already up. Carol, honey, is something wrong?"

"Well, yes and no."

"Where are you? Are you calling from the White House?"

"No, I stayed back at the ranch to clear up some problems with Steve, one of the wranglers."

"I watched on TV when James was getting off Air Force One and you weren't with him, but I thought that you might have gotten off the plane later. Why aren't you in Washington with him? What is it, honey? You can tell me. You can always confide in your mother."

"I know, Mother. I thought I'd better tell you before you learn it from the press. I'm leaving James."

There was a long silence on the other end of the line. Finally her mother spoke. "Carol, are you sure you want to do this? Do you realize the implications? You are about to turn your life upside down. And what about James? It could ruin him politically."

"I think James will be fine. I have to think about my life."

"Why are you doing this? I know you haven't been happy the last couple of years, but you have a very good life and you should realize it and be thankful. Many women would give anything to be the First Lady."

"Mother, I don't have a good life. I don't have my own life. Everything I do is for James and the White House. Do you realize what I have to do as First Lady? I am an ambassador when foreign officials visit and I entertain the wives of heads of state. I am the official hostess for the White House, coordinating all of the parties and galas, and I'm in charge of the household in general with a hundred staff members, making sure everything runs smoothly. This is a huge job and do I get paid for it? Do I even get credit? No. The American people get two for one. What would they do if James weren't married? They would have to hire someone to do all of this and pay them."

As she was telling her mother these things she thought about how demanding her job was. It required twelve to fourteen hours of her time each and every day, seven days a week organizing and attending various social and political functions.

"And then I have to campaign with James," Carol continued, "spending endless days and nights away from home, giving speeches, shaking hands a million times until my hand starts to feel like a piece of wood, always smiling and having to be upbeat when I am really feeling lousy."

Carol thought about the dinners on the campaign trail. The menu read much like a Texas-style barbeque—chicken, spareribs, potato salad, baked beans, and bread, lots of bread. She would fill her plate with all of the highly caloric foods so that it would appear that she was thoroughly enjoying every morsel, then try to eat as little as possible. And she was constantly dieting to compensate for the campaign cuisine.

"All of this to get James reelected. Mother, I'm a private person. I love being at home with my family. I love cooking and gardening, having the time to take a walk. Do you realize, if I want to take a walk, I have to put it on the schedule so that the Secret Service can approve a walk plan?"

"And what do I get for all of this? Constant criticism. If I cut my hair too short, I'm not feminine enough. If I let it grow too long, I'm a siren. They even criticize my clothes. When I dress conservatively, I'm frumpy. If I wear a gown from a high-fashion designer, I'm called extravagant."

Her mother's voice broke into her thoughts, "Carol, you must have known all of this when you agreed with James to run for office.

Why are you backpedaling now?"

"I'm not backpedaling," Carol said in defense of her decision. "And those aren't the main reasons why I'm doing this. It's because I don't believe in what James stands for anymore. He has changed and he is getting in way over his head. Washington is an ugly place and there are ugly things happening there, and I can't go along with these policies, like the war in Iraq and killing thousands of people."

"You were always an idealist. But if you carry through with this, it could be to your detriment. I don't support this, but I will always be there for you. I love you and I am very worried."

"Don't worry, Mother, I'm going to be okay. I have to be true to myself first. I cannot live a lie."

"Have you filed the papers yet?"

"No. Not yet. I'm calling Marshal Dale today, and I'll try to see him tomorrow. I know tomorrow is Saturday, but if I tell him it's urgent, hopefully he will see me."

"Oh, I'm glad you're calling Marshal. He's a very good lawyer. I still think you're making a mistake, but you've always been strong headed, and you're not going to change now. I love you. Just keep in touch."

"I will, Mother. I love you, too."

And as she hung up the phone, her thoughts went back to the many nights she and James had talked late into the night about the problems with Congress and getting the defense budget approved and about foreign policy and how to deal with the Middle Eastern conflict between the Israelites and the Palestinians. He always listened to her views, but when it came down to it, her opinions meant very little to him or anyone else for that matter. And then, when the war had started, he stopped listening to her altogether. She felt that there was an unstoppable freight train going through Washington, and her viewpoint and tens of thousands of Americans viewpoints were meaningless.

She called her dad in Phoenix and received a similar reaction from him.

Her dad said, "Carol, be careful. This could be very dangerous for you. These are powerful forces you are dealing with, and if they think you are messing things up for them, they could take extreme measures."

"I know, Dad, but I don't think they'll do anything to me. The people of this country wouldn't put up with it."

"The people wouldn't even know. In fact, you shouldn't even be talking to me from this phone. They are watching you. Call me back from a pay phone."

"I can't call you back today. I'll call you later in the week."

"Just be very careful. I love you and I don't want to see you hurt."

"I will, Dad. I love you, too. Thanks for the advice."

She hung up the phone and went back to the bedroom to dress for a shopping trip into town. It was now 10:30 and she would be in Fort Collins by noon. According to standard operating procedure, she notified the Secret Service that she would be going.

About an hour later, Carol was driving down Main Street in Fort Collins with her agents following behind. She pulled up in front of Hal's Hamburgers and went inside to get some lunch. The Secret Service parked the black car in front of the restaurant and waited for her. While inside, Carol went to the restroom where there was a pay phone and called her attorney. When she dialed, the receptionist answered.

"I'd like to speak with Mr. Dale, please."

"I'm sorry, he's with a client right now. Can I have him call you?" the receptionist said.

"Let me speak with his secretary, please."

"One moment," she said with decorum.

Carol fiddled with the cord on the telephone and looked at the door behind her to see who was coming into the restroom and then down at the dirty floor where paper towels were strewn everywhere. A couple of minutes later another woman's voice answered. "Hello, this is Kristine. How can I help you?"

"Kristine, this is Mrs. Walters. I need to talk with Marshal. I know he is with another client, but this is very important. Can you please get him for me? It will only take a couple of minutes."

"Normally I wouldn't do that, but I will for you, Mrs. Walters. How's the president doing these days?"

"Fine, he's doing fine."

A few minutes later a deep male voice came on the line. "Carol, what's happening? Are you in some kind of trouble?" Marshal said with concern.

"Not exactly. I just need to see you. I can't talk about it on the phone. Could you make some time for me tomorrow? I know it's Saturday, but this can't wait another day."

"Well, my grandson has a soccer game in the morning but I guess I could come into the office in the afternoon. Let's say 1:30?"

"Perfect. I really appreciate this."

"How's the family and how is that husband of yours, you know, the president?"

"Everyone is healthy and James is doing well. Thanks again, Marshal. I'll see you tomorrow."

She hung up and then called her college roommate, Karen, in Denver and told her that she was coming to Denver on Saturday for business and asked if she could spend the night.

Andrew and Alison

Hey, Ali, I've been waiting for you. What took you so long?"

"I was late getting off work and then I played Ann Landers to Jody." Alison slid into the booth next to Andrew and ran her hand over his thigh. Andrew turned to her, kissed her on the cheek and smiled. "She's getting a raw deal from Dawson. I tried to clue her in that he's a loser."

"Always the little mother."

"I care. I hate to see her taken advantage of. This guy is sleeping around with half a dozen other women and he tells Jody she's the only one, and she believes him."

"How do you know he's sleeping with half dozen other women? Come to think of it, that doesn't sound too bad."

"I know some of the other women," Alison said as she disregarded his last statement.

"What's your brand of pizza? I would've ordered for you, but I thought I'd wait until you got here."

"Food and sex. That's all you think of," Alison winked at Andrew. "You know what I like, you should've ordered."

Andrew looked up from the menu, "You're changeable sometimes and I didn't want to take a chance. Vegetarian, sausage, pepperoni or all of the above."

"Vegetarian. Let's order half vegetarian and half pepperoni. I know you love the meat."

"You've got a deal."

The waiter returned and Andrew ordered the pizza and a

pitcher of Coors beer.

"Jody will have to fend for herself some day. She's only your roommate and she's a big girl now."

"There is some truth in that, but I like Jody and I don't want to see her get hurt."

"If it's not this guy, it'll be somebody else. She's going to have to figure it out for herself."

Alison stared straight ahead, not wanting to meet eyes with Andrew. The waiter brought the pitcher of beer and two iced glasses. Andrew poured a glass for Alison and then squeezed her hand.

"You okay?" he asked.

"Yeah, I'm all right."

"No, I don't believe you. Something's wrong."

Alison took a long drink of her beer. "Andy, are you seeing other women?"

Andrew looked down at the table for what seemed like a very long time.

"Would it matter if I were?"

"Yes, it would matter."

"I thought we were just friends."

"We are friends. But I want something more than that. If I am going to give my time and my body to you, I want some kind of commitment."

"Oh, the big C word," Andrew looked away from Alison.

"I don't think you're taking me seriously."

The waiter brought the steaming hot pizza on a round metal tray and set it down in front of them.

Andrew cut a piece of the vegetarian pizza for Alison, put it on the plate in front of her, then he took a piece of the pepperoni and put it on his plate and took a long drink of his beer.

"Let's talk about this later, okay."

"Sure. But I do want to talk about it. It seems like we say we're going to talk about something and we never do."

They started to eat the pizza and drink more beer. After Andrew had finished all of his pepperoni pieces and Alison all but one of the vegetarian, Andrew turned to her, touching her hand, "Let's go back to my place."

"We always go to your place. I'd like to go to my house for a change. Jody's gone out with that creep, Dawson, and we'll have the house to ourselves."

Andrew agreed, paid the bill and they left.

"Do you want to walk? It's only a couple of blocks," Alison said.

"I have to let Joe and Darryl know," Andrew said, referring to the two Secret Service men assigned to him.

"You always have these guys following you?"

"One of the joys of being part of the first family."

"Guess you can't have very many secrets," Alison said as they walked over to the Ford Bronco parked in front of the pizza restaurant.

"You've got that one right."

Andrew talked to the two men in the Bronco for several minutes and then he turned to Alison, "Let's go."

Holding hands, they started walking north on Broadway and then turned onto Walnut, with the Secret Service in the Bronco following slowly behind them. Fortunately there was very little traffic on Walnut. The sky was clear and the evening had started to cool down, so Alison pulled on the jeans jacket that she had tied around her waist. Andrew put his arm around her, "Are you cold?"

"A little. It's not very far."

They walked the rest of the way in silence. Reaching the walkway that led up to Alison's house, Andrew again took her hand and led her to the front door of the fifties ranch house. Alison turned the knob and found it to be locked, so she searched in her purse for the key and, finding it, unlocked the door.

"Hey, Jody. Are you here?" Alison called out as they walked into the living room furnished with thrift shop furniture. An oversized couch with an off-white slipcover dominated the center of the room with an old mission-style coffee table and a antique end table holding an old crystal lamp sitting on a doily. It was unmistakably a house occupied by females in the attention to detail and neatness.

Hearing no answer, Andrew put his arms around Alison and kissed her deeply on the lips and the neck, "I think we have the house to ourselves." He took off her jacket and started to pull her sweater over her head. Alison stopped him and led him to the couch.

"Andy, we still need to talk about this."

"About what?"

"Yeah. See, you've forgotten already. About our relationship."

"Ali, I haven't forgotten. But let's go into the bedroom first and then we can talk."

"No, we're going to talk right now," Alison said firmly.

Andrew pulled back from Alison and crossed his arms in front of him, "I thought you liked it like this. You're free to see other people."

"I don't want to see other people, I want to see you," Alison looked straight at Andrew. "You know, Andy, we're spending a lot of time together and I would like to think that it is leading somewhere." They both sat down on the couch and Alison pulled her knees up to her chest while Andrew sprawled his legs out and laid his head back.

"You still have a couple of years of undergraduate work and then law school. I graduate next spring, but there aren't any jobs out there so I guess I'll keep on going to school. We just don't know what is ahead of us. And it doesn't look very good right now."

"That's no excuse. Think about if couples during the depression of the thirties decided not to get married and have children, you might not be here right now. Your grandparents wouldn't have had your parents and. . . ."

Andrew sat up and looked at Alison. "Marriage? Is that what you're thinking about. Having kids? Ali, I'm not ready to settle down at this point in my life. Everything is too jumbled. My parents, my career, school. I'm just not ready."

Alison lowered her legs off the couch and turned to face Andrew. "I understand what you are saying and that's okay. Maybe it's not time to talk about marriage, but if you are going to be sleeping with me I want to know that I am the only one."

"Oh, that's what this is about. Ali, you are the only one. I don't have time for anyone else right now, you are taking up all of my spare time."

"You're making it sound like a chore," Alison said with a frown on her face. "Don't you love me?"

Andrew laughed. "Yes, I love you. I didn't mean for it to sound like that. Don't be so sensitive." He pulled Alison over to him and started to kiss her on the mouth and Alison melted into his body. "Now where were we when we came in?"

The Saga Begins

Saturday morning arrived much too soon for Carol. As had been her habit lately, she awoke before her 5:30 A.M. alarm went off. This was not going to be an easy day, she thought as she lay in bed for another few minutes.

She then got up, showered and dressed in clothes that would make her appear to look like her housekeeper—Levis, a blue sweatshirt and sneakers. She was about the same size as Nancy, so she could easily pass for her. She then called Paul Bartello, one of her Secret Service agents. The phone rang five times and Carol hoped they wouldn't answer. Luck was not with her.

"Can we help you, Mrs. Walters?" Karl answered the phone with a sleepy voice.

"Karl, I'm sorry to disturb you at this hour. I just wanted to tell you that I'll be staying in all day today. I have the stomach flu and I don't want any calls."

"Sorry to hear you're not feeling well. We'll take any calls for you. Is there anything else we can do?"

"No, not right now. I'm sending Nancy to the store to pick up some ginger ale and Pepto-Bismal. I know I'll be better tomorrow, thanks."

Carol then walked out the service entrance in the back of the house and got into Nancy's green '95 Honda Civic hatchback to drive to Denver. She had made these arrangements the day before with Nancy and felt confidant that she could be trusted. Nancy had worked for the Walters family for eight years. She told Nancy to tell anyone who asked that she was not feeling well and would be in bed most of the day. She didn't want the Secret Service to know where she was going and with whom she would be meeting in Denver. She thought James would be occupied with the heavy campaigning this week, and she would be back at the ranch tomorrow before anyone noticed.

Carol drove out the long driveway, through the gate and onto the main road just as the sun was peaking over the hills to the east. Once on Highway 25, the freeway going into Denver, Carol began to relax and think that she had made her escape. Intrigue and lies were not in her bag of tricks, but this was the only way to prevent the Secret Service from following her.

It was 7:00 A.M. by the time Carol arrived at the outskirts of Denver, even though she drove the speed limit most of the way. She certainly didn't want to get a speeding ticket. She turned off the freeway onto Interstate 6 toward Arvada where Karen lived. She was going to leave some of her things there, and then she and Karen were having breakfast together.

Karen's house was in an older neighborhood with stucco bungalow-style homes on a street with large trees standing guard. She drove into the driveway, got out of the car and went up to the front door and rang the bell. It was a couple of minutes before Karen opened the door, dressed in a terry robe, just out of the shower.

"Hey, Carol. It's so good to see you. Come on in." Karen hugged Carol. Slim and about the same height as Carol, Karen's dishwater blond hair was cut in a short bob and her blue-gray eyes could be piercing at times.

"It's good to see you, too."

"Why don't you go into the kitchen and grab a cup of java. I'm going to get dressed and then we'll go over to Le Peep in the Town and Country shopping center for breakfast."

"Sounds good to me." Carol walked through the living room and into the kitchen to get her coffee, then took it back into the living room and sat down on the sofa. She picked up a *Newsweek* magazine laying on the coffee table. James' face stared back at her from the cover and she shivered. She just couldn't get away from him. Twenty minutes later Karen walked back into the living room, dressed in gray flannel slacks and a burgundy paisley shirt.

"Ok, I'm ready. Sorry to keep you waiting, but I see you're reading about that fabulous husband of yours."

"Yeah. Fabulous husband."

"You want to take my car or yours. But that's not your car. Whose car are you driving?"

"It's Nancy's car. Mine is in the shop," Carol lied. "Let's take yours. Can I put my, uh, Nancy's car in the garage?"

"Sure. You are so mysterious," Karen laughed.

"No, I don't think so," Carol tried to sound nonchalant.

"I was just joking. It's really good to see you. We have so little time together these days. You being the First Lady and all."

They jockeyed the cars around and got into Karen's blue Ford Bronco and drove to Le Peep. Once seated at a table, Karen ordered scrambled eggs and whole-wheat toast and Carol ordered French toast.

"So how is life at the White House these days. Hey, why aren't you there?"

Carol explained that she was taking care of some business at the ranch.

"Is something wrong, Carol? You look kind of peaked."

"Things are not totally as they should be, but I can't talk about it right now."

"Why the secrecy?"

"I just can't tell you right now. You have to trust me. But when the time is right, I will fill you in. Now, tell me, how's work going?"

"Work is as hectic as always. My caseload increases in a down economy. I am working on a case right now where this woman was terminated for not wanting to work overtime. She's 59 years old and having a hard time finding another job."

"Can an employer do that?"

"Technically, no. But proving it is another story."

"That's rough. There aren't any jobs out there. Did you know that we've lost four million jobs in this country in the last three years, and I don't think we're creating any new ones except in the defense industry? It's understandable that she can't find work. What kind of work does she do?" Carol interjected.

"She's a programmer and was on salary, so they weren't paying her overtime and she refused to come in to work weekends when they asked her. She said that she had to look after her granddaughter. I guess her daughter was in some kind of trouble and she was helping out. But her boss told her that they had too many projects and they needed her to work sixty hours a week. Of course they just laid off three programmers in her group, so she was supposed to pick up the slack. They hadn't laid her off because she was paid the smallest amount. Employers trying to squeeze as much as possible."

"The tech industry has been hit hard by this recession. Do you think she'll win?"

"We're approaching this from the age discrimination standpoint. That's the only hope we have. Yes, I think she will. But labor laws are changing fast and the worker has very little clout these days."

"This is what happens in a recession," Carol said.

"I know. Too many people chasing too few jobs. And then these companies are outsourcing jobs to India and China. They pay them six thousand instead of sixty thousand to improve the bottom line."

"And the CEOs win with the big bonuses. There is no fairness. Not to change the subject, how's your love life these days? Are you dating anyone?"

"My love life? Non-existant. I don't have time for dating right now. My career is too important and I'm perfectly happy with the single life. The last guy I was dating dumped me because I was always working and never had time to go out with him, and I don't blame him."

"Well, let me tell you, being married is not all that wonderful."

"I thought you were in love with James."

"I am. I was. I'll explain later."

"Carol, this all sounds so ominous."

They finished breakfast and then drove back to Karen's house.

"Bring your bag into the house. I have the guest bedroom ready for you," Karen said.

"Thanks. I want to change clothes before I go downtown. I'm going to do some shopping and then I have an appointment with my attorney at 1:30. I should be back by 4:00. Do you have plans for dinner? I could stop by the store and pick up some salmon and we could eat in tonight. I'll even pick up a video; what's your pleasure?"

"That sounds perfect. I won't be home until about 7:00, if you can wait that long for dinner. And a video, your choice."

"7:00 is fine with me. I'll see you then."

"This will be just like having a wife, uh, husband, whatever, to come home to." Karen decided not to press Carol for any more answers to her questions, but the fact that Carol was seeing her attorney raised a flag.

The Campaign Trail

The motorcade of Secret Service, unmarked police cars and limousines wound it's way from Sky Harbor airport to 24th Street north to Van Buren. The Republican rally was to take place at the Civic Center with a $2,000-a-plate dinner at the Hyatt Regency Hotel across the street. Like all other events, the rally was by special invitation only, and if you had the money, belonged to the Patriot party and supported James Walters, you could attend the dinner.

The streets were empty of any other traffic and no pedestrians were allowed within a five-mile radius. Two or three motorcycle cops hugged every street corner and local police cars patrolled the streets to ensure the security. As the entourage came closer to the Civic Center, there were perhaps a hundred men and women carrying placards and shouting, "We Love Walters" over and over again with Fox News Channel 10 and Channel 12 TV camera crews filming. Attractive female reporters, holding microphones, were reporting the arrival of the president, who was making an appearance in their community.

About a mile and a half away there was a very different kind of demonstration that the TV cameras never saw. Pushed together behind temporary fences, one thousand to fifteen hundred people had gathered. They carried placards, but the message was not the same. "Stop the War" and "Stop Killing Iraqi Children" were carried by some of the people. Others carried signs saying "Stop Power Plant Pollution" or "Save Trees for Our Grandchildren". And then some of the signs said, "Women Have the Right to Choose". These were not anarchists and they were not the hippies of the sixties and seventies; they were office workers, 65-year-old women, housewives, students and some children. The riot police almost outnumbered the crowd, dressed in black uniforms with bulletproof vests and black riot helmets, and they carried automatic guns and nightsticks. They were pushing back the crowd to make sure that they stayed within the boundaries of the fencing, and because it was a relatively small area, the people were packed in like cattle in a stockyard and there was a lot of pushing and jostling to get the signs in the air so they could be seen. But there was no one there to see them. The press had been kept away and the motorcade would not be driving by. President James Walters, it was reported, totally disliked dissent, so whenever an opposing demonstration was planned, the people were always herded into a designated area far from the president and far from the main event where the press would be reporting. It made him angry to see these demonstrations and he oftentimes would lose his temper and shout obscenities.

"Damn those protestors. They should be all rounded up and put in jail to rot for the rest of their lives," James had said.

As the people were milling about, one of the policemen fired a rubber bullet at an older, overweight woman who was trying to get out of the barricade. It hit her in the stomach and she fell to the ground. The crowd reacted by jeering and pushing at the police, and the police retaliated by using pepper spray on the crowd and the mayhem began.

About this time, one lone photographer from the *New Times*, a tabloid publication, had managed to dodge the tight security and was taking photos of the scene unraveling before him. The police, in the process of wrestling with the woman who had fallen and another woman who was her friend, had little time to deal with the photographer. They had both of the women on the ground and were handcuffing them in preparation for arrest, and it was all captured on film. Eventually other policemen closed in on the photographer and tried to take his camera away, but he was a slippery sort and was able to dodge between them and escape into the alley behind.

Back at the Civic Center, several thousand people had gathered to hear President Walters speak.

"I have served you well in the last three and a half years, but we are at a pivotal moment in the history of this country. I have waged the war against terrorism and made this great country safer with the new Homeland Security Agency." President Walters spoke from the podium and the crowd clapped enthusiastically. "I have passed a bill that provides prescription drug assistance for the elderly and the poor. And I have lowered your taxes. You now have more money in your pocket to spend or save." The applause arose from the crowd. "And this is creating jobs and turning the economy around. The Democrats don't have a plan; we do and we will, with the help of the Patriot and Republican House and Senate, implement that plan." More clapping. "We will insure that there will be jobs for the loggers in allowing them access to our forests to harvest and thin the trees to keep them healthy and free of fire." Applause. "Hundreds of jobs are being created in your state by defense companies." More applause. "This is the greatest country in the world, but we will have to work hard to keep it that way. If you want to see this country safe, if you want to protect your freedoms against dictators like Saddam Hussein, we are the party for you. We are dedicated to eradicating weapons of mass destruction around the world." Applause. "We will continue the long war against al-Qaeda until every one of them is brought to trial, convicted and put away forever." More clapping. "We are committed to you, the people of this country and we will work for you in the next four years."

And with the final words of a very short speech, President Walters left the podium, surrounded by his aids and Secret Service men to make the trip across the street to the Hyatt Regency.

After the usual campaign fare of chicken and rice, shaking hands and patting backs, James retired to the Presidential Suite very late that night. He would stay one night in Phoenix, make a brief appearance in Tucson, a Democratic stronghold in Arizona, and then fly on to California, another state where the Democrats held the majority. The midterm elections two years ago had given the Patriots seats in the Senate and the House, but they had lost twenty state governors, and Arizona was one of those states where that occurred.

James took off his clothes and hung them neatly in the closet. He put on a terry robe over his boxer shorts and lay down on the bed thinking of the events of the day. Picking up the phone, he dialed the number at the ranch. There was no answer. He would try again in the morning. James was exhausted. The sixteen-hour days of intense work, speeches, talking to people, shaking hands, always a smile on his face for the photo ops was more than he bargained for. He really hated it. He preferred to be home, spending the evening by the fireplace and in bed early. But he had to admit that he loved the excitement of the crowds, the ovations he received and the challenge of convincing the public, in spite of his poor performance, that he was the man to lead them for the next four years. And he was somewhat dismayed that, no matter what he told them, they believed him, even though he was sometimes stretching the truth.

Appointment with Attorney

Carol changed into a lightweight wool, tan pantsuit with an ivory, mock-turtleneck silk sweater. She wore very conservative gold button earrings, her watch and her wedding rings. It was eleven o'clock when she left Karen's house, and so she decided to stop and do some shopping, but because too many people recognized her, she walked out of the shopping center, got back into her car and headed for downtown Denver. It was nearly one o'clock by the time she pulled into the garage of the Bank One building on Lincoln Street, and after parking the car on the third floor, Carol took the elevator to the tenth floor where the Dale, Goodsen and Battersby law firm occupied the entire floor.

She opened the massive glass door to the office suite and entered. As this was Saturday, there was no receptionist and Carol just sat down in one of the dark-blue velvet upholstered chairs to wait. Carol looked at her watch. Ten minutes had gone by, but then Marshal walked into the reception area. Athletic and trim at five feet eleven, his graying hair was the only indication of his sixty-two years.

"Carol. It is good to see you. Let's go to my office. Would you like some coffee or Evian?"

"Water would be fine. It's good to see you too, Marshal. Unfortunately most every time I do see you, I am having some kind of trouble. But, then you are accustomed to that, I would think."

"That is true." He led her back to his office and then went to get the water for Carol. Upon returning he took his seat in his black leather executive chair behind a massive oak desk piled with neatly stacked folders and papers. "What can I help you with, Carol?"

"Marshal, I'll come right to the point. I want to divorce James and I want to file this week. I've made up my mind. The sooner the better."

Marshal stared at Carol for a minute. "I remember when you two were married. I was at your wedding. Are you sure about this?"

"Yes, I am sure."

"I'm not going to try to talk you out of it, but wouldn't it be prudent to wait and think this over more carefully? This is not your ordinary divorce. If you waited until after the election. . . ."

"You're just like everyone else. No, I have thought this through and I want to do it now. So let's start drawing up the papers. How soon can we get it filed?"

"I can get it done by Friday or the following Monday at the latest. This is not a community property state, so you might have a battle on your hands. Is your name on the deed to the ranch?"

"I don't think so. The land was a gift from James' father. My name is on the deed to the house."

"Do you want to claim part of the ranch land as yours?"

"Yes. I helped build our ranching business and I am entitled to half of it."

"Are you going to ask for additional interim support money?"

"No, I have some money of my own and I think I'll be okay. Andrew has a trust fund that he can use for college. And then we can sell the ranch, and our savings and other holdings, if they are divided evenly, will give me enough until I can get my career back on track."

"You realize this could ruin him politically? He's at the pinnacle of his career and it could really hurt him."

"I'm aware of that, but James has an innate ability to survive and I am sure he will be fine. I have to take care of *me* and that is what I am going to do."

"Will you be going back to teaching?"

"No, I think I am going back to school, law school that is."

"Good choice. I think you would make an excellent lawyer."

"Thank you. You can send the papers to me at the ranch for a signature as soon as you have them. I won't be going back to Washington. Thanks for your help. I realize that this is going to be a battle, but hopefully we can minimize it. James will be preoccupied with campaigning in the next couple of months, and it will be difficult for him to fight two battles on two fronts at once."

"You are more political than I thought, Carol."

"I just want to get this done."

"I will send you the papers as soon as I have them processed."

"Thanks."

Carol shook Marshal's hand and walked out of the office. She took the elevator down to the third level of the parking garage. There were two men and a woman in the elevator with her, and they looked at her curiously but were too timid to speak to her. Carol never knew until she became First Lady how much she treasured anonymity.

She retrieved her car, drove out of the parking garage and onto the streets of Denver, got on the freeway and headed back to Arvada and Karen's house. It was still fairly early. She thought she could stop by an Arby's and pick up a garden sandwich and then she would pick up the food for dinner tonight along with the video. And if she got back early enough, she might have time for a nap. Freedom. She hadn't known freedom like this in three and a half years and she liked it.

"Carol. Are you here? Anybody home?" Carol raised her head from the soft down pillow. Was that Karen already? What time was it? Seven o'clock. She'd been sleeping for three hours.

"Karen, I'm in here. Just closed my eyes for a few minutes."

"Gosh, I thought you'd have dinner all ready for me," Karen cajoled.

"I will. I'll get up right now and start the grill."

"Relax. I'm joshing you. Let's have a glass of wine. Merlot or chardonnay or I have this wonderful sauvignon blanc."

"The sauvignon blanc sounds wonderful."

"In fact, I am doing the cooking and you are going to be the guest tonight."

"I'll go along with that, too."

Karen opened the wine, poured two glasses and took them into the living room, and Carol joined her. Karen's house was decorated in the California mission style with a large brown leather couch and love seat in the living room. Beside the couch was an oak end table in the same style with a fringed scarf on the top and a Tiffany lamp. It was a masculine look, but Karen's touches of a vase of fresh flowers and floral paintings on the walls softened everything, making it more feminine.

"So, friend, are you going to tell me what this is all about or do I have to ply you with alcohol and pry it out of you?" Karen searched Carol's eyes.

"I might as well. You'll know soon enough. I'm divorcing James."

Carol watched as Karen's eyes widened. "I know. Everyone is shocked. I mean everyone I've told so far—Mother, Dad and Andrew."

"And James. Have you told James yet?"

"Yes. I told him yesterday."

"And what did he have to say about it?"

"He's not happy, of course. But I can't be concerned about that."

"Why would you want to do this? Has he been unfaithful to you?"

"No. As far as I know. It's nothing like that."

"You've found another man who caters to your every whim?"

"No. I haven't looked at other men. I don't have time."

"His career. What about the elections?"

"I keep hearing this echo. What about the elections? Well, the elections are not important in the scheme of things. Let me try to explain this to you, and I'm thinking you will understand better than everyone else. You're a woman and a realist."

"I know I'm a woman and I like to think I'm a realist. But because I am pragmatic, I am concerned." Karen sipped her wine and was starting to feel quite mellow.

"I'm sure you must be aware of what is going on in Washington and the impact it is having on this country."

"Yes. Although I have to admit that I've been so busy, I haven't paid a lot of attention lately. The war in Iraq isn't going so well. Right?"

"That's one problem. But while the country's attention is on the war, a lot is happening behind the scenes. The environmental regulations governing power plants has been weakened, the environmental laws for the national forests have been thrown out and the new laws are weakened to allow unfettered logging. Corporations no longer have to clean up their own toxic waste; the taxpayer does that now and the list goes on."

"I've been reading of some of this in the newspaper and on the Internet. I heard about cutting off the United Nations funding for family planning because China was forcing women to abort babies."

"That's right, and when they do this, poor women in third world countries suffer. They are no longer providing family planning counseling or educating young women on reproductive issues, and these women have no access to birth control. Millions of babies will be born only to die of malnutrition, and mothers will die in childbirth, many of them leaving orphans behind."

"But can't the Senate override these decisions?"

"After the midterm elections, the Patriots gained a half dozen seats, and they won't go against the president. And the Republicans and some of the Democrats have been siding with the president. I don't know if they are afraid of this powerful group or maybe they are all making money from the war or something. I just don't really know. And that is why I am leaving James. I vehemently disagree with everything that is going on in this administration today. If I stay married to him, then I would have to support his agenda and the Patriot's, and I don't." Carol finished her wine and got up to fill her glass again.

"I thought you and James were on the same page."

"I thought we were, too. Something has happened to James. It's like he's been taken over by some unseen force. He doesn't listen to me anymore. We can't even talk about it without getting into a huge battle. There's an inside group of people running this show and they tell him what to do. I think he is in so deep now that it would be impossible for him to get out. He was bought and paid for by the corporations, the oil industry and others. They tell him what to do and he does it. The bills he's signing and the policies he's making are not good for the country and the American people."

Carol took another sip of wine and watched to see Karen's reaction.

"Why do you care? Why don't you just play the game along with everybody else? Why do you want to make trouble for yourself?"

"Because I am a member of the human race and I do care about my fellow man. Because I come from a middle-class family and I understand the plight of the common person."

"But you could just go along now and come out punching later. You'd have the recognition and the money."

"Karen, people are dying in Iraq. Sure, Saddam killed and tortured many of his own people, but now we are killing and torturing them. Men, women and children. Civilians. Families.

Thousands of them."

"The people seem to like him. The polls say that he has a sixty percent approval rating. I have been paying attention to that."

"I think the polls are skewed. The questions they ask will most always bring a positive answer. Like how do you think the president is handling the war on terror? Most people would say that he is doing a good job. They are constantly making noise about capturing this al-Qaeda operative and that terrorist suspect. If you're not aware, and most people are busy just like you, then you would think he's doing a great job."

There was silence as Karen absorbed all of this. Carol continued, "This administration is scripted, packaged and sold. They've hired public relations firms, advertising firms to sell their agendas. They have the best and they spend millions of dollars doing this."

"But they all do that, don't you think?"

"I'm sure they do, but not to the extent that James' administration does. Do you know when they hold town hall meetings, they carefully screen the audience to make sure that they are going to agree with the president. No dissenting allowed and what, may I ask, was our country built on? Dissent. The Boston tea party. Revolution. This is what has made our country great."

"Wow. Fascinating stuff. But, Carol, what does all this have to do with you? Even if you divorce him, you can't stop these things from happening. And if you stay with him and ride it out, you could divorce him after James is out of the White House and you'd have a lot more money and you could do what you like."

Carol gave Karen an icy stare.

"I told you I'm practical."

"I can't do that," Carol said.

"Do you think they'll let you divorce James?"

Carol hadn't thought about this before. "What do you mean, will they let me? I am an independent person, a citizen of this country. You think they would try to stop me?"

"They might. There is a lot at stake here. These are powerful people and there's millions, no billions of dollars on the table here. I'm not going to try to talk you out of this, but as a friend and an attorney, I would proceed with extreme caution."

"I will. I'll watch my back. I don't see how they could stop me, though."

"People have been killed for less."

"Are you trying to frighten me out of doing this? Because that is even more reason for me to go ahead with it."

"Carol, you haven't changed a bit. Same stubborn person I knew in college. I don't mean that in a negative way. You're my friend and I don't want to see you get hurt. Do you have a good attorney? One you can trust?"

"Yes, Marshal Dale. He's a friend of the family, my family, and he's handled legal problems for us before."

"Maybe you should get someone who specializes in divorces, a real shark. I know Marshal and he's a good attorney. . . ."

"Marshal is a friend of the family and I trust him. He will have my best interest in mind."

"I hope this works out for you, Carol. I am worried for you. Just remember that I am here for you if you ever need help. We haven't been friends all of these years for nothing."

"I appreciate that. Don't worry. I'll come out okay. And then I'm thinking I will go to law school and do what you do, help people with problems."

"You are an idealist, but I love you for it. Now, let's fix some supper before I get too drunk."

Karen and Carol went into the kitchen. Karen grilled the salmon and Carol prepared a salad and they sat down to the sumptuous meal.

Nancy was in the kitchen cleaning the oven and thinking about Carol. She thought about how unusual it was that Carol had asked to borrow her car. Carol had confided in her how confined she felt since becoming the First Lady and how she just wanted to steal away for a day of shopping, and Nancy wanted to help her out. But now she was worried. Would she get into trouble for this? No, she reasoned, Carol was her employer, not the Secret Service. Still, she was having second thoughts.

This was Saturday and Carol had been gone since early yesterday morning and, so far no one had inquired about her. Nancy reasoned that Carol had made a clean getaway and she would be home tonight and no one will have noticed. She heard the front doorbell ring and hoped someone else would answer the door. It rang again and then she remembered that she was the only one in the house at the moment. She went to open the door. Looming before her were Carol's two Secret Service agents, Karl and Paul.

"May we come in ma'am?" Karl asked.

"Uh, sure, come on in," Nancy stuttered. These guys always intimidated her. She led the two men, wearing dark slacks, white shirts and ties, into the living room.

"We would like to talk to Carol. Will you go and get her?" Paul asked, staring straight at Nancy.

"She's not feeling well and is not receiving guests today."

"We are not guests, miss, we are her agents and we need to see her, now," Karl said insistently.

"No. I'm following her orders. She said she didn't want to be disturbed by anyone."

"Look, the president, her husband has been trying to call her and can't reach her. He is very worried about her. Now be a good girl and bring her in here so that we can see that she is all right," Karl continued to press her.

"I can't." Nancy looked around the room as if she were looking for a way out of this. If she lied to them, she would be in trouble. If she told the truth, she would still be in trouble.

"What do you mean you can't? Are you saying she isn't here?" Karl looked at Paul knowing this wasn't getting them anywhere.

"No, I'm not saying that." Nancy was visibly upset.

Paul stepped closer to Nancy. "You can tell us. Where is she? The president needs to know," Paul softened the tone. "If she's not here, we need to know. Her life could be in danger. There are really bad people out there who are enemies of the president, and if they could find a way to harm the president in any way, they would. They could do this by hurting Carol. So, you have to tell us where she is."

Nancy stepped back. She thought for a few minutes. When he put it this way, it made sense for her to tell them. She would be saving Carol's life. But then Carol might be really angry with her and she could be fired. But Paul and Karl weren't going to leave without an answer.

"She went shopping," Nancy said dejectedly, thinking, how did I get myself into this.

"Where did she go? Did she take your car?"

"I don't know exactly where she went. I think she said Denver, but I don't know where in Denver." Nancy was telling the truth. "She told me that she just wanted some time on her own. Mrs. Walters has been under a lot of pressure and a woman needs time to herself."

Karl looked at Paul. They had to get her back; it was their job to know where she was at all times. "Paul, you call the president. I will get some help down here. We have to find her."

"I was just trying to help."

"You didn't do anything wrong," Karl said, trying to appease her in hopes of getting more information out of her. "When did she say she would be back?"

"Today. She left yesterday morning and was planning on staying overnight."

"Did she tell you where she was staying?"

"No. I have no idea."

"You can tell us. We aren't going to punish you."

"I don't know. I would tell you if I did."

"Paul, check every hotel in Denver and see if she is registered."

"She could have used an alias and she's most likely left the hotel by now."

"You're right. I'll have to call the president and let him know what is happening here. This is not going to be pretty." Karl knew that his job could be on the line for letting Carol slip away like this. This was good duty and he didn't want it to end.

"Why don't you just wait until she comes back? She should be back by this afternoon," Nancy said in earnest.

Paul looked at Karl and said, "We can't do that. We have to find her."

Carol's cell phone started ringing. She pulled off the freeway onto a side street, and by the time she had gotten to a safe place, she had missed the call. She looked at the number of the last incoming call and saw that it was from Nancy and she called her back.

"Nancy, you called me?"

"Yes, they were here looking for you."

"Who was there?"

"The agents. They wanted to talk to you."

"And what did you tell them?"

"I'm sorry, Missus Walters. I had to tell them that you'd gone shopping."

"Did you tell them where I'd gone?"

"I just told them that you'd gone in to Denver. That's all I said. They said that you could be in danger, and I started to worry about you."

"It's okay, Nancy. I'm not angry with you. I shouldn't have put you in this position. I'm on my way home. You can tell them to stop looking for me."

"I did. I told them to wait. That you'd be home this afternoon. They're checking the hotels. They're calling the president. I'm so sorry."

"It's okay, Nancy, don't worry about it. I'll see you later this afternoon."

Carol drove back onto the freeway. It was eleven o'clock on Sunday morning and she would be back at the ranch by early afternoon. She had taken her time this morning. She and Karen had a leisurely breakfast in Karen's kitchen in their pajamas. They had talked for about an hour before Karen decided that she really needed to get in to work to get a head start on the Monday morning workload. Carol then put on her jeans and a dark blue sweatshirt, packed up the few personal things she had brought with her and left the house, driving slowly through north Denver.

Carol stopped at a shopping center in Longmont and strolled through the indoor mall window shopping and watching the people. She often thought lately that she would like to be just a common person, not the First Lady of the land. Now she was going to make that happen, but she knew she would never be just that ordinary person. She wondered how people would remember her. Would they think she was a horrible woman for deserting the president in his time of need? Or would they think of her as a very brave person, who stood up for what she believed in spite of the possible consequences? Would her actions change the course of history, causing James to lose the election and bring the Democrats into power? And, most importantly, was this her motive for divorcing James? She didn't want to believe that she was doing this for political reasons, but if

James lost the election, she wouldn't be sorry. She didn't believe in what James and the party stood for anymore. In fact, Carol had never been a member of the party before she married James. Her parents had always been Independents and Carol followed suit, voting for the person she felt most qualified. When she started dating James and then was considering marriage, she didn't think too much about James' political affiliation. Weren't the parties pretty much the same? Then the Patriots party split from the more moderate Republican party and they recruited James to run for the presidency. They had the backing of some very powerful groups with a lot of money behind them. James, of course was flattered that he had been chosen and jumped at the chance to run for president, and Carol was excited, too that she was a part of this. But as she saw the policies they were making, she began to have reservations about this new party and the administration. And it wasn't until the last midterm election that she began to truly see what the Patriots party stood for and it wasn't for the good of the people of this great country. It was a party of power and greed, and Carol wanted no part of it.

Carol turned off Highway 25, turning north on 287. She observed the automobiles around her. Was she being followed? And then she wondered what was ahead of her when she returned. No doubt she would get a tongue lashing from the Secret Service. They constantly worried when she was out of their sight.

She turned onto the road leading to Mountain Sky Ranch, driving through the old wooden gate with the ranch branding insignia in the shape of the silhouette of three mountain peaks on it. Her eyes were drawn to the ranch house where there were about ten more cars than usual. Had James come back to get her? She hoped not. She drove up close to the house, and Karl and Paul burst out the front door followed by Nancy and some other men she had never seen before. Apparently James was not here.

"We've been very worried about you, Mrs. Walters. Where have you been?" Karl gave her that very stern look when he was angry with her.

"I just went into Denver to see a friend and do some shopping. Is that a crime?"

"You know the rules, Mrs. Walters. You are to let us know where you are at all times and we are to accompany you on shopping trips. In other words, you are not to go anywhere without us. Do you not understand that?" Paul was almost yelling at her. They were undoubtedly in trouble with their supervisor and the president.

"Do you realize this might have been an international incident? You could have been kidnapped and held for ransom. There are bad people out there who would like to do harm to your husband and this country," Karl chimed in.

I guess they don't really care what happens to me she thought, just national security and my husband.

"Hi, Nancy. I brought your car back. I'll drive it around back."

"No problem, I'll do that. I am so sorry, Mrs. Walters. I had to tell them."

"Don't you worry. You did the right thing."

Carol pulled her one small overnight bag out of the car and walked up the steps and into the house. She ignored Karl and Paul and all of the others. They were right. There was a danger going off alone without the Secret Service, but she no longer cared about such things. She wondered what would happen once they all found out about the divorce. Does the Secret Service cover divorced spouses for life? She hoped not. But there was no precedent for this. A First Lady has never divorced a sitting president.

She took her things to the bedroom and then went to her office to check for messages. The first seven messages were from James, then a message from Karen and one from Andrew. The messages from James were all pretty much the same, asking, no, demanding to know where she was and when she was coming back to Washington. She played the message from Karen.

"Carol, are you all right? They called here for you. I didn't know what to tell them. I said you had been here and left this morning. I hope you're okay. Call me if you need me."

"Hi, Mom," Andrews voice came from the answering machine. "I'm just calling to see how you are. Call me when you get in. I love you."

Just as she had finished listening to her messages the phone rang. It had a very pregnant ring. Carol hesitantly picked up the receiver.

"Hello, this is Carol speaking."

"Carol, where have you been?" James roared. "I have been so worried about you. Karl called me and said that you were missing."

"I wasn't missing. I just went shopping."

"It doesn't matter what you were doing, they couldn't find you. Do you realize the trouble you've caused?"

Carol was silent. She wasn't ready for another lecture.

"Don't do that again, do you hear?" James said.

Carol picked up a pencil and started to doodle on a notepad. She was being treated like a child.

"When are you coming back to Washington?"

"Remember, I told you last week that I would not be coming back."

"Carol, I'm in Texas campaigning. I'll come up there tonight and let's talk about this."

"We can talk about it. But I'm not changing my mind."

"I'll see you tonight." James hung up the phone.

The sun was just setting in the cloudless sky in the west behind the corral when the presidential caravan came rolling down the rode of the Mountain Sky Ranch. The lead car, a black Lincoln

Navigator bristling with antennas, pulled up to the portico leading to the veranda of the main ranch house and parked. Three others followed suit, including the black Lincoln Town Car carrying the president. As the president opened the back door of his car, the Secret Service all exited their vehicles and stood at the ready to protect him. Carol watched the spectacle from behind the curtain of the spacious ranch house living room.

James leapt up the steps to the front door and, opening it, walked into the foyer.

"Carol, are you home?"

"Yes, James. I am here. I'm in the living room."

James opened one of the French doors and walked into the room. His eyes met with hers and they both stood for a moment.

"Won't you have a seat?" Carol offered as if she were meeting him for the first time. James accepted and sat on the oversized tan leather couch while Carol sat in the large oriental chair next to the couch.

"I had no idea this was happening," James said as he looked at his wife.

"I know that. You are in a different world now."

"I thought maybe you'd change your mind. You know what this will do to me don't you?"

"Politically? It doesn't matter. I have to do what is good for me not what is good for you."

"I love you, Carol. I always have. You are the mother of our child. Don't do this."

"I have to. I have to preserve my life and keep my personhood. I have been merely an extension of you for the last four years. I have a lot to offer this world and I want a chance to do that."

"But you could if you stayed with this. Don't you understand that?"

"No, I don't think so. If you look at other First Ladies throughout history, they have been ostracized for thinking for themselves. Hillary when she tried to introduce health care reform. Eleanor Roosevelt was successful in standing up for women's rights and became a diplomat, but many people ridiculed her for doing so. And Ladybird Johnson contributed greatly with her roadside beautification program, but most other First Ladies have played the traditional female role of running the household and acting as a super-hostess. I want more. I want a say in our government. I know what this nation needs and I want to be able to have a chance to make this country and the world a better place to live for everyone."

"You weren't the one the people elected. They elected me to represent this country."

"How arrogant. That's exactly what I would expect you to say. Just because they elected you doesn't mean that I don't have ideas too, and I want to be able to express those ideas and have a chance to make a difference in this country and the world, and I don't want to have to do it through you. Do you understand that?" Carol was standing now and pacing back and forth in front of James.

"And why can't you do that? Who's stopping you? Certainly not me."

"Your party is stopping me. My views on how this country should be run are diametrically opposed to the Patriots party, your party's views. I want a world of peace. I don't want my son to die in some far-off country from a mortar shell."

James interrupted her, "Well, that's never going to happen. I'll see to that."

"You're missing the point. I don't want anybody's son dying that way. We can settle differences diplomatically by talking with our heads and mouths instead of guns."

"Carol, you are naive. It is a mean world out there and some countries won't listen to words. Guns are the only way."

"I don't think so. I also want to see a country, a world where a good education is available to everyone. Where everyone at least has a chance at a good job, one where they can make enough money to support a family and buy a house and have a vacation. And if they can't get a job, if they are mentally ill or sick in some other way, they don't have to beg on the street for handouts. Do you realize that many of the homeless people on our streets today are veterans? That is shameful."

James closed his eye as if he was trying to close his ears, he didn't want to hear this.

"And I want to see a world where the beautiful forests and lakes and streams will be preserved for my grandchildren and their children to come. This is not the same world your party envisions."

"Won't you reconsider?" James was begging now. So unlike him.

"I would reconsider under one condition." Carol sat down again and looked directly into James eyes.

"And what is that?"

"If you would not run in this election."

"Are you mad?" James was off the couch now, pacing. "I can't do that. I have an obligation to the party and the people of this nation and I have to carry through with it."

"What is more important, our marriage and our life together or being president?"

"Carol, you don't understand. You don't know what it is like. I have so many enemies; I have to watch my back every minute, literally. I can't even trust my own cabinet members or the vice president. They would all stab me in the back if they had a chance. I have no friends, you are my only friend and now I'm losing you, too."

"Then step down. We can go back to the ranch and repair our marriage and get on with our lives."

James was silent for several minutes and then he said, "I have promises to keep."

"I've filed the papers. You should get them in a day or two."

"Oh." James paused for a moment and looked straight at Carol with pleading eyes. "You know I thought we had a pretty good life together. I thought we were partners."

"We did have a good life until you became president. Then things started to change and not for the better."

"But this is only for eight years. After that we can name our ticket. We are going to be wealthy beyond your wildest dreams. We can have anything we want."

"Is that why you became president? For the money? What about the people of this country who've lost jobs? What about the soldiers who are fighting and dying in the Middle East? I thought you cared about people. That's why I can't support you and your effort in Washington."

Carol got up from her chair and walked over to the large window looking out on the mountains to the west. Then she turned back to face him. "You know, James, I can't sleep with you anymore. I can't make love to you knowing the decisions you've made are responsible for people dying. And I can't live a lie."

James lowered his head and thought about what Carol was saying. "If we hadn't invaded Iraq, many more people would be dying."

"Do you really believe that?"

"Yes, I do."

"And that's why I can't be with you anymore."

"Look, Carol, we have to keep very quiet about this. How many people have you told?"

"Only those closest to me—Andrew, my mother and dad, and my lawyer of course." She didn't mention Karen because she didn't want her dragged into this.

"Well, this sounds final. I have to go. We are flying on to

California tonight. California has the most electoral votes of any state and if we can lock them in, we will have the opposition beat." He walked toward the door and then turned to Carol. "Maybe you'll change your mind."

"No, James this is final. I won't change my mind."

As James walked out the door, tears welled up in her eyes and spilled down her cheeks. This was the beginning of the end of her life as she knew it. And what would her future be? She admitted to herself that she was just a little frightened. She got up and went into her office to call Andrew.

"Are you okay, Mom? I was worried. I called earlier and Nancy said you had gone into the city."

"So is everyone. Yes, I'm fine. I went to Denver to see my lawyer and have the divorce papers drawn up."

"You're really going through with this?"

"I said that I was. Yes. Your dad knows. In fact he was just here. He's not happy, but I can't help that."

"Please call me often and let me know how you are doing. I hope this works out for you and for Dad. You know I care for him too and I don't want to see him hurt."

"He's very strong. And politically, I doubt this will affect the election that much."

"Take care of yourself and be careful. I'll try to come to the ranch this weekend. Love you."

"Love you too, Andrew."

Carol looked out of the window at the cerulean sky and the red glow on the mountains in the distance. She was tired. She got up to go into the kitchen to see if she could put together a light supper. And then she was going to bed where she could finish the mystery she had been reading for about a month now. Maybe that would take her mind off all of the week's events.

When she reached the bedroom, she put on her pink and blue

flannel pajamas. James never let her wear them when he was there. In fact, he did not like to have her wear a nightgown, but Carol always did because she felt uncomfortable sleeping nude. Now she could wear her flannels whenever she pleased.

She pulled down the covers, and Buffy and Opal jumped onto the bed before she climbed in. Pulling up the pink satin down comforter around her, she opened her book and started reading. Ten minutes later, her eyes were closing and she turned off the light and snuggled in for the night.

Secret Service

How could you let her get away from you? You know that your boys are to stay with her at all times. Do you realize the trouble we're in? This could have been an international incident. Anything could have happened. A terrorist could have taken her and held her hostage."

Chief Agent Mark Bowerman sat in Director Nick Hopkins' office listening to the tirade and nodding his head in agreement.

"Yes, sir. I know, sir."

"But if you know, why did you let it happen?"

"I don't know, sir. She just slipped away. I talked with Karl and Paul and they said that she told them she was sick and was going to stay in bed for the day. And they believed her. And then they thought better of it and decided to check it out and she was gone."

The Secret Service Agency, a special services agency, has been assigned to protect the presidents and their families since 1894 when they began part-time protection of President Grover Cleveland and then assumed full time responsibility after the assassination of President William McKinley. The agency was first created July 5, 1865, in Washington to suppress counterfeit currency. They now assumed full responsibility for the protection of the president-elect, the president and his family while he or she is in office, and the vice president. The protection is continued for former presidents and their families for life.

"I'm warning you, Bowerman, if this happens again, I'll have your head."

"Yes, sir. It won't happen again. I'll personally see to that.

Cabinet Meeting

After a quick tour of California, making stops in Los Angeles and San Francisco and then traveling further up the coast to visit two liberal bastions, Portland and Seattle, President Walters arrived back in Washington late Wednesday evening. He was exhausted from the campaigning but also from the visit he had had with Carol. How would this divorce affect the election and his career? How would the public see this if his wife were not supporting him? And if she weren't behind him, would it be perceived that she also was not supporting his party's agenda? He was very worried, but he knew he had to get some rest. After checking his messages he retired to their bedroom at 10:30 and read for a while before falling asleep.

At 5:30 A.M. the alarm pierced the silence like a Duluth foghorn in summer. James pulled himself out of bed, stumbled into the shower, dressed and went downstairs to the Oval Office from the presidential apartment. Entering the office, he thought about how he belonged here. When he was a young boy he had always told everyone that he would one day be president of the United States of America. And now, here he was living his dream. Of course, it was true that he came from a long line of politicians, and his family had money, so it wasn't such a stretch for him to believe that he could achieve this. His father had served one term as president in the late eighties and before that had been a Republican Senator from Colorado. His grandfather had been a judge and then governor of Colorado. James certainly had a leg up.

He looked around at the office. The sun was shining in from the south lawn through the large windows framed by the gold, floor-length drapes. The large round area rug, the centerpiece of the room, was of a starburst design in gold, yellow and blue tones with the eagle seal of United States in the center. Each president designed his own rug and he thought his was one of the better ones. The walls were a pale yellow and the two Queen Anne occasional chairs in front of the fireplace were upholstered in blue and ivory silk. The room exuded history with portraits of former presidents; one of George Washington hung over the fireplace mantle and a portrait of Abraham Lincoln by the door. Busts of Winston Churchill and Abraham Lincoln stared at him from tables near the fireplace.

Each president additionally decorated the room with his own paintings and pictures of family members. James, a collector of the Cowboy Artists of America, had brought several paintings from the ranch and one of them was hung in the Oval Office—*The Cowboy* painted in 1880 by John Wade Hampton, depicting a lone cowboy riding a chestnut horse through the sagebrush at sunset. There were photos of his father and his grandfather, whom he revered greatly, and an ornate, silver-framed family photo of Carol with Andrew on a Colorado ski vacation.

James sat down at the massive, dark-mahogany desk called the HMS Resolute. Both Theodore and Franklin Delano Roosevelt and every president since had used it. He was preparing for a cabinet meeting at 8:00 A.M. The agenda this morning included reports from the secretary of defense concerning the war with Iraq, the growing problem with North Korea threatening its neighbors and the United States with nuclear attacks, a report from the secretary of commerce on the state of the economy, and reports from the Department of Security concerning the war on terrorism domestically and abroad.

President Walters looked at the antique clock on the mantle over the fireplace. It was five minutes before eight, time for the meeting to begin. James was seldom late and he chastised others who were.

The president walked into the Cabinet Room from the Oval

Office. A large, full-length portrait of George Washington greeted him as he entered the room. Since the president is the last one to enter the room, all of the cabinet members were already assembled around the large oval table that had been a gift from President Nixon. They rose to greet him as he seated himself in his chair in the middle of the table with Vice President Jason Martin sitting across from him, Secretary of State Josh Dean to his right and the Secretary of Defense Charles Robertson on his left. The chairs in which the cabinet members sat were quite special in that they have plaques on the back inscribed with the prior office or offices held by each member. It should be remembered that each cabinet member is in line to take over the presidency should something happen to the president. The vice president is first in line, of course, and the secretary of transportation would be something like fourteenth in line for the presidency.

"Good morning, Mr. President," Vice President Jason Martin greeted him, and everyone in the room parroted his words.

James sternly looked around the table to see if everyone was accounted for. "You may all be seated."

"I called the meeting this morning to discuss some very important issues facing us and the nation in the next couple of months leading up to the election. The economy is still not performing as we would like it and we need some answers for the public. The war in Iraq is bogged down with guerrilla fighting, soldiers continue to be killed at a rate of one a day on average. How do we explain this since we told the people that this would be a short war? And nuclear issues are heating up in North Korea. We are considering an attack on military bases there in hopes of curtailing their ability to send a nuclear device across the water."

"Do you think it wise to start another fray this close to the election?" Charles Robertson said as he looked around the table for support.

"I tend to agree with Chuck," said Josh. "We have two major

conflicts going right now, Iraq and Afghanistan. And we're working on the peacekeeping mission in Liberia. We would be stretching the military and ourselves pretty thin if we started another conflict. And what if we aren't successful?"

"We won't fail. We had a meeting with Struthers and Wiley last week. Chuck you were there. The intelligence is showing us exactly where the missile launchers are located. It's a sure thing," James said.

"Don't we have to get the buy-in from the Hill?" asked Josh.

"This is a national emergency. We don't have to get Congress involved. Getting the go ahead from them would take another two months anyway," said James.

"If we don't act on this, we'll look weak in the eyes of the world and the people of this country," said Jason. "I believe the Pentagon already has its orders and is making plans to move ahead. This is a done deal."

"I can't imagine losing on this one. This will only increase our image in the world as the dominant force. We will be taking out Pyongyang's nuclear facilities and that will make the American people feel safer," said James. "This is a win, win. No more discussion needed."

The others in the room remained silent. The President had spoken.

"Tom, I need a report from you on Homeland Security," James continued. "There are rumors in the media that we are not fully prepared in case of a terrorist attack on our home soil. How did that information leak to the press?"

"It's partially true, Mr. President. Are you aware that many states have suspended the alerts because they are too costly? They don't have the money in already-insufficient budgets to cover the cost. They are coming back to the feds and asking for more money and we can't give it to them," Tom said. Tom Wiley, fifty-six years old with a stocky build, ruddy complexion and gray around the temples, had been appointed by the president to head up this new government agency that encompassed the FBI, the Coast Guard and several other agencies in order to have more control of national security in the case of another terrorist attack. James made this a high-level cabinet position for Tom.

Jason spoke, "We don't have the money. The states are going to have to figure it out for themselves."

"It was Congress that voted for this bill and the executive branch, you, Mr. President, signed it. They felt that you were pushing this and didn't really have any say in it and now they're feeling pretty helpless," Tom said.

"This is making us look bad. We're not going to solve this one today, but Tom, I want you to work up a story on this that you can give to Stanley. Something that puts a positive spin on it," Jason said.

"Warren, I would like your report on the state of the economy and a projection for what we can expect in the next couple of months. The reports don't look good. What can we do to make this look better?" James asked, looking down the table where the secretary of the treasury was sitting.

Warren Kennedy, a long-time friend of James, had been hand picked by him for this very prestigious and high-profile job. Before coming on board with this administration, Warren, at the tender age of thirty-five, had been CEO of Synergy, a large international company that brokered energy. Although he was not from the financial world, he was a go-getter and had good business sense. His Hollywood good looks and trim cycling body, didn't hurt him either.

"Yes, Mr. President. We've been limping along the last couple of months. Durable goods sales are up four percent over last year at this time. Factory inventory is down and it will be just a matter of time before manufacturing increases to meet the demand. I don't know what another war is going to do to this, however. Consumer confidence seems to drop when we have war."

"Let us worry about that. It will be over before they know it and then the public can get on with their spending," said James. "The main thing right now is making sure that we have a positive outlook for the next three months at least."

"It's jobs that they're worried about. Bankruptcies have jumped twenty percent in the last year alone. Foreclosures are running about the same," said Warren.

"If we can let the people know that the economy is growing, jobs won't be that far behind. It always takes a while in a recovery for the companies to start hiring again," said Jason.

"There's this problem about jobs going offshore," said Warren. He took a sip of water from the crystal glass in front of him. "You know, the IT jobs and accounting jobs. We lost two million white collar jobs last year to India and China."

"That can't be good for our tax base," Josh interjected.

James, looking annoyed at Josh, said, "People are just going to have to retool. We are living in a global market, and the people in India and China have a right to those jobs. After all, they've trained for them."

The silence around the table was as thick as Cheddar cheese. Eyes were down and looking at notes and twiddling pens and rolling the edges of paper. Finally Warren spoke again.

"I understand that, Mr. President, but the people of this country may not see it that way. They are concerned about earning a living wage to support their families, and when the people in India and China are willing to work for a fraction of the salaries here, we have a problem. Especially since the cost of living in this country is so much higher. You do understand that, Mr. President?"

"Warren, put together a task force to study this and I want you to report back to me in a month with your results. In the meantime, it is critical that the public perception of the economy be a positive one. Get with Stanley and write up some press releases to the effect that the economy is growing by four percent," said James.

"That's all for today. Thank you all for coming. Remember, we have to keep this on track," said James.

Everyone rose from the table and started to leave the room. Josh and Jason approached the president.

"Mr. President, we'd like to have a meeting with you in private," Jason said.

"Sure. What's this about?" James asked curiously.

"Let's go back to the Oval Office," Josh said. "We've asked Terry to join us."

The three of them walked back to the Oval Office. James was even more curious now. Terry, chief strategist to the president, entered the room. James took his seat at his desk while the others pulled up chairs to be near the president.

"You know how Washington is, Mr. President," Terry said. "Rumors fly around this town like kites in a March wind." Terry, 42 years old, had the temperament to go along with his carrot red hair and Irish freckles. He had been with the FBI before joining the Walters team and he was a political whiz when it came to strategy.

"You'll have to explain what you're talking about, Terry. Give me a clue." James looked at the three men, seemingly unknowing of what they were about to confront him.

"It's about Carol," Jason said. "It has been almost three weeks since you got back to Washington. And people are asking where the First Lady is. It is unusual that she should not be back here with you by now. Are the two of you having problems?"

"No. No problems," James scratched his nose and looked away from everyone.

"You sure about that?" asked Josh.

James got up from his desk and started to walk around the room. The others turned in their chairs, eyes following him as though they were making sure he wouldn't escape.

"No, I'm not sure. I guess I'd better tell you all. You'll find out later anyway. Carol's divorcing me."

"Good God! What'd you do to deserve that? You foolin' around on her?" Terry exclaimed, blue-green eyes open wide.

"No, I've been faithful. Although I've seen women that I would like to have, but I've never acted on it. No, it goes deeper than that."

"We can't let this happen," Jason said. "You have to stop her. Tell her to wait until after the election."

"I did. She won't."

"Did you know this was coming?" Terry asked. "You must have known that things were not right with you and Carol."

"I should have. The signs were there. We were arguing a lot and then she seemed to be pulling away from me. But I've been wrapped up in this election and taking care of matters of state—Iraq, the economy and all. I thought it would just blow over. But it didn't."

"Why don't you ask her to go to a marriage counselor?" Josh said. "That way you could delay and maybe save your marriage, too."

"No, that's not a good idea," said Terry. It could be leaked. And any word that Carol is divorcing you is going to go against you. Do you realize what this could do to the election?"

"I do. And you are right; marriage counseling is out of the question. Anyway, she's adamant about this. Remember when I went back to the ranch this week? Well, we had a big argument, and I lost. I begged and pleaded and she's not going to change her mind. In fact she's already filed the papers. Not much I can do about it at this point."

"There is a way around this. Let me talk to Frank over at the Bureau," Terry said.

"What does that mean, Terry?" James was concerned about bringing in Frank Karwoski, who was the head of the FBI.

"We just have to keep this under wraps until after the election.

And I think I have a way to do that," Terry said.

"You aren't going to do anything to hurt her, are you?" James was sorry that he had told them. But he really had no other choice.

"No. We won't hurt her. I promise you that we'll take the best of care of her."

Terry glanced around the room at the others and they shook their heads in agreement.

Three hours later, James was sitting in the Oval Office reading the daily briefings when his secretary rang him.

"Yes, Connie, what is it. I'm very busy."

"There is someone to see you, Mr. President. He says it is very important."

"I don't have any appointments scheduled. Who is it?"

"He's from the District of Columbia District Court. Do you want to see him?"

James lowered his head. He knew what this was about and there was no escaping. "Send him in."

Connie opened the door and motioned to the process server to enter the Oval Office, and the sandy haired, freckled, thirty-ish man dressed in baggy khaki pants and a denim shirt with a red tie entered the room and approached the president. He handed him a thick envelope and said, "Are you James K. Walters?"

"You know who I am," James said contemptuously.

"You have been served." And then he turned to leave the room, but just as he was walking through the door, he turned to the president and said, "I'm going to have quite a story to tell my grandkids."

James looked dumbfounded. She could have done this in a better way, he thought. This was not fitting for the president of the United States.

Infidelity

Jason rang the doorbell of the red brick townhouse on R Street in Georgetown not far from Montrose Park. It was late, past 10 o'clock. The streets were wet and shiny from an earlier rain shower, and pungent earth aromas permeated the air. Jason, 56 years old, hair still dark brown, the little he had left, a narrow nose and thin lips, had been secretary of state under James' father and a long-time friend of the Walters family.

"Come on up," a feminine voice said over the intercom. "The door's open."

Jason pulled on the door and walked up to the second floor. An older building that once had been a single-family home in better times was now divided into two apartments, one on each floor. The wooden stairway, well worn from use, was narrow and dimly lit with one wall sconce light at the top of the stairs. He labored up the stairs, holding onto the banister as he went as if he might fall if he didn't. At the top he turned to the left, saw the open doorway and walked into the apartment.

"I am so glad you're here," Nicole said as she enveloped him into her arms. "I was worried about you. You said you would be here by nine and it's now ten. No matter. Come in. What would you like to drink? Wine, Scotch, anything you want."

"Nicky, I can't stay long. I told Diane that I would be home by 11:30," Jason said as he kissed her deeply, running his hands over her lithe body and inhaling her essence. "You are beautiful. I think about you all day and long to be with you."

Nicole, or Nicky as Jason called her, pulled herself away from him and walked over to the bar, her pink silk kimono open in the front revealing her small bare breasts and black silk bikini panties. Her straight, jet-black hair cut in a short bob with bangs falling over half her face certified her Eurasian ancestry. Twenty-seven years old, Nicole Yang was an attorney with Louis, Beckett, Harper and Johnson, one of the most prestigious law firms in Washington specializing in litigation, representing many in the House and the Senate. She had met Jason at one of the many Washington parties one fall evening two years ago, and they had been seeing one another ever since. Jason was attracted to her sharp wit and entrepreneurial spirit. Her body wasn't bad either.

Jason collapsed on the blue velvet sofa. "What a day this has been. Oh, I'll have Scotch on the rocks. You won't believe what I found out today."

"What? I'm dying to hear? Tell me," Nicky said as she brought the drinks and set them on the coffee table in front of them. "Anything can happen in this town. That's why I love living here."

"You love it here because there is a ton of lawyering to do. There is more litigation in Washington than any city in the world. Everyone in Washington has an attorney standing by just in case they get sued."

"Tell me. What's happening," Nicky said as she lifted a glass of chardonnay to her cinnabar red lips and nestled close to Jason.

"You have to promise not to tell anyone. Do you promise?"

"Yes, of course. I promise."

"It could ruin him if people knew this before the election."

"Tell me," Nicky was becoming impatient.

"Carol, the First Lady, is divorcing the president. You know how he has been back in town for three weeks now and she stayed back at the ranch?"

"That doesn't mean anything. Maybe she had a legitimate reason to stay behind. Like taking care of family business."

"He told us today. He came right out and told us."

Nicky sat up and her eyes got very big. "Did he tell you why she's divorcing him? Has he been messing around?"

"No to both of your questions. He wouldn't tell us why. He said it was very deep. And, he said he hadn't been unfaithful to Carol. And I believe that. He's kind of a square guy that way."

"But why would she do this? She has it made. Many women would give anything to be in her place. I don't get it."

"I don't know. I can't get into her head. All I know is, if this gets out, it could be the end of the Walters presidency," Jason said as he caressed Nicky. "Let's go into the bedroom."

They walked to Nicky's bedroom, arms around one another. The decor was minimalist like the rest of the house. There was only the large super-king-sized bed and a postmodern teak dresser. An arc light hung over the bed casting shadows on the oyster walls, and an O'Keefe painting, the Miracle of Flower, hung on the opposite wall. Nicky took off her gown and laid down on the bed, anticipating Jason's body next to hers. Jason carefully removed his shirt and unbuckled his belt, pulling it out of his pants. He then unbuttoned his pants, slid down his zipper and let them fall to the floor, removing them with bombast. His striptease continued as he slipped his silk paisley boxers down over his hips and crawled onto the bed next to Nicky. Their bodies melded together in a symphony of notes playing on one another, touching, probing until they became one, and with the rhythm at first slow and deliberate then crescendo, Jason played Nicky like a fine instrument. Nicky arched her back and her joy was his.

They stayed entwined for a time, relishing the pure pleasure that each felt. Finally Jason pulled himself away from Nicky and laid alongside her, feeling the release that he had been waiting for all day.

"Jase, I want you to stay here with me. I want us to be together for always."

"Sweetheart, you know that's not possible. I wish it were. If I didn't have my two children. . . . Maybe when they're through with college."

"You always have some excuse. You couldn't love Diane anymore or you wouldn't be here with me."

"I have great respect for Diane. She's a good mother."

"But what about me? Do you expect me to be waiting for you, spending holidays alone while you're with your family? What about us?"

"Nicky, you know things happen for a reason. What if James lost the election? Or what if he was impeached? I'm next in line for the presidency. That would change everything."

"You wouldn't want that to happen, would you? I thought James was your friend. You don't wish your friends to have failure." Nicky pulled the pale-gray satin sheet over her breasts.

"In this town nobody has friends. It's everyone for himself."

Middle of the Night

It had been one week since Carol had returned from seeing her attorney in Denver, and her life was in chaos. James called her daily, badgering her and still attempting to get her to abandon the divorce. Additional Secret Service men and one woman had been assigned to her, and they were watching her every move. She had begun the task of determining the assets and the settlement she would ask for. Every day was another step toward her freedom, but it didn't come without a price. The stress level had risen two hundred percent and most of her nights were sleepless. This night was no exception. Carol slept fitfully for about an hour and then looked at the clock beside her bed. It was only 12:30. It seemed like she had been in bed for hours. This was going to be another long night. She decided to get up and take a couple of sleeping pills. She knew if she was sleep deprived she couldn't function and she had to be alert during the day. Her plan was to temporarily move away from the ranch where she could have more privacy. Her lawyer had told her that if she did move, she could possibly lose any rights to Mountain Sky Ranch, but she was willing to take the risk. Money was not important to her; at least not at this point. As a couple, they had accumulated considerable wealth over the years, and she felt that she was entitled to half of it, so she was reasonably sure that she would be financially secure when this was all over.

She stumbled into the bathroom and turned on the light. Looking into the mirror, she saw a stranger's face. There were dark shadows under her eyes, the lines on her forehead were more pronounced and her skin was grayish yellow. She felt old and haggard. Is this what divorce does to a person?

She groped in the medicine cabinet looking for sleeping pills and finally found them hidden behind a large bottle of aspirin. It was not her habit to take sleeping pills. Normally so tired by the time she went to bed, she didn't need them, but tonight was different. She walked out of the bathroom, leaving the light on, and went back into the bedroom. Carol swallowed the two tablets with some water from the glass she kept on the nightstand beside her bed. She crawled back into bed with thoughts of what lay ahead of her and finally dropped off to sleep.

Carol thought she must have been dreaming. She'd heard a noise, footsteps. She felt a needle go into her arm and then her body, floating into another realm, was being lifted by three men, their grim mask-like faces illuminated by the light coming from the bathroom. They were looking at her and they called her name, "Carol, it's all right. We're here to help you. We won't. . . ." Everything went black. The light had gone out.

Dad, where's mother?" Andrew asked, phoning his father from the ranch. He'd tried to call his mother a dozen times the day before and, unable to reach her, decided to drive down to the ranch. When he got there, he questioned Nancy. She'd started crying and told him she didn't really know where his mother was, but that an ambulance had come the night before last. She'd seen the lights and looked out the window to see three men pushing a gurney into the vehicle, and after closing the doors, it took off down the road to the main highway.

"Andrew, your mother is sick. We had to put her in a care facility."

"Sick? What's wrong with her? I talked to her a couple of days ago and she was fine."

"Your mother's had a nervous breakdown. I called her on

Wednesday night and she was very groggy. She said she had taken sleeping pills and she wanted to die. So I had her committed to a psychiatric hospital for a month or two."

"I don't believe you. What have you done with her? Where is she? I want to see her."

"I can't tell you where she is right now. She's in a safe place and she'll be all right. You are not to worry about her. We have the finest doctors taking care of her. Trust me."

"This is your doing. You want her out of the way before the election so the public doesn't find out about the divorce. I should have known something like this would happen. I'm going to find her. And, Dad, I can't believe you would go along with this. I have totally lost respect for you. I thought you were better than this. Now I know why Mother wanted to divorce you. You've sold yourself to the devil."

Andrew slammed the receiver down. He put his head in his hands and wept, the tears falling onto the Oriental rug, like so many splashes of rain. He cried until he couldn't cry anymore. His mother was in danger and he couldn't help her. And his relationship with his father was all but over. He saw for the first time what his mother had been trying to tell him, that his father was a power-hungry person who would do anything to further his cause. In Andrew's mind, this was unconscionable.

After what seemed like a very long time, Andrew wiped his eyes with the sleeve of his sweatshirt, got up out of the chair in his mother's office and walked down the hallway to his parent's bedroom. He carefully looked around the room, trying to take in every detail. The bed had been made up. Nancy had probably been in here cleaning up. His eyes went to the nightstand and he saw a glass half full of water and beside the water glass what appeared to be a package of pills. He walked over to the nightstand and picked it up. It was an over-the-counter sleeping pill called Simply Sleep. It had contained 24 tablets, but most of the packets had been opened, with the empty packets still on the nightstand and only two pills remained. He went into the bathroom and found a bottle of Prozac beside the washbowl. The prescription had his mother's name on it with instructions to take twice daily when needed for relief. This is strange he thought. Prozac is prescribed for people with severe depression. He had never known his mother to need medication of this sort. Nothing else seemed out of the ordinary. Her pink toothbrush was still in the bracket beside the medicine cabinet and the plush salmon-colored terry towels were neatly folded on the rack.

He left the bathroom and walked back into the bedroom, searching for anything else out of the ordinary. He opened her walk-in closet to see if anything was different there, but being that he hadn't been around the house in a few years, he didn't know what he was looking for, and her clothes were all neatly hung on the rack, shoes in the shoe packets and sweaters carefully folded in the drawers.

Walking down the hall to the living room, he saw that Nancy was there, vacuum cleaning the carpet.

"Nancy, can you think of anything else about Wednesday night? Did you see a name on the side of the ambulance?"

Nancy jumped in surprise. "Oh, I didn't know you were here. Yes, I did see a name, but it was dark and I couldn't make out what it was."

"What did the men look like and how were they dressed?"

"They were big, I would say all three over six feet. And they wore white pants and coats. I couldn't see their faces. I'm sorry, Andrew. Is your mother going to be okay? I talked with your dad and he said that she's had a nervous breakdown and they had to take her to the hospital for treatment. This is just terrible. I know your mother has been very upset lately, but I didn't think it would come to this."

"Don't worry, Nancy. I am sure Mother is going to be fine."

"You must be awfully worried about her."

"I am, Nancy. I didn't know she was sick either." Andrew was not going to let on to Nancy that he thought his mother had been kidnapped.

"Are you going back to school today or will you be staying the night?"

"I don't know what I'm going to do."

"That's understandable. This must be quite a blow for you. If you are staying the night, I will prepare your room for you."

"Thanks, Nancy. I think I will stay tonight. We're fortunate to have you."

Carol opened her eyes and looked around the room. She felt as though she had been asleep for twenty years; her body ached and she was dazed. There was an IV in her left arm with clear fluid dripping, drop by drop, one drop every second. The room was austere but clean. The walls were painted a light pink with the customary non-descript beige tile flooring. Her bed was the standard hospital bed with guardrails on the side and a button next to her hand for raising and lowering the top part. As she began to think more clearly, she realized that her hands were tied to the side rails with cotton cording and she couldn't move her arms. The TV over her bed was turned on and a daily soap was in progress with the usual drama playing out. My life is like a soap opera, she thought. She turned her head and saw a very large bouquet of daisies, pink carnations and yellow roses on her nightstand. Just then a middle-aged nurse, with gray hair in a bun and dressed in a starched white nurses uniform, entered the room.

"How are we feeling this afternoon, Mrs. Walters?" she asked.

"Where am I?"

"You are in one of the finest nursing centers in the area."

"But where is that? And how long have I been here?"

"You've been here about three days and I thought you would never wake up. You sure took a lot of those sleeping pills."

"I only took two sleeping pills. Now, tell me where I am. Untie my arms; I need to get out of here." Carol struggled to raise her head but was unable to get very far.

"Now calm down. You're going to be here for a few weeks. We can't release you until you've had some therapy. It is very serious when someone tries to kill herself."

"I did not try to kill myself or anyone else." Carol raised her head and tried to pull her hands out of the restraining cords. "Has my husband called? I want to talk to my son."

"The flowers are from your husband. Aren't they beautiful? You are so lucky to have such a wonderful husband."

"My son. I need to talk to my son. Where is the phone? These rooms don't have telephones?"

"It's going to be all right. We can't let you talk to anyone just yet. But it's going to be all right." The nurse assured her as she injected a yellowish white solution into the IV and Carol slowly slipped back into the twilight zone once more. As she slipped away, she heard the actress in the soap opera accuse another woman of killing her husband.

News conferences are held almost daily in the White House press briefing room called the Brady Briefing Room, named after James Brady. The 9:45 briefing, called a "gaggle" and held for the press corps and White House staff, is on the record but not televised. The official briefing is held on camera at 12:45. The briefing room had been a swimming pool built for Franklin Roosevelt, until Nixon's presidency when it was redesigned to become the theater-like room it is today where each reporter is assigned a chair with his or her name on it. The press uses this room throughout the day.

Royal-blue draperies frame the plaque behind the podium, and when the president speaks, a different plaque depicting the White House is used along with a special podium named the Blue Goose. Today the president would be speaking.

Stanley Thompson entered and took his place at the podium as the TV cameras focused on him.

"Good afternoon, ladies and gentlemen. The president will speak to you today, and he has a special announcement to make."

James entered the room and took his place at the podium as all of the press stood up.

"Good afternoon," he repeated. "I have come here to make an announcement. I am sorry to have to tell you that the First Lady, my wife Carol, is very ill and is in a care facility until she recovers from her illness. She has a team of fine doctors and we have every hope that she will recover completely and return to a normal life, but it may take some time."

There was a hush among the reporters and then the questions started coming.

"What is her illness?" Bob Johnson of Associated Press queried.

"She has had a slight mental breakdown. I found that she had been taking antidepressants, and last week she took more than the usual amount of sleeping pills. As I was concerned for her life, I thought it best that she be hospitalized where she can be monitored and have the therapy she needs to get well again."

"Had you known about this for some time now?" Andrea Evans of the Washington Post asked.

"I had noticed that there was a behavior change, but I thought it was due to the pressure of the upcoming election."

Jack Wallace of the *L.A. Times* asked, "Mr. President, we are very sorry to hear this. Can you tell us what hospital she is in?"

"No, I can't tell you that at this time. It is located in one of the western states however. That's all for today. Thank you all for attending."

"What is the status on the war with Iraq?" Joseph Forman of the New York Times asked as the president exited.

"That's all for today. We will hold another news conference tomorrow. Thank you again for attending." Stanley Thompson had again resumed his position at the podium.

With that statement, the press literally ran from the room to call or email this vital piece of news back to their respective newsrooms, and the briefing room was empty and peaceful once more, belying the commotion that had occurred only moments before.

As James left the briefing room, the vice president, Jason Martin, and the secretary of state, Josh Dean, grabbed James.

"James, we need to talk to you. Can we go into the Oval Office?" Jason asked.

"Sure. What's up? Did I say something wrong?" James said on the defensive. Since people criticized him often, he never knew where it would be coming from.

"No, you did fine under the circumstances," Josh said.

Once they were settled, Josh took the lead.

"Your son, Andrew, is missing. We can't get a line on him. He has withdrawn $200,000 from his personal account and he is nowhere to be found. What do you make of that?"

"I think he's going to try to find his mother and break her out of the nursing home. He's a smart kid. You're going to have a tough time keeping track of him, but I don't think he'll be able to find her," James said.

"You have to admit, he's a threat. If he should happen to get to her and get her out, our plan would go to hell," Jason said.

"And if the press gets to her, you can kiss this election good-bye," Josh added.

"Why do you say that? Look, we've already established that she's nuts. Even if she talked, no one would believe her anymore. She has no credibility. But I don't think that's going to happen. Andrew is going to make a great attempt at a rescue, but I don't know that he will be successful," James countered.

"And, if he is? What is the backup plan?" Josh asked.

"We don't need a backup plan. You gave me your word that you wouldn't harm her, and I expect you to stand by your word. We'll just keep her under wraps for another two months and then the election will be over. Whatever happens then won't matter. End of discussion."

Josh and Jason filed out of the Oval Office, looking worried, and James called up his agenda for the day to see what was next on his calendar.

If this was important news for Americans, the newspapers were not aware of it. The majority of the papers across the nation printed a small article on the back page of the main news section. Only the Washington Post, The LA Times, The Sacramento Bee and the New York Times found room on the front page for this story.

"First Lady taken to hospital after taking overdosing of sleeping pills."

And the gravity of it was greatly played down. She would be in therapy and back in circulation, good as new, in a matter of weeks. This was not an unusual event. Most people could relate. The First Lady was only human after all. Just what the administration was hoping for.

Andrew turned off the TV. Watching the news conference was very disturbing to him. He still didn't believe that his mother had overdosed on sleeping pills. In fact, he knew it was a lie. She was too much into life. Sure, she had been under a lot of stress with the campaigning and the election. And being First Lady was not a walk in the park, but his mother was strong and was dealing with it in a positive way. She had not been depressed that he had observed and was facing every one of her problems head on. It had to be the divorce and politics. They, the party, were not going to let her ruin the election, so they were putting her away for a couple of months to keep her quiet.

He knew one thing for sure, he had to find her and get her out of wherever she was. He felt that her life depended on it.

Since she had disappeared, the Secret Service had been on his tail constantly. Andrew was going to try to drop out of sight for the next month or so. He had called his roommate on that fateful day when he found out that she was missing to tell him that he would not be coming back to school this semester and that he would contact him from time to time to get any important phone messages. He dropped all of his classes, notifying his professors that he had a family emergency to deal with. They were very understanding.

He then called Ali to tell her that he would be gone for a while.

"But, where are you going?" Ali wanted to know. "And why are you doing this?"

"I can't tell you. And if anybody asks you questions about me, tell them you just don't know. I'm sorry, Ali, I wish I could tell you more."

"What about us? Is this your way of telling me to take the highway?"

"No. Absolutely not. I do care for you and I will be back. But I might not contact you during the time I am gone, so you'll just have to trust me. I don't want to say this, but if you want to date other people, then you should do that. But I promise that I'll come back and we'll see where we are then."

"I love you, Andy. There, I said it. And I will wait. I don't want anyone else."

"You know, Ali, I love you, too. I hope this all works out for the better, and I think it will. Hang in there and I'll call you as soon as I can."

He also called his grandparents. He didn't want to worry them, so he told them that he was dropping school for the semester and was getting a job and that he would call them when he had news. James had already called them, and it was strange the way his grandparents were seemingly so accepting. Andrew's grandfather was the only one to raise any questions at all. He guessed his grandmother was getting old or too busy. He thought, that's the American way—totally trusting and believing.

Withdrawing money from his college account, Andrew got an apartment in Denver under an assumed name, and he took a part-time job as a waiter to help with expenses. He bought an old dark-blue Ford pickup, the kind that a lot of people drive in the Denver area, so he would blend in. And he attempted to change his appearance by growing a beard and cutting his shoulder-length hair. Working three hours a day at his waiter job, he spent the rest of the day devoted to the search.

The only fact that he knew at this point was that she was in a care facility in one of the western states. Not a lot to go on. There were twelve western states, excluding Alaska and Hawaii. Was Texas a western state? He guessed it was; they had oil and cowboys. And as for a care facility, it could be a psychiatric hospital, nursing home, or drug rehab center—how many of those were there in the western states? This was going to be a monumental task.

He started with a process of elimination. He thought he could rule out Alaska and Hawaii right away. They would not likely take her to Washington, Oregon or Idaho. It was doubtful they took her to Montana, Wyoming or Utah. And if dad had anything to say, Texas was out. So, that left Arizona, Colorado, Nevada or California. He didn't think it would be Colorado because that would be too easy and Arizona was just too hot. It had to be Nevada or California. He decided to start with California and southern California, because Dad and Mother were partial to the Palm Springs area, vacationing there occasionally. Andrew was impressed with his own deductive thinking and was spurred on by this.

He decided to limit his search to the Los Angeles area south to Palm Springs. San Diego was a possibility, but he would stick with the LA vicinity. Huge, he thought. His momentary elation quickly turned to despair. But he kept marching along.

Now, as to the type of facility. He decided to rule out hospitals in general. That left drug rehab centers and nursing homes. It just made sense to him that they would take her to a nursing home. There were so many of them and it would be easier to hide someone in a nursing home.

Time to get on the Internet. Andrew booted up his laptop computer and clicked on the icon to bring up Internet Explorer. He then went to his favorite search site, Yahoo, and typed "nursing homes" in the search fields. This brought up another page with a list of options, including a "Yellow Pages: find nursing homes near you." He clicked on the text and another page came up with a lot of advertising and more search fields, this time city, address and zip. He decided to enter "Palm Springs" to see how many he would get. One hundred; there were one hundred nursing homes in the city of Palm Springs.

Then he wondered what was he going to say when he started calling. He couldn't ask for Mrs. James Walters, the First Lady. Undoubtedly they were not going to divulge that she was there at all, even if she was. Again, he felt dejected. He was just flailing at thin air, stabbing in the dark. He guessed he could call and pose as a state or federal agency and ask how many people were admitted around the first part of September and their age and gender. That might tell him something.

He knew this was going to be difficult, but he felt that it was critical that he pursue it. He had no trust for the people who were responsible for this happening to his mother. They were desperate. There was a lot at stake.

"You say he's not at school?" Chief Agent Mark Bowerman yelled. "Where is he if he's not at school?"

Joe Parks and Daryl Hansen, the two Secret Service agents assigned to Andrew, sat in chairs in front of the chief's desk looking at one another and then at the chief and shrugged. "We don't know at this point," Joe said.

"You don't know. You fucking don't know. What are the taxpayers paying you a hundred K a year to do?"

Joe and Daryl shifted in their seats. "We'll find him. We talked to his roommate and he told us that he'd gone down to Mexico for a few weeks. We'll check all of the flights and find out where he went and go and get him," Daryl said.

"No. I am taking you off this detail. I want you both to stay here in Washington for a while until further assignment. That's all for now."

Joe and Daryl got up and walked out of Mark's office. Mark picked up the phone and punched in the number for Frank Karwoski, director of the Federal Bureau of Investigation.

"Frank, Mark here. As you might already know, we're having a problem with the President's son."

"We're already on it. We're interviewing some of his friends, his roommate and one of his girlfriends."

"Good, good. I thought you might be. He's a smart kid and he gave my boys the slip. That's why I called you."

"We've had orders from above and you know what that means."

"Yeah, I know. Let me know if you need help from my people. That's all for now. Bye."

Alison Under Fire

The only thing that Alison hated about bartending was walking through a nearly deserted parking lot at 1:00 A.M. after the late shift. She didn't mind the smoke or the noise, she often saw many of her friends and the money was good. She could make a hundred and fifty dollars in an evening for six hours of work. Not a bad hourly rate. But the walk to her car late at night always made her feel uncomfortable, so much so that she would often ask one of the male bartenders to walk out with her.

This night Alison was closing out the cash register and she was the last to leave. It had rained earlier in the evening and there were puddles everywhere. She looked up to the sky and watched the moon play hide and seek with the last of the storm clouds, outlining the edges with silver. She had jumped over the last puddle before reaching her car when she saw the two men come out of the shadows and rush her. One on either side, they held her by her arms, one of them covering her mouth with his gloved hand.

"Don't scream. We just want to talk with you," the taller man said. They were dressed in black shirts and pants with black ski masks concealing their heads and faces.

Alison struggled and kicked and dug her nails into one of guy's arms, but they held her tightly. They lifted her bodily into the back of a panel truck that had appeared from nowhere and set her down on a dirty mattress. The man who was not holding her mouth put a blindfold over her eyes and pulling her hands behind her back, binding them with a nylon cord.

"If you promise not to scream, I won't gag you," the shorter man said.

Alison shook her head up and down, saying yes, and the hand was taken away from her mouth.

"Who are you? What do you want with me?"

"We just want to ask you some questions. We won't hurt you if you cooperate."

"What does that mean?" she asked.

"Shut up. No more questions. We're taking you for a little ride."

Alison fell over on her side, her face plunging into the musty smelling mattress as the truck turned sharply out of the parking lot. She was trying to get her bearings as to which way they were headed, but she lost her sense of direction in the windowless van.

"Where are you taking me?"

"We told you to keep your mouth shut," the large man slapped the side of her face hard.

She felt the truck take another sharp turn. They traveled for what seemed like an hour or more, but was most likely only twenty minutes on a paved road and then turned off onto a rutted dirt road. After maybe another half hour, the truck came to a stop and the two men got out of the back of the truck, and Alison could hear them talking to others in the front cab. She twisted and pulled and tried to get her hands free, but they were tightly bound and the men were returning.

Picking her up off the mattress, they carried her into a small building and placed her in a chair in the middle of the room. They removed the bindings from her hands and bound her legs and upper body to the chair. She wasn't going anywhere, not without the chair anyway. The men removed her blindfold and Alison was blinded by a very bright light bulb hanging close to her head, but as her eyes adjusted she could see that she was in a small, sparsely furnished room with whitewashed walls and a bare wooden floor. Three men in black clothing surrounded her.

"Where is he? Just tell us where he is and we'll take you back."

"Who are you talking about?"

Another hard slap to the cheek throwing her head back against the chair. "You know, Alison, you know who we're talking about. Now be a good girl and tell us where he is and we'll let you go home."

"I don't know where he is."

"Didn't he call you before he left school?" the man to the right said.

"Yes, he called me. But he wouldn't tell me where he was going. He just said he was dropping out of school for the semester and that was all. I can't tell you anymore because I don't know anymore," Alison started sobbing.

"I think we'll leave you here to think about it for awhile." The men left the room talking among themselves.

She heard them talking in the next room, and then she heard a cell phone ring and some very loud voices. She twisted and tried to move her arms but she couldn't, and she was losing feeling in her hands with the cord cutting off the circulation. She knew that it would do no good at all to scream; they would only come back in and slap her around some more. She was so tired. She had started work in the afternoon, and because it was Friday and a very busy night, she had worked straight through to closing with only a couple of small breaks to go to the bathroom. Closing her eyes, she tried to shut everything out and her head drooped and she drifted off to sleep.

Alison didn't know how long she had slept. Her body ached and her mouth was dry; she needed a drink of water. The door burst open and the same three men rushed back into the room and circled around Alison. She could tell that they were angry.

"You are going to tell us. You do know where he is."

"Please give me some water. I am so dry."

"When you tell us, we'll give you some water. Now you be a

good little girl and tell us exactly what he told you."

"All I know is that he was leaving school. I think it may have had something to do with his mother going into the hospital. He seemed to be kind of upset when he called. He told me that he was going away for awhile and I wouldn't be hearing from him."

"Was he breaking up with you?" One of the men asked.

"No, he said that was not the reason."

"Have you heard from him since that call?"

"No, I haven't heard from him at all."

"What about his roommate? Have you talked to him?"

"No, I've been really buried with work and school. I figured that, when Andy got ready, he would call me." Alison paused. "Please give me some water."

"Al, go get her some water."

Al left and the rest of the men followed.

Alison heard them whispering in the next room and strained to hear what they were saying.

"I think she's telling the truth," the short man said.

"I think so too. What are we going to do with her now?" the large man spoke first.

"We're going to take her back to her car," Al said as he came back with a blue plastic cup of water.

Al walked back into the room where Alison was held captive and walked over to her, holding the cup while she drank.

"Look, girlie, we think you know more than you're telling us. We had orders to kill you if you didn't talk, but for now we're going to take you back. And if you say anything to anyone about this, well I wouldn't guarantee your health for very long. And we will be watching you."

Alison gulped the water, her eyes wide with fear. She shook her head up and down, acknowledging every word.

The Patriots Convention

The frenzy had been building all week. Delegates and the media started arriving the day after Labor Day and continued to arrive up until the start of the convention. A tent city was set up around the convention center to serve as headquarters for some 1,500 journalists from around the world, and photographers and reporters streamed in and out of the tent openings like ants from an anthill. New York hotels were overflowing and restaurants were doing a booming business with lines of people waiting out on the sidewalks of New York. And there were parties every night and tours of the city, the museums and art galleries. The delegates and party members stood out from the local New Yorkers in their gaudy red, white and blue clothing, straw hats and buttons, and banners with words like "Walters is Our Man", "Walters Works for US", "Walters the Patriots' Patriot". The conventioneers were everywhere, and they were boisterous and raucous and enthusiastic.

Wednesday, September 8, was the first night of the convention, and the delegates and press convened in one of the largest meeting halls in New York City, Madison Square Garden. The Garden, as it is known among locals, was first built in 1879 and had been rebuilt three times to become the meeting hall that it is today with the capacity for 20,000 people. Elvis, the King of the Garden, played there in 1972, Sinatra in '74 and Joe Frazier defeated Muhammad Ali, punching out fifteen rounds in August of '71. Now the Patriots would be punching it out in '04. Except there were no contenders for this fight. James Walters, the incumbent president, was the sole challenger and Jason Martin was along for the ride, hopefully for another four years. And so this was merely a protocol, a ritual ceremony to honor the head of the Patriots party, James Walters.

Speakers paraded before the delegates, praising President Walters and Vice President Martin for the accomplishments of the past four years and talking about the vision for the next four. The Speaker of the House, Dan Gillespi, the senate majority leader, Jack Turner, James' brother George, the governor of Colorado, and many others all extolled and aggrandized ad nausea to an audience completely caught up in the words of the moment. But this is what political rallies are all about, and the conventions held by the now three political parties were the largest of all.

Conspicuously missing from the activities were Carol and Andrew, although no one seemed to question early on in the week as they would not normally appear until the last night of the convention, after the roll call and the official outcome of the convention had been decided.

The night before the roll call, President James Walters spoke to the faithful Patriots. The hall was all lights and music and balloons, ticker tape of every color imaginable. There were three large screens that projected the image of the president to all in bigger-than-life, Mt. Rushmore fashion and speakers to project his voice so that all could hear. It was the circus of circuses. The president came before the audience and everyone rose to their feet in adulation. The clapping and cheering went on for twenty minutes until finally James raised his hands like a Zoroastrian prophet and there was quiet.

"I stand before you tonight, humbled to receive your adoration but energized in knowing you support me and the Patriots party. We have come far in the last four years, but we have much to accomplish in the next four," James said. Applause for another two minutes, then James again raised his arms, "My only regret tonight is that Carol, your First Lady, is not here to share the joy in my heart and see and hear your enthusiasm. We pray for her to be well soon." More applause. "We are winning the war on terrorism. We are winning on the economy. We are winning with education. And we are winning the war on crime in this country." Applause, applause. "We will bring peace and democracy to the Middle East, we will have more jobs for Americans, we will provide prescription drug benefits for the elderly and for everyone, and we will continue to improve our schools."

More sound bites and more applause. "But in order to do this, I'll need your help. We are in this together; we are partners in bringing about a better world, a better country. So I am asking you for your continuing support and hard work. Together we will make this happen."

The speech continued another twenty minutes with applause every two minutes. As James ended his speech, balloons of every color dropped from huge nets fastened to the ceiling of the hall, and strobe lights danced in time with the band playing Rocky, and the crowd went wild.

Outside the hall it was a different story. Mobs of protestors stormed up the street toward the Garden, and hundreds of riot police with full riot gear pushed them back with rubber bullets, pepper spray and night sticks. Hundreds of people, men and women, young and old, were being arrested and led off to paddy wagons to be taken to jail. And while some of the press attempted to cover the event outside the hall, they, too were driven back and arrested along with the protestors.

Carol is Captive

Life in the nursing home was becoming routine for Carol. After three more days of being drugged every time she got angry and upset, she decided to cooperate and they stopped the drugs. The IV was removed; she was eating regular meals, getting up out of bed and walking about her room freely, although she still was not allowed out of the room unaccompanied. They had told her that she would be taking part in group therapy sessions, but that wasn't happening at this point. This was most likely because someone in the group might recognize her.

There was one large window in the room with the shade pulled down at all times. She figured that her room was on the east side of the nursing home because the sun always shone on the shade early in the morning. She peered behind the shade to see if anything looked at all familiar to her. The landscape was similar to Colorado in that it was very dry, but there were palm trees and cactus plants and she saw an orange tree across the street. At midday the sun was blazingly bright. She figured that she was somewhere in the southwest, maybe Phoenix, Arizona.

"We must keep the shade down at all times." Nurse Jackson had come into the room again.

"I would just like some sunlight," Carol said.

"If you're good, we'll take you out on the patio tomorrow for a little walk."

"That would be nice." Carol felt powerless.

"I have a menu for you to select your meals. Then you can take your bath and I'll bring you some reading material."

"Thank you." Carol took the sheet of paper from the nurse and searched for the name of the nursing home. It had been clipped.

"You seem to be in better spirits today."

"Yes, I'm feeling much better, thank you."

A cleaning person knocked on the door and then entered to clean the floors and the bathroom and to dust as she did every day.

"It's such a lovely day. I love the weather here. Do you live in this city?" Carol tried to make conversation.

"Yes, ma'am, I do," the woman said hesitantly.

"What city is this?"

"I'm not supposed to talk to you," the woman answered.

"I was just wondering where I was."

"I was told not to talk to you," she said and went about her business of cleaning and then left the room when finished.

Nurse Jackson returned. "Have you completed your menu selection?"

Carol felt like she was being treated like a child. "Yes, I have. Here it is. Would you bring me a newspaper?"

"Sure, I can do that. Now, you step into the shower and get all cleaned up and I will bring your newspaper to you."

Carol went into the bathroom and took off the blue robe and the blue and white print hospital gown that had been provided for her. Her personal clothes had been taken from her. She turned on the water and adjusted the temperature to her liking and then got into the shower. She soaped her body with great care and let the water wash over her as if a great cleansing of her whole being was taking place. Then she got out of the shower and used the lotion provided to her, lovingly applying it all over her body. She was a prisoner, but she was being treated reasonably well. She thought about other prisoners throughout history—the prisoners of war during WWII and the Vietnam War and the Jews in Auschwitz and the atrocities they endured. She was, like them, a prisoner. She dried herself, put on a clean hospital gown and walked out of the bathroom.

Nurse Jackson appeared again. "You're all cleaned up, I see. Now don't you feel better?" She was so damn cheerful. "I brought you a paper."

She handed Carol a copy of *USA Today.* Carols heart sunk. She was hoping for a local paper. She searched for an address label but there was none.

"Do you think I could have some regular clothes? I am well enough to be up and around, and I would like to have something besides a hospital gown. Just a pair of jeans and a t-shirt would do."

"I'll see what I can do. I'm not guaranteeing it, but I'll try. You look to be about a size six or eight, is that right?"

"Yes, I am a size six normally, but I don't like my jeans to be tight, so size eight would be fine and a medium top or shirt. And some real shoes, if I could have some sneakers, that would be wonderful."

"I'm afraid we won't be able to get the shoes. You can continue to wear the slippers from the nursing home. Are they not comfortable?"

"No, they're fine," Carol acquiesced.

The nurse left and Carol went over to the window and raised the shade to let some sunlight in and settled into the large upholstered chair in the corner to read the newspaper. The paper was dated Saturday, September 11, 2004, and the headline read *James Walters to Lead Again; Patriots Behind Him 100%.* Carol opened the paper and saw an article entitled, *First Lady Doing Well after Breakdown.* She started to read the article.

First Lady Carol Walters is responding well to medication and therapy in a rehab hospital in southern California after it was discovered that she had overdosed on sleeping medication at the Walter's Mountain Sky Ranch outside of Fort Collins, Colorado. Her housekeeper discovered her on September 4 and called 911, bringing the paramedics.

What lies, she thought. But at least she knew more about where she was. Or maybe she did, she could not be sure of anything anymore. Maybe they had lied to the media.

Andrew returned to his apartment from his waiter's job at the Hungry Horse restaurant. He was exhausted but had to continue to make calls in his search for his mother. He reviewed the list of nursing homes he had already called in Palm Springs, and he had almost come to the end of the list. What city should he try next? There were so many small cities in southern California and each would have twenty or more nursing homes. Was he going about this the right way? But he didn't know of anything better at this point. Should he hire a private investigator? But that might alert the Secret Service and the FBI. He was very unsure at this point and very worried that he might not reach her in time.

The Demonstration

It had been advertised as the largest antiwar demonstration in all history. It was Saturday, September 18, 2004, and through the magic of the Internet, there were protests planned around the world. Events were planned for San Francisco, New York, Dallas and every major city in the United States with smaller protests on college campuses throughout the nation. In Europe and the Far East, protests were going on in London, Paris, Oslo, Tokyo, Cairo and many other cities abroad. But Washington would attract the largest number of people. President Walters and many of his staff and cabinet members planned to be out of town that day. James left for Camp David early Friday to spend the weekend, taking Harry, his cocker spaniel, with him.

The protestors started to arrive in the Capitol on Thursday and by Saturday they were gathered as close to the White House as they could get, spilling over into Lafayette Park across Pennsylvania Avenue. They carried placards saying "No Blood for Oil", "Make Peace, Not War" and "Bring our Soldiers Home Alive, not Dead," and they danced and paraded from the grounds of the Capitol and along the National Mall back to the Smithsonian. It was, for the most part a peaceful march, with the exception of a few who broke down some of the barricades and ended up face down on the grass with police handcuffing and arresting them. And even though this was a serious matter, there was an air of festivity, with people singing and chanting, forming conga lines singing "Give Peace a Chance". There were others, particularly women, who carried signs asking the First Lady to intervene for them, knowing full well that she was not able to. They called themselves Mothers Against Wars (MAWS) and they were very vocal about not sending more sons and daughters to fight unnecessary wars.

The press estimated that there were 70,000 people marching, but those who were there, and had been to events in that space before, said that it was more like 500,000 people. They were all ages, from all walks of life—nuns and clergy, families, and professionals, along with students. This was mainstream America.

NBC News interviewed the national security advisor, Tom Wiley, who said, "It shows the rest of the world how freedom works in the United Sates. We welcome these peaceful demonstrations as an expression of American freedoms."

It was Sunday, and Andrew logged onto Yahoo and noticed the item on the Saturday demonstrations. Being an advocate for peace himself, he was happy to see people expressing their opposition to the war. He felt that war seldom solved anything and brought about the killing of many innocent people along with soldiers.

Searching new cities for his mother, he had about exhausted the possibilities in Palm Springs and began looking at nursing homes in San Bernardino and the Loma Linda area. There were thirty nursing homes in the San Bernardino area and twenty-one listed in the Loma Linda area.

He started with the Golden Valley Nursing Home on 1527 Canyon Way in San Bernardino. Dialing the number, he waited about ten rings before someone answered.

"Golden Valley Nursing Home, how can I help you?" a woman finally answered.

"May I please speak with your director? My name is David Nelson and I am with the Federal Medicare program."

"One moment, I will see if she is in."

Andrew waited again for what seemed like a very long time. He thought about the responses he was getting when he called. Hardly anyone questioned him about his credentials and they gave him information willingly for the most part. He often had difficulty reaching the right person, and then when he would find out who the right contact was, that person was sometimes either not available or too busy to talk with him and he would have to call back, which was very time consuming, and time was not on his side.

"This is Jane Ferris, what can I do for you?" Another woman finally answered.

"My name is David Nelson and I am with Medicare in Washington, D.C. We're trying to get an idea of how many people have been admitted to nursing homes over the past month. This is a national study to help the Medicare program make projections for future use of nursing care facilities," Andrew said with an authoritative voice.

"Just wondering why you are calling on Sunday," Jane asked with some skepticism.

"We have a huge workload and short time period in which to get this done, so we are working almost around the clock. Sorry to bother you on Sunday."

"That's all right. Let me get my records. Do you want me to send you something?" Jane asked.

"No, you can just give me the information over the phone. I need to know by gender and age if you can do that."

There was silence for about five minutes and then Jane returned. As she rattled off some statistics, Andrew listened carefully to the genders and ages admitted in September. There had been twenty-three admissions to the nursing home that month, but none of them were younger than age seventy-five. He would have to keep trying.

The Nursing Home

Carol had begun to garner trust from the nurses, doctors and aids at the nursing home and was gaining new freedom to move about the facility in the week and a half that she had been there. She had done this by cooperating completely with every rule, every demand they had imposed on her. Nurse Jackson sent an aide to buy some clothes for her, and she could now dress in jeans and a t-shirt; no shoes yet. Being allowed to leave her room, with a nurse at her side, she could take short walks in her area and was even taken outside onto the patio to sit in the sun and enjoy the garden. However, she was isolated from the other residents; her only contact with humans was with the nursing home personnel and the resident psychiatrist, Dr. Anne Molear. Carol was scheduled to meet with Dr. Molear two times a week, on Tuesday and Thursday, for one hour at 10:00 A.M.

Since this was Tuesday and it was 9:45 A.M., Amy, one of the aides, knocked on Carol's door and entered.

"I'm here to take you to Dr. Molear's office for your counseling session. Are you ready to go?" Amy inquired.

"Yes, I'm as ready as I'll ever be." Carol dared not to question why she was seeing a psychiatrist. She knew she was not mentally ill and she had not taken the pills, but she would play the game until she somehow was able to free herself from this horrible nightmare.

They walked down the hallway to the doctor's office. There were two old women in wheelchairs along the side by the wall. One woman was sleeping, her head hanging over the side of the chair with her mouth open. The other old woman, with grayish, wrinkly skin hanging from emaciated arms, reached out to Carol with a bony hand and said in a scratchy voice, "Take me home. I want to go home. I want to go home."

I want to go home too, Carol thought. She continued following Amy along the hallway until they came to the doctor's office. Amy knocked on the door and said," Dr. Molear, I have Mrs. Walters here to see you."

"Bring her right in," Dr. Molear said as she rose from her desk. She was about the same height as Carol, five foot five, in her mid-fifties with short silver-gray hair, dressed in a white doctor's coat over a white crepe blouse and a black mini-skirt. She wore very little jewelry—diamond-stud earrings, a diamond wedding ring on her left hand and a Rolex watch.

Carol entered the office and reached out to shake the doctor's hand.

"I am happy to meet you, Mrs. Walters."

"I am pleased to meet you, too, although I would like it to be under different circumstances."

"I understand. Please come in and be seated." The doctor motioned her to an overstuffed, amethyst-colored leather occasional chair as she seated herself in an identical chair opposite Carol. The room was paneled with mahogany, and there were floor-to-ceiling bookcases on one wall. The other walls were painted a deep mauve, and there were two Norman Rockwell-like paintings on the wall opposite the bookcases—one of a little girl playing with a cocker spaniel in a field of flowers and another of a small boy catching his first fish from a tree-lined stream. It was a comfortable room and again Carol thought about being home.

"Carol, I would like you tell me about your family. Tell me about your parents and what your life was like when you were a child."

"You know I didn't take those pills. There is nothing wrong

with me. I am just trying to divorce my husband."

"Yes, I know, but I need your cooperation. We will progress much faster and maybe you will be released if you cooperate."

Carol thought this over for a few minutes and decided that this would be the thing to do. She could think of nothing better than getting out of this nursing home or where ever she was.

"My parents were very loving. I grew up in a pretty normal family. My dad was an engineer with Coors and he worked very hard and was seldom home. But I adored him and spent time with him on weekends when he had time. My mother was a stay-at-home mom; took care of us and the house, and she worked hard, too. She was very involved in volunteer work with the church and she was a PTA president, so she was busy, but she always had time for us, my brother and me."

"Did you get along with your brother?"

"My brother was eight years older than me. No, we didn't get along very well. In fact, we fought a lot. He was always hitting me and trying to get me into trouble. But that was when we were younger. We're pretty much friends now."

"And your parents divorced? How old were you when that happened?"

"How do you have this information?" Carol was incensed.

"We were given some history on you. I can't divulge the source."

Carol settled back. She had to cooperate. It was the only way.

"Yes, I was thirteen when that happened. I was devastated. I loved both my parents and I couldn't understand why they couldn't be together anymore."

"Do you know why they divorced?"

"No, I'm not really sure. Mother must have had her reasons. They didn't fight a lot. I think my mother wanted more excitement in her life. Dad wasn't real demonstrative. I think she wanted excitement. And I don't think she understood him and who he was."

They continued to talk about Carol's childhood for the rest of her allotted hour. Then abruptly, Dr. Moreal said that her time was up and she would meet with her again on Thursday.

"When am I going to get out of here?" Carol asked as she was leaving.

"I couldn't tell you that. We'll see how you're doing in a couple of weeks."

As she was leaving the office, she noticed a notepad on the doctor's desk. It read From the Desk of Dr. Anne Molear, Village Mountain Nursing Care, Redlands, California. So, this is where they had taken her.

Alison's Misstep

Alison slowly opened her swollen eyes. The sun was beating down into her car. How long had she been there? She tried lifting her head off the back seat and then she slumped back down. Her whole body ached, she felt sick to her stomach and she was so tired. Was this a bad dream, or had strange men really taken her for a ride. The bruises on her arms told her that it was no dream. Again pulling herself up, she got out of the back seat and fished for her keys in her purse. The sun was directly overhead; it must be about noon and people were hurrying about, and gladly for her, they were not paying much attention to her. She thought that she must look terrible.

Opening the door, and with difficulty sliding into the driver's seat, Alison put the key in the ignition and turned the motor on. She slowly and carefully eased her car out of the parking space and drove out of the parking lot. She felt like she was drunk; they must have given her drugs. She couldn't remember. She remembered the light bulb shining in her eyes, the man with the black ski mask slapping her face. She looked in the rearview mirror at her face. She looked like she had been in a boxing match; there were bluish-green circles under her eyes and a black and purple bruise on her right cheek.

Finally reaching the driveway of her house on Walnut Street, she parked in the driveway, got out of the car, unsteadily walked up the walk and opened the front door. Jody, her roommate was sitting on the couch in the living room, eating a sandwich and watching a soap opera on the tele.

"What happened to you? You look awful," Jody exclaimed.

"I fell down. I was hiking and I fell down this cliff," Alison mumbled as she walked quickly through the room, heading toward her bedroom.

"It looks worse than that," Jody said as she followed her. "Looks like somebody beat you up."

"No, that's not what happened. Jody, stay out of this." Alison pushed Jody out of the room and closed the door.

"Okay, Ali, whatever you say. I'm worried though," Jody said on the other side of the door.

"Don't worry; I'll be all right. I can take care of myself."

Alison took off her jeans and shirt, wrapped herself in her pink chenille bathrobe and laid down on the bed, trying to think about what she should do. She had to tell someone, but if she did, would they come after her again? Who were these thugs and why would they do this to her? This obviously had something to do with Andrew. Was Andrew dealing drugs? No, Andrew was not the druggie type. In fact, he hated drugs. Maybe this was about his family, maybe having to do with his mother being taken to a rehab center. That had to be it.

She reached for her cell phone.

"Sean, this is Ali. I need to talk to you. Can we meet somewhere, say in about and hour," Alison said breathlessly.

"Hey, Ali, what's up? Sure. Where do you want to meet?"

"At Hamburger Heaven over near the Union Center. I'll see you."

Alison walked through the old wooden swinging door of Hamburger Heaven. She had since showered and put on a clean pair of jeans with a white blouse. She covered her bruises on her face as best she could with some concealer that she kept on hand for the few blemishes that she might have on her usually flawless, creamy complexion. She looked around the restaurant for Sean and saw him sitting in the very last booth and she walked over to join him.

"Alison, sit down. Would you like a beer?"

"No, just coffee. I have to work tonight."

"What's going on? You don't look so good. What happened to you?"

"What's going on? That's what I'd like to know," said Alison as she tried to avoid the other question.

"What're you talking about?"

"Can I trust you?"

"Sure, of course."

"You must not tell anyone what I am about to tell you. Promise?"

"Yes, I mean no . . . I won't tell anyone. What is it?"

"Some goons met me at my car last night and took me for a little ride and they roughed me up a bit."

"Oh, Ali. I'm sorry. Are you okay? Did they . . . uh did they. . . ."

"No, this wasn't about sex. They wanted to know where Andy was."

"And?"

"I couldn't tell them anything. I don't know anything. Who do you suppose these guys are? And why are they so intent on finding Andy?"

Sean had a blank look on his face. "I don't know."

"Have you talked with him since he left?"

"No, I haven't heard a word, although the FBI contacted me and asked me some questions. You do know that his mother was taken to a rehab center?"

"Yes, I saw that on CNN. Strange isn't it. I didn't know that she was having mental problems. Andy never mentioned it."

"Yeah, but his mom might have been really stressed out with the war and the election. I think just being in Washington could drive anyone crazy these days."

"No, I think there's something else going on here. But I can't put my finger on what it is."

"Are you going to the police?"

"No, I'm really afraid. They said, if I talked to anyone, they would kill me. But I just couldn't keep this to myself. I had to talk to someone, and I felt I could trust you."

"I think you're right. There is something rotten here. But there's nothing we can do about it. I think this is bigger than any of us would imagine. Andy is smart and strong, and he'll come through this. In the meantime, just keep your head down and don't talk to anyone else and I promise I won't say a word. And if you need someone, I'm here."

"Thanks, Sean. I knew I could count on you."

Alison sat quietly for a few minutes, mulling over everything.

"Why did they come after me like that and not you?"

"I don't know, Ali, I really don't know. Maybe because they thought they could. You're a girl and more vulnerable and easier to bully."

"I'm not a girl, I'm a woman. But you're probably right."

They both sipped their coffee in silence.

"I have to leave. I have to be at work in an hour and I have to go home and change first. Let me know if you hear anything, especially if you hear from Andy. I miss him so."

"I will. Be careful, Ali. I don't think Andy would ever forgive himself if something happened to you."

The Debate

The pace was picking up in Washington with the election less than two months away. After the convention in New York, James took the show on the road, traveling from one state to another and then back to Washington and off again to Ohio, Indiana, and Pennsylvania, historically Republican states. And then on to Iowa, Minnesota and Wisconsin, states where he thought the Democrats might have an edge. It was Monday, September 19, and James had come back to Washington to prepare for the upcoming debate in Boston on the 22nd. He met with Terry Fleming, Vice President Martin, his press secretary Stanley Thompson and some of the members of his cabinet. Terry, the president's chief strategist, had worked with his father and Ronald Reagan and was a political pro when it came to election time.

They worked through the night and on into the morning of the 21st. James then went back to the White House apartment to rest before flying to Boston for the debate. He slept for nine hours. When he woke, he looked at his alarm clock. It was four in the afternoon and he was due to leave for Boston at seven that night. Fortunately his flight would wait for him even if he were a little late. He would fly in on Air Force One and spend the night at the Hyatt Regency Boston located in downtown Boston. The next day there was a luncheon planned with the Patriots women's caucus and then on to Clark Athletic Center at the University of Massachusetts in Boston where the debate was scheduled to take place.

James boarded Air Force One on schedule and walked back to the executive suite as the flight crew greeted him.

"Good evening, Mr. President. It will be a very short flight tonight. We thought about flying you up there on Marine One, but that would not be very comfortable," Captain Gary Rider said. Gary had been with the presidential aircrew for twenty years, and he looked the part of an airline captain—five foot ten with silver hair, neatly trimmed, an honest stare and an easy smile.

"You've got that right. And how would we get all these people up there?" James said, referring to his staff and cabinet members and the press. Just the thought of flying to Boston in a helicopter made him shudder. But he knew that it was a big deal to fly the Big Bird. Every trip was a military mission. The airspace has to be cleared and the airfield where they land is hand checked for debris and devices. The 230-foot-long Boeing 747 is taller than a five-story building and longer than a city block, and it is equipped with anti-missile devices and a shield. The aircraft has sleeping quarters for the president, a small infirmary in case of illness with a full-time nurse, and an executive suite called the flying Oval Office. There are eighty-seven telephones on board, of which twenty-four are encrypted. A C-141 Star Lifter flies along with Air Force One, carrying the president's bulletproof limo. The Football, a sealed suitcase with instructions to launch a missile attack, is always on the flights and passed off to a high-ranking Marine when they land.

"We were pulling your leg, Mr. President," Gary said.

"Are Terry and Jason on board yet?" the president asked the head purser, Jimmy Watkins, as he laughed a nervous laugh while brushing past the captain.

"Yes, I believe they are in the conference room, Mr. President. Let me know if you need anything," Jimmy said.

"Thanks, Jimmy." James continued on to the executive suite, leaving his luggage, and then headed straight to the conference room.

As he entered the room, he saw that Jason, Tom, Stanley, Charles and Terry, part of James' inner circle, were already seated at one end of the executive-size conference table.

"Good afternoon, Mr. President. I trust you are well rested?" Terry spoke first.

"I am. This campaigning is very draining."

"We know. If it's any consolation, we are all feeling it," Jason said.

"I'll be glad when this is over," James said.

"It's never going to be over. We have to be in perpetual campaign mode to maintain the edge. That's just the way it is. Fortunately we have more money than they do. And you are in office. It is easier for the incumbent, and you have Air Force One. That's an advantage in itself," Terry said.

"I know. Let's get started." James sat down with the others.

"We need to go over some of the questions that might come up in the debate," Terry said as Air Force One left the runway in a powerful climb into the night sky.

"By the way, how is Mrs. Walters doing?" Stanley asked.

"She's doing very well, thank you. She's in therapy and making good progress. I expect she will be out of the hospital soon."

"We are happy to hear that. Everyone was shocked when they heard about her illness. It just wasn't like her to do that, but I guess extreme stress does strange things to people," Jason said with sincerity.

"I wouldn't have thought that about her either, but humans are unpredictable sometimes. Now let's get to these questions," James said.

The rest of the short flight was devoted to the three of them grilling James and examining his answers, anticipating the questions that might be asked and attempting to find the right words to sway the voters to their side.

Air Force One landed at Logan airport, just outside of Boston, at 8:30. James was whisked away in the presidential limo to the downtown hotel. The evening's activities included dinner with Massachusetts Patriot party officials and then it was back to his room, to bed early to get ready for the next day's marathon of activities.

Sleep did not come easily for James, and he was glad for the wake up call from the front desk at 6:00 A.M. He dragged out of bed and went into the bathroom. Looking in the mirror he barely recognized himself. Who was this person staring back at him? He hadn't had those puffy bags under his eyes before he became president. The dark circles, where did they come from? His hair had not been that gray before. He started to shave and came to the realization that there is a price to pay for being the president. He had aged ten years in the three and a half years he had been in the office of the presidency.

After showering, James pulled on his silk boxer shorts, put on a powder-blue Armani shirt over his bulletproof vest and his navy blue pinstriped $14,000 Armani suit. That's as much as some people pay for an automobile, he thought. Now for the tie, should he wear a red tie or a yellow one? He decided on the red. He looked in the mirror again. Not a bad transformation. The clothes do make the man, he thought as he slipped into his Bruno Magli shoes.

The luncheon with the women's caucus was held in the main ballroom of the Hilton Hotel. Maryanne Banter was the leading state woman in the party, and she came forward and introduced James.

"Ladies and gentlemen . . ." Maryanne paused. "I have to say gentlemen because there are some here today." Giggles were heard in the mostly female audience. "I am honored to be able to introduce to you this afternoon the leader of our nation and the Patriots party, the president of the United States of America, President James K. Walters," Maryanne said as she blushed. A short, stocky woman in her late sixties, she then stepped away from the podium as James came forward, planting a kiss on Maryanne's cheek while the audience stood and clapped enthusiastically.

He gave the same stump speech he had given a thousand times in as many cities, promising more money for education, a prescription drug program for seniors and the privatization of Social Security. He had memorized it by now. Everyone clapped wildly and then the luncheon of Cordon Blue chicken with saffron rice and asparagus tips was served. James wondered why this seemed to be the menu every time he attended one of these functions. At 2:00 P.M., James and his entourage left the Hilton for another reception and then it would be back to his hotel to rest again before the debate.

The Lincoln Town Car carrying President Walters arrived on the campus of the University of Massachusetts promptly at 6:00 P.M. In preparation for the debate, students and volunteers had placed red, white and blue banners at the entrance to the campus and on many of the buildings to welcome the candidates. The Town Car pulled up to the side of the Clark Athletic Center and Secret Service agents lined the street to the entrance of the building. Two blocks away, about 100 students were carrying anti-war placards and marching in their small, designated area out of sight and sound of the president and the TV cameras.

James' opponent, Elizabeth Baker, had already arrived and was having makeup applied, as James would, to enhance her looks for the telecast to the worldwide audience. Elizabeth, the first woman to be nominated for the office of the president of the United States, a Democrat, was running on developing alternative fuels, thereby creating jobs and improving the economy, providing medical insurance for every American, and more social services for families in need after the long duration of unemployment. Millions of people were without jobs and unable to feed their families, so many that it was necessary to set up food centers in every state for families, not unlike the soup kitchens of the thirties depression era.

In addition to being televised to the nation and Europe via satellite, CNN would be broadcasting the debate over the Internet to the widest audience ever in presidential election history.

Nearing the 7:00 P.M. starting time, the two candidates sauntered onto the brightly lit stage of the auditorium and took their places at the podiums. James, tall and self-assured, surveyed the small audience that had gathered, and Elizabeth maintained her calm look of authority, reading notes and glancing periodically over her glasses around the auditorium. Betty, as she preferred to be called, wore a bright-red wool gabardine Christian Dior suit, conservative classic gold earrings, bracelet and black pumps. She was an attractive woman in her mid-fifties, her ash blond hair cut in a stylish bob with deep blue eyes that were compelling, if one had the chance to meet with them. She was a convincing candidate and James had his work cut out for him. It was evident that people liked Betty.

"Welcome to the first of the three ninety-minute debates between President James Walters and Elizabeth Baker. I am Samuel Warren, of "The News Place" on PBS," Samuel opened the program. "The debates are sponsored by an independent presidential commission and will be conducted with a predefined format agreed upon by both candidates. I have a series of questions that I will ask each candidate. We may not get to all of them, but we will try our best. I have selected the questions and neither of the candidates nor anyone else has prior knowledge of the nature of these questions. Each answer to a question must be limited to two minutes, and the rebuttal must not exceed one minute. As your moderator," Samuel continued as he scanned the audience, "I reserve the right to follow up on a subject, with the answer again not to go over two minutes. The candidates will not be able to speak directly to one another. There are to be no opening statements, but the debate will allow for closing summary statements by each candidate."

Warren, a veteran TV host and announcer, well known among those who were avid PBS fans, at sixty-two years, with gray hair, a face strong-boned face and a large nose, had a commanding presence about him. "We have a small audience here tonight. They are not here to participate, but to listen and applaud when appropriate."

"I want to welcome Elizabeth Baker, the Democratic nominee for the presidency, and James Walters, the incumbent president now serving our country. Elizabeth has asked that I call her Betty and so I will do that. Betty and James have chosen straws and James will answer the first question."

The audience applauded.

Warren: "President Walters, our country is experiencing record unemployment, I believe somewhere around eight percent. What would you do to alleviate this? And what would the cost be, if any, to the taxpayers?"

Walters: "I would continue with a tax cut. If you get money into the hands of the people, they will have more to spend, bringing profits to corporations, stimulating manufacturing and thus creating more jobs. We would start with the capital gains tax, which is double taxation at its worst, and then the marriage tax. I would also increase the tax deduction for each child to $2,000 from the $1,000 that it is today. Families would have more money in their pockets to buy clothing and feed their children. Our families are this nation's most important asset, and we need to help them make ends meet any way we can. And when goods and services are in demand, companies will start hiring again and our economy will have a chance to recover and move on to the prosperity we all want and need."

The audience responded once more with applause as Samuel nodded toward Elizabeth.

Baker: "I think we can do better than that for the people of this country. First of all, our downturn is partly cyclical and partly due to policies put in place by this current administration. If we look at this as a short-term problem and get money into the hands of the people who will spend it, we will see a quick turnaround of this unstable economy. I would cut the payroll tax immediately. This will provide relief for the middle and lower income people, not the wealthier people who are the ones concerned with capital gains. They don't need it. They won't spend it. It is the middle to lower income people who really need this tax relief."

Warren: "Betty, would you agree with rescinding the marriage penalty tax and allowing a larger tax credit for children?"

Baker: "Yes, I would agree with these measures. The majority of the people fall into the middle and lower income groups. In fact, it is the middle-income wage earner who bears the brunt of the tax burden in this country. We need to bring tax relief to this group more than anyone else or they will cease to exist."

The applause this time seemed to be louder and longer.

Warren: "President Walters, this country has been waging a war against Iraq for the past year and a half. When we went into this, you promised this would be a war of short duration, but it hasn't turned out that way. We now have other Arab countries fighting against us; we've had terrorist attacks on our soil recently. How are we going to get out of this and can we win this war in the Middle East?"

Walters: "We are winning this war. Initially we were predicting that the campaign would last ninety days, and then we would go in and clean up. Well, that didn't happen. War is unpredictable. We have the finest people in the military over there and I am confident that within the next six months we should be able to wrap this up. We were not prepared for the Arab people coming together as they did, working against us. Saudi Arabia has always been our ally and now they have broken with us and sided with the Iraqis. We will prevail in this conflict, however, and bring peace and prosperity to the Middle East."

Baker: "Of course it was a mistake to attack Iraq in the first place. We were warned. But we did and now we have to deal with it. I propose bringing U.N. peacekeeping troops into Iraq, thusly creating a lower profile of U.S. troops so that we look less like an occupying power. They are more qualified than we are to do this. We did not have the support of our allies, and it doesn't look like we will get it now that we are so mired down. Nobody else wants to get into this mess. Saddam Hussein is in hiding and, even though he is not visible, he is still powerful. This was going to be a hornet's nest from the get go and it is. Let's not lose any more of our young peoples' lives over this."

Thundering applause from the audience. Elizabeth, Betty, won another round.

Warren: "How soon will the area stabilize after we pull out?"

Baker: "It could be a long time. As far as the oil is concerned, we need to move ahead with programs to develop alternative, renewable resources. They exist already. We just need to retool, and in doing so, we could create thousands of quality jobs for people in America. We could even export the technology to other countries instead of guns and war machinery. And getting off petroleum products will have another benefit; people will be healthier. People will not suffer from asthma as much and the cancer rate will go down. And lastly, think about not having to deal with the Middle Eastern countries anymore. It just makes sense."

Another round of applause.

The debate continued on past the 90-minute limit. The topics discussed included Social Security, Medicare, prescription drugs, education in this country, separation of church and state, and the most contentious issue of the evening, abortion rights. Pundits would evaluate the evening after it was all over and say the James won the debate, but if measured by the enthusiasm of the audience for Betty, she clearly had an edge.

Carol Calls Andrew

Carol turned on the television to watch the presidential debate. She was getting the *USA Today* newspaper every morning now and had read about the live telecast from Boston. She would be able to watch the entire three hours of the debate due to the fact that she was on the West Coast and there was a three-hour time difference. The debate started at 7:00 P.M. eastern daylight time, which was 4:00 P.M. Pacific daylight time where Carol was. The nursing home required her to be in bed, with lights out, promptly at 9:00 every night, much to her dislike.

Seeing James again sent a shiver up her spine, knowing that he could have been complicit in her kidnapping. Instead of hating him, though, she pitied him, but she was also fearful of James and the people surrounding him in his administration. She felt that he had somehow gotten in over his head and couldn't get out. Either he was being threatened or they could be bribing him. She wanted to believe that it was the first scenario, although even that was a dreadful thought. Carol had read about a Democratic senator from North Dakota being killed in a plane crash, and there was some speculation that he may have been murdered. Senator John Collins had been flying in a small, chartered airplane to Minot to campaign for reelection when his plane went down just five miles from the landing strip. The aircraft was very capable with an experienced crew and the weather conditions were near perfect. Unfortunately with no black box, and the plane with its passengers were burned beyond recognition, the investigation could not prove that there was foul play. But it had been a month before the midterm elections and the Democrats, although trying to stay in the race by bringing back a former senator from the past, lost to the Patriots by a thousand votes, giving the Patriots another seat in the Senate. Would these people kill for power and money? She thought they would.

If this were true, James' life could be in danger, all because he wanted to serve his country in the highest office in the land. But she couldn't worry about that. She had to take care of herself, and she was in more danger than anyone right now. Her divorce, if the news got out, would upset the status quo in the Patriots party and throw the election to the Democrats. This had not been her intention, necessarily, although it would probably be a good thing if that happened. But there was a tremendous amount at stake for this administration. Gaining control of the region in the Middle East and the oil in Iraq would bring billions of dollars to the oil companies involved. Those in the administration who had affiliation with defense companies, and there were half a dozen, were making obscene amounts of money from the war and the rebuilding of Iraq. This was money that was being stolen from the taxpayers; money that would not be used in the United States for education, health care and other social programs. Millions of people were without work, being laid off from closed manufacturing plants, and the crime rate was rising to twenty-one percent and already crowded jails were bursting at the seams.

Carol was pleased with Elizabeth Baker's answers in the debate and she thought she had definitely done a good job. She also thought that having a woman in the White House would bring the divided country back together and mend the rifts with our allies and other countries in the world, gaining respect for the United States once again.

After an hour and a half of watching, Carol had had enough. She turned off the TV just as her dinner was being brought in to her. She had the aide put the tray on the table by the window and raised the shade halfway to bring some light into the room. The menu for this evening consisted of meatloaf, mashed potatoes, green beans and a Jell-O salad. Desert was chocolate pudding with whipped cream and a cherry on top. Pretty basic food and high in calories, so Carol was careful to not overeat, as she was not exercising like she normally would and she didn't want to gain weight. She had to stay lean and mean and healthy.

After eating dinner, she took off her one t-shirt and her jeans and put on her pajamas to get ready for bed. What else was there to do? She had talked her nurse into buying her a Tom Clancy novel and she was almost looking forward to an evening of reading in bed.

The next morning at 6:00 A.M., nurse Jackson knocked on the door and entered her room. "Time to get up, Mrs. Walters. Did you sleep well last night?" She asked the same question every morning.

"Yes, I slept as well as I could. What's on the agenda for today?"

"It's Thursday and you have a counseling session with Dr. Molear at 10 o'clock. You can take your shower, and breakfast should be here soon. Let me know if you need any help."

"I think I'll manage. I do need more clothes. I've been wearing this same t-shirt and jeans for over a week now. Do you think you could do that for me?"

"I'll try, Mrs. Walters. Or we could just send them to be laundered."

"Yes, I guess we could do that; however, I am getting tired of wearing the same clothes every day."

"Now, now," nurse Jackson said in a patronizing way. "I'll talk to somebody about it." And she left the room.

Carol went into the bathroom and took off her pajamas. She opened the shower door and turned on the water, adjusting it until it was just the right temperature; she liked it a little on the warm side. She then entered the shower and let the water pour over her face and her body. She stood there, reveling in the feeling of the water caressing her body. After several minutes, she didn't know how many, she squeezed a dollop of the herbal shampoo into the palm of her hand and rubbed it into her hair and massaged and scrubbed until she felt satisfied that her hair was clean. She then took the washcloth and put some of the Dove soap on it and, starting with her arms and her shoulders, she washed and massaged her skin, washing her breasts with loving care as her nipples became erect. She slowly washed her belly and then her buttocks and moved her hands to wash her legs and her feet. She thought about how little time in her adult life she had devoted to taking care of herself. To love herself. She was always taking care of Andrew or James, working with him on the ranch and seeing to it that the house was clean, the kitchen well stocked with food, dinners ready on time, and of late, taking care of the White House and the many duties that that entailed. It occurred to her that if she didn't take care of herself, who would? And if she didn't take care of herself, how could she take care of anyone else?

She heard the door to her room open again and she moved from her reverie to turn off the water, stepping out of the shower to towel herself dry. Putting on her clothes, she walked out to see that her breakfast had been placed on the table, along with the morning newspaper. Sitting down at the table, Carol glanced at the headline on the front page of the newspaper. In bold print, PRESIDENT WALTERS CLEAR WINNER OF FIRST DEBATE.

Winner, my foot, she thought. And she drank some orange juice and slowly ate one of her poached eggs and one piece of toast with grape jelly. The coffee was not very hot and not of the fresh-ground variety that she liked most, but it would have to do. She thought about how, two years ago, she would have been cheering for her husband, but that had all changed. For him to win would be to lose.

Carol sat by the window with the shade raised just enough to let some sun in and read her Clancy novel for the next two hours until it was time for her appointment with Dr. Molear. Promptly at 9:45, the aide knocked and opened the door.

"Are you ready, Mrs. Walters?"

"Yes, I am ready." And they walked down the hall and around the corner to Dr. Molear's office.

"Good morning, Carol. How are you feeling today?" Dr. Molear greeted her.

"All things considered, I am feeling well. And you, Dr. Molear?"

"Yes, I am quite fine, thank you, although I did not sleep well last night. Come in and sit down here."

Dr. Molear motioned her over to the same leather chair that she had been sitting in for the last three sessions.

"Carol, I would like to talk about your relationship with your husband. How did you meet your husband?"

"We met at the school where I was teaching. James came to give a talk on civics to the children."

"When you saw him for the first time, what were your thoughts?"

Carol thought for moment. "I don't know. I guess I thought he was an up-and-coming senator, and he was a handsome, likable guy."

"Did you know that day that you would be dating him?"

"Dr. Molear, where is this going? No, I didn't. I wasn't a groupie if that's what you're referring to. And I'm not a manipulating person. He was as much interested in me as I was attracted to him."

"Now, calm down. I am just wanting to know if you felt a connection when you first saw him."

The door flew open. "Dr. Molear, you have to come with me now. One of our residents is really sick. She tried to commit suicide," the aide blurted out.

Dr. Molear quickly left the room, leaving Carol alone. She looked around the office. She was annoyed with the questions that Dr. Molear was asking. She felt that her private life was being put under a microscope and she didn't like it. Then she spotted the cell phone. She went over to the desk, picked up the phone and dialed her son, Andrew's number.

After four long rings, her son's roommate answered "Hello, who is this?"

"Sean, this is Mrs. Walters. Listen carefully; I can only say this once. Tell Andrew that I am in Redlands, California, at the Village Mountain Nursing Care. Call Andrew. . . ."

The aide who had summoned Dr. Molear was back and he grabbed the phone from her hands.

Trouble for Alison

Hey, Alison, aren't you going to work tonight?" Jody asked late one afternoon as she was getting ready for a date. "You haven't been working very much lately, did you inherit some money or something?"

"No, I'm not feeling well. I think I'll stay home in bed today."

"There's something wrong. Do you want to talk about it? I'm your friend, you know."

"No, nothing's wrong. I'll feel better soon."

Jody, Alison's roommate had noticed that Alison had changed since that fateful afternoon when Alison had come home with bruises on her face, and she was concerned.

And Alison realized that she was not the same person after her abduction. She had trouble concentrating on her schoolwork and she started missing work, calling in sick, saying she had a migraine, the flu, cramps, anything she could think of, especially if it was a late-night shift. Every day was becoming a struggle. Every day Alison was looking over her shoulder, wondering if she was being followed, being watched. Would they take her again? She was also concerned that they might find out that she told Sean about her kidnapping, and she knew that these guys meant business.

Worrying that this was going to cause her to fail in school and maybe lose her job, Alison went to the doctor to see if there was a medication that might help.

"I can give you a prescription for an antidepressant, but it will most likely make you sleepy," said Dr. Mendez, one of the physicians in the school infirmary.

"I hate taking medication, but I don't know what to do. And I'm having trouble sleeping at night, too."

"Has something happened to you that would cause this?" the doctor asked.

"No, I can't think of anything," Alison lied. She couldn't tell him or anyone else for fear *they* would find out and come and kill her like *they* said they would.

"Something going on in your family? Did your boyfriend dump you? You were dating Andrew Walters weren't you?"

Everyone on campus knew that Alison was dating the president's son.

"Do you want to see a counselor?"

"No, I don't think that would help at this point."

"I'll go ahead and give you two prescriptions, one for sleeping and one for help with depression. I want you to take the sleeping pills only when you absolutely have to, and I am suggesting that you take the antidepressant on a daily basis until you feel that things are evening out, and then I want you to check back with me in a month."

"I hate taking this stuff. I've never taken sleeping pills before and antidepressants? It's a crutch."

"No, not really. A lot of people take them."

"But I'm not a lot of people. Isn't there a better way?"

"Exercising will help. Do you work out?"

"Not really, but I think I will start. Thanks, doc, I appreciate it."

Alison went to the pharmacy and had the prescriptions filled, but she didn't take the antidepressant and only took a sleeping pill when she felt she absolutely couldn't get to sleep. There was a gym on campus and she started working out every day and was beginning to see a difference within a week's time. She also started hiking again. Hiking was her first love, but she had done little of it since Andrew had gone. This was the one thing that they had done together every week, and they had had a special place past Centennial Park off of Sunshine Canyon Drive. It was rocky and steep in places, but it was a good workout and not far from the campus. And, so, every day that she was not working the late shift, she would drive out to the canyon, hike for an hour or more and then drive back feeling recharged. Her feelings of paranoia started to lessen, she was able to concentrate on her studies, and was missing work less often.

On one afternoon hike she stayed longer than usual to watch the sunset over the mountains, wishing Andrew were there to enjoy it with her. It was almost dark by the time she got back to her car. She got into the car and drove away from the trailhead parking area and onto the main road. Immediately a truck approached from behind with its lights glaring in her rearview mirror, temporarily blinding her. Alison tried to pull away, but the truck moved up closer and bumped her car, causing it to lurch forward. Panic set it. Alison stepped on the gas but there was a sharp turn ahead, and with the truck closing in behind her again, she lost control and her car tumbled over the edge and into the canyon below.

One week later, Sean opened up the *The Denver Post* as he was having his morning coffee. He saw the headline on page five: "College Coed's Car Crashes in Canyon." He read further. "Alison Moffet's car was found in a side canyon off of Sunshine Canyon Drive. Alison was pronounced dead at the scene apparently from injuries sustained in the crash. A hiker in the area spotted the crashed car and notified authorities. . . ."

Tears streamed down Sean's face. "Damn. Damn," he said again. "Why did this have to happen to Alison?"

A New Strategy

The same group was gathered in the executive conference room aboard Air Force One on the return trip to Washington that late night on September 22. The huge airplane slipped up through the scattered clouds, climbing into the night sky with great power and ease. A half-moon, white with promise, shone down on the great bird in the sky to belie the turmoil within.

"We have to stay away from domestic issues altogether," Jason implored.

"And how do we do that?" James said.

The debate had not gone well for James. It was obvious by the end of the evening that Elizabeth Baker was dominating by keeping to the message of addressing the issues of a faltering economy, loss of jobs for the middle class and other domestic problems in the country.

Terry, being silent for some time now, spoke up. "By talking up the war and the fight on terrorism. If the people are convinced that we have done a great job in protecting them against terrorism and that no one, no administration can do this as well as we can, they will support us. We can't be concerned with the domestic issues right now. We will not win that battle with Baker. Addressing social programs will mean spending more money and the deficit is already skyrocketing. We could lose many of the conservative Republicans who have been supporting us in the war effort."

"Terry's right," Charles, the Secretary of Defense interjected. "The ordinary citizen in this country is more worried about protection against terrorism than anything else and we have to play on that.

That is what will get us reelected."

"We've done a great job in this area. We've created the Homeland Security Agency. We've captured hundreds of al-Qaeda in Afghanistan. We've ousted Saddam from Iraq. We need to concentrate on the positive."

James looked around the table with skepticism. "What do I say when I'm at the podium and questions are being fired at me about the unemployment rate, about factories shutting down? What do I tell them?"

"You tell them that the economy is fundamentally sound and that it is recovering. I think we will see evidence of that in October. And then talk about your economic measures of lowering taxes to put more money in people's pockets and then shut up," Terry said.

"I agree. Our strong point is the war. People have always rallied around the president during wartime. As long as we are at war, we will be heroes and this war is not going to be over for a very long time. Saddam is out. We will bring democracy to Iraq, and we will have control of the majority of the oil in the world. The American people will be bowing down in the streets to us. You know how they love their SUVs," Charles said.

"Charles is right. Keep to the war message and we'll be fine," Stanley parroted.

"What if we aren't heroes? What if this war drags on and we have more terrorist attacks on our soil. We know that Homeland Security is not yet prepared to handle suicide attacks in this country. All it takes is one or two suicide bombers in shopping malls and a couple of restaurants, and people will stop shopping and the economy will continue to spiral downward. Then manufacturing would cut back and more jobs would be lost. Do you see what I am getting at? It doesn't take a missile from Iraq to take this country to its knees." James was clearly worried.

"What if, what if, what if. . . . You could go on saying that all day long. Do you want to be reelected? If you do, then you need to keep to the war and security message. It doesn't matter after that. Once we are reelected, we are golden. If we can maintain and even gain in the Senate and the House, then we will have a mandate. We can have another four years to put our military programs in place and cut taxes again. The people will not have a choice then." Terry was close to yelling at the president, his face red and his veins bulging out on his temples.

"Most of the manufacturing is overseas anyway. When was the last time you bought a pair of shoes made in this country?" Jason said, as he looked James straight in the eye.

"That's the problem. Manufacturing has gone offshore; IT and other white-collar jobs are going to India and China. What kinds of jobs will be left in the U.S.?" James drank his Evian water from the crystal glass in front of him. "How can the economy ever recover if there aren't any jobs. And that tax base is gone forever."

"But this is good for the corporations, keeping labor costs low. With a high unemployment rate, the worker has little bargaining power and companies can hire people for less money. The jobs that used to pay sixty to seventy thousand are now paying half that, and this improves the bottom line. As far as the workers are concerned, they're going to have to retool. Healthcare jobs are plentiful, and as we become more of a service economy, they'll have to move into these kinds of jobs," Jason said.

"You can't go ballistic on us now. You are in this and you will do what we say. And in the end we will all gain from this," Terry said looking at the president in earnest.

"And another thing, Mr. President," Stanley said in a softer tone, "we have the media on our side. I heard the broadcast on Fox News before we left tonight and they said that you are clearly the winner tonight."

James looked around the table, but he was silent now. Yes, he was in this. To a degree that he knew he couldn't turn back. He was sacrificing everything for power and money. And in the end, he didn't even have the power. The political machine had the power and they were dictating to him what to do, and if he did not want to follow orders, he would be out. He realized that now. His marriage was gone; his relationship with his son was gone. What price had he paid?

Terry, Jason, Stanley, Charles and Tom left the conference room, stomping out with great pomp. James went back to his bedroom area and sat down in a large leather chair by a window. He looked out at the clouds, viewing the tranquility below him, knowing that underneath that layer of clouds were the people of his country. People who trusted him, many of whom were hurting now for lack of work, people who were fearful and counting on him and the government to protect them. Was he betraying them? And he knew something else. The people in this country are not stupid and they would know the truth when they see it and that is what really frightened him.

Jason, Terry, Charles and Stanley walked back through the area of Air Force One where the press held court. Several of the reporters were on their cell phones calling in to further report on the debate, while others were pounding away on their laptops, hoping to meet the deadline for tomorrow morning's papers. They continued on back to the VIP area where only the cabinet members and friends were allowed. Jason sat down in the plush, camel-colored leather seat and motioned Terry to join him.

"Terry, I am really worried about James. I wonder if he really has the balls to go through with this," Jason said looking directly at Terry.

"Oh, he'll be all right. I think he's upset about Carol, to tell you the truth."

"That's just what I mean. If he's not concentrating and looks ambivalent, this is going to come across to the public. I am very concerned."

"What do you suggest we do about it. He is the duly elected incumbent president. We can't just remove him from the election," Terry said, his Irish temper showing.

"No, I guess you're right."

"Jason, I've never heard you talk like this before. We're a team. We have to support the president one hundred percent. It's the only way. And if we see him cracking, we're gonna prop him up and help him to go on."

"If something happened to him. . . ."

"I don't know what you're saying, Jason, but I don't like it."

As Jason got up from the seat and walked back to the special seat assigned to the vice president, there was a little bump in the airplane and he grabbed onto the bin handle above him and then sat down.

Situation Room

There was a somber tone in the situation room this late September morning. The President and his staff had returned from the debate in Boston to find the war in Iraq was turning even more ugly and fighting in Afghanistan had escalated. With troops now in Colombia and the Philippines, the military was being stretched thin and battles were being lost on a daily basis. In addition, North Korea was becoming more of a threat, Pakistan was threatening to attack India with nuclear weapons, and Japan and China were getting into the fray as well.

The large room, dimly lit with huge maps on two walls, a strategy board on another, could be called the war conference room or command center in Washington. James, the vice president, Jason Martin, the secretary of defense, Charles Robertson, General Donald Struthers, chief of the United States Central Command, and other lesser generals and officers had gathered for an emergency meeting to try to address the problems of the moment.

"The Kurds are vying for control in the north, attacking the Turks and our troops. The two bombings yesterday killed 25 people and injured 150 more. We need to defuse these battles. They are taking away from our main objective of securing the country. Saddam's men are still out there sniping away at our troops on a daily basis, even though he is in custody. And the Republican Guard has gone into hiding among the residents of Baghdad. We think they occasionally appear and shoot at our men in the city," Donald reported.

Saddam had finally been captured the week before, much to the relief of James and everyone involved in the war, and it had given James a boost in the polls.

"What is the situation with the Shiite and Suni Muslims in the south?" Charles asked.

"We are holding these areas, but with guerillas coming out at night and attacking our troops in this area, we're losing one or two soldiers a day, and last week we lost ten in Tikrit with a firebomb. The area around An Nasinyan along the Euphrates still remains to be a problem," Donald said as he pointed out the areas with a laser pointer on the large, brightly lit map.

James was strangely silent as this dialogue was taking place.

"What about the oil fields? Have we been able to secure the oil wells yet," Vice President Martin asked.

"We can't get in there to get the job done. When we send people in there to do the work, the guerrilla fighters come out and snipe at them and we've had casualties here also," Donald continued. "And add to this the problems we are having in Afghanistan and Colombia, not to minimize North Korea and the Philippines, Mr. President, I think we have to come up with a better plan. We're in over our heads right now, stretched pretty thin."

James snapped to attention. "No, we aren't. We just have to keep working all the fronts. I think North Korea is bluffing right now; they're not going to attack the U.S. China won't let that happen. So we'll shelve our earlier plan to attack their nuclear facilities. And as far as the Philippines are concerned, we did not send our men in there to fight. They are only there to advise the Philippine military on how to search out and eradicate Muslim extremists. That eliminates two problem areas right there."

"Now our only objective in Afghanistan is to secure the area along the pipeline and maintain control of Kabul, and so far, we are doing that, am I correct in this assumption?" James stared at the other men seated around the table.

"We are, but I think it is just a matter of time before we lose that control. The Taliban is back in full force and the Warlords, who were on our side a couple of years ago, are now fighting against us," Donald pointed out. "And another real problem that we need to address is the morale of our troops. We've had 200 military go home on leave and never return; gone AWOL. This is serious. We've had twenty-two suicides and another 1,000 soldiers sent home with psychiatric problems. If we don't rotate these troops out of there soon. . . ."

"Look, they knew what they were getting into when they signed up. They knew they could be sent to war. Most of them were looking for a way to go to college on the cheap," James said.

"That may be true, but you need to understand what it is like over there. In other wars, soldiers had some downtime. In this one they are watching their backs twenty-four by seven. It gets pretty intense."

There was silence around the large mahogany table, and heads were looking down, as if these men, many who had never seen combat, were putting themselves in the places of the men and women fighting in these faraway places of the world.

Charles broke the calm, "We need to have a massive rotation out of Iraq. We'll call up as many National Guard troops necessary to do this and bring these people home for some R and R. And then we also need to consider the draft."

"The draft? We can't do that. It would kill us in the election," Jason stood up with his hands on the table.

"I agree. We can bring back the draft, but after the election," said James.

"The immediate problem at hand is securing Iraq so that we can get our contractors in there to start rebuilding, getting the electricity up and going with some reliability. You do know that some of the causalities in the last few months have been civilian U.S. contractors?

When other contractors see this happening, they don't want to go there and you can't blame them," said Jason. "Once we get the infrastructure working, I think the attacks will start to decrease. Once the Iraqi people see that we intend to do good things for them, they will start working with us and help in the fight against these rebel insurgents."

"Just who is responsible for these attacks?" asked James.

"We're not sure to be truthful. We thought once Saddam was caught, the attacks would decrease. But that hasn't happened. If anything, they've increased and the intensity has increased also. The attacks are more professional, if you will. Like an outside group, maybe the Taliban or al-Qaeda is in there working with other insurgent groups," said Donald. "We're seeing suicide bombers like in the West Bank, and that is something new and very hard to control as Sharon already knows. When we were in the heat of war, we were unable to adequately secure the borders, and I think terrorists came in from other countries in the region to fight the jihad for Islam. It just complicates things more. And another point here; until we can guarantee a safe Iraq, the elections cannot go forward there, and our promise of bringing democracy to the country will fail."

"You are right. We are committed to making Iraq a safe country. We told the world that we were bringing democracy to the Middle East and, by God, we are going to do that," Jason said with fervor. "Charles, I want you to go to the United Nations next week and get them involved. They can help us with setting up the Iraqi elections. Now, we have Japan sending in some troops and we're going to go ahead and rotate some of our soldiers out, getting some fresh people in there. I want to see things improving in the next month."

"And if it doesn't?" asked James. "What then? We can't have this mess for the election."

"I agree, but I think we will see an improvement soon," Jason answered.

The men discussed other world issues for the rest of the meeting and then broke up with everyone leaving the room and going on to other meetings and appointments for the day. As James was walking out of the door he called to Jason.

"Jason, would you come to my office. I would like to talk to you."

"Be glad to. What's this about?"

"Let's go to my office."

Both of the men walked down the hallway and turned into another in the West Wing heading for the Oval Office. When they reached the office, James seated himself at his desk and Jason pulled up one of the upholstered chairs in front of the desk and sat down.

"I have been hearing strange rumors lately and I am concerned," James started the conversation.

"Rumors? What kind of rumors?"

"That you are questioning my authority in the Executive Office."

"I don't know what you're talking about."

"I'll come right to the point. That you would like to see me out of the way."

"The only question that I have, is are you up to the task? Are you tough enough for this job? You sometimes seem ambivalent, even frightened. If that should come through to the people, you will lose all credibility. You're going to have to remain strong. And I am wondering if you can do that with your family problem with Carol." Jason looked strait into James eyes.

"What is happening there? Is she going to get better? You must be devastated," Jason continued.

"Carol will come through this. She's a strong woman. And devastated, yes, I am, but I can still do this job and do it well."

"Maybe you should step down temporarily. Just until things quiet down and you know Carol is safe."

"No, absolutely not," James said with resolve. "I guess you want my job, is that right?"

"No, I don't want your job. You have one of the toughest jobs in the world and I don't want it."

"Well, if you continue to question my authority, I'll. . . ."

"You'll what. There is nothing you can do. Everyone knows that I am the brains in this administration. That you are the rookie."

James eyes narrowed and the veins on his neck stood out. "Jason, I am going to warn you just once. If you continue to challenge me, I have the ammunition to bring you down and I'll not hesitate to use it. Trust me."

"What are you talking about?"

"I'm talking about your late night visits with your little female lawyer friend. I'm sure Diane would be very interested."

"This is nonsense. I don't know what you're talking about. I think it's time to end this meeting. I'll see you in the cabinet meeting tomorrow morning." And with that said, Jason promptly got up and walked out the door.

James turned to the window and looked over the manicured south lawn of the White House. He had struck a nerve, but he also felt very isolated. With Carol, his trusted ally, gone, he was alone and he didn't know whom he could trust anymore.

Andrew Gets the Call

Andrew was carrying a large tray of dishes when he felt his cell phone vibrate. He delivered the last tray to the table that he was serving and then went back to the kitchen to check his phone. Seeing one message from his roommate, Sean, Andrew walked into the men's room, hoping for privacy. Two men were standing in front of urinals and a third was washing his hands. He turned and walked back out and continued on out of the restaurant, almost running to his truck. He unlocked the door and sat down and punched in the number in Boulder.

"Hello," Sean answered after about five rings.

"Sean, this is Andrew. You called me? What's up?"

"Your mother called. Just a couple of hours ago."

Andrew's heart jumped. "What did she say? Did you talk to her?"

"Yeah, I did."

"What did she say?"

"It was hard to hear her and she was cut off, but it sounded like she said that she was in Redlands. In a place called Mountain Ridge Nursing Home or Mountain something nursing care."

"Didn't you write it down? This is critical."

"Yeah, Andy, I did, but I couldn't hear her very well. The connection was poor and then it went dead. But I am sure about the mountain thing and I know she said Redlands."

"I'm sorry, Sean. Didn't mean to yell. This is so important. You just don't know how important. Thanks for taking the message and thanks for calling."

"It's okay, pal. I hope everything is all right. I heard that your mother was in the hospital or something. Is she going to be okay?"

"Yeah, she's going to be fine. As soon as I . . . well, I can't tell you any more right now."

"I guess you heard about Alison."

"No, I didn't. What about her?"

"Her car went off the road and crashed into a canyon. A hiker saw the crashed car off of Sunshine Canyon Drive. She evidently died of injuries from the crash. I'm sorry, Andy."

"Oh, no. That can't be. She just wouldn't do that. She was a good driver. How could she crash her car like that?"

"You know she called me and we had coffee. She told me that some thugs kidnapped her and roughed her up. She was really frightened. They told her that if she mentioned a word to anyone about it, they would kill her. Maybe it wasn't an accident."

Andrew was silent.

"Oh, Andy, one more thing."

"Yeah?"

"The FBI was here. They asked a lot of questions."

"So what'd you tell 'em?"

"Just what you told me. That you were taking a break from school and I didn't really know where you'd gone. They were pretty persuasive, but I kept my mouth shut."

"We'd better hang up. No doubt the phones are tapped and they're listening to every word we're saying right now. Thanks for your help. I probably won't talk to you for awhile."

Tears streamed down Andrew's cheeks as he turned off his cell phone. How could this happen? He really loved Alison and he had even thought about marrying her. But now she was gone and it was his fault.

Andrew went back into the restaurant and nearly collided with one of the other waiters as he was going to find his supervisor to let him know that he was leaving for the day. He told him that he had a family emergency. He then went back to his truck, got into it, revved the motor and drove as fast as the speed limit would allow. The five-mile drive to his apartment seemed to take forever, but because the traffic was light this time of day, ten minutes later he pulled into the parking area of the Sun Down Apartments where he lived temporarily. He got out of the truck, raced up the stairs to his second-floor apartment, fumbling with the key, finally entered and went straight to his computer.

It was 2:00 P.M. in Denver, mountain daylight time. It must have been about 10:30 Pacific daylight time when she called, 11:30 Denver time. He quickly got on the Internet and went to the nursing home page that he had been using for his search. He entered Redlands in the space for "city". There was a Redlands in Colorado and Redlands in California. He wondered if she could be in Colorado. No, they would not leave her in this state. He pulled up a list of nursing homes in Redlands, California. There were thirty-four and only two had names with mountain. There was the Desert Mountain Rehabilitation Center on West Mountain View and the Mountain Village Nursing Care center on East Via Linda.

Andrew's heart was still pounding, the palms of his hands sweating as he dialed the number of the Desert Mountain Rehabilitation Center. He asked for the director or someone in charge. A woman by the name of Sara Goldstein answered and when he said that he was with the Federal Bureau of Nursing Homes, she seemed agreeable to talking to him. He then asked how many people had been admitted in September and to give him a list for each day by gender and age. Sara searched her records and rattled off some numbers to him. No female his mother's age had been admitted on or around September 5. He thanked her and hung up the phone. It has to be the Mountain Village Home, he thought.

He punched in the number of the Mountain Village Nursing Care center. Again he asked for someone in charge.

"Hello, Mountain Village Nursing Care, this is Patty Simpson, how can I help you?" a cheerful voice answered.

"My name is Thomas Morgan and I am with the Federal Bureau of Nursing Homes in Washington. We are trying get a handle on how many people have been admitted to nursing homes in the last several months so that we can design our federal programs to meet the needs of an aging population."

Patty was very agreeable. "Yes, I can get that for you. Give me your address in Washington and I'll send it to you."

"I would like the information over the phone. If you can imagine gathering this information for thousands of nursing homes and I just have the West coast. If you could just give me one month's data, say for September?"

"I guess I could do that. Just a minute, let me pull up my records on the computer. Yes, September."

And she rattled off the numbers, ages and genders. As she got to the fifth and sixth of the month, Andrew held his breath.

"September 4, we admitted one male age 80 and three females ages 80, 83 and 85. September 6, two males ages 75 and 79, and one female aged 56. We sometimes have younger people convalescing from surgery that is probably why the woman of 56."

Bingo. That had to be her. He raised his hand in victory as he listened politely to rest of the data and then he thanked her very much and hung up the phone. He went back to the Internet to find the closest airport to Redlands and determined that to be the Ontario airport. He then went to Expedia.com and found that United Airlines had a flight at 8:05 P.M. He hoped there was a seat for him and there was.

By tomorrow morning, he would have his mother out of the nursing home and in a safe place. If he could just figure out now how he was going to achieve this. And then he would have to find a safe and secure place for her where they, the CIA or FBI or whoever else, wouldn't find her. He still had some things to work out, but he was pleased with his progress.

United Airlines, Flight 475 landed at Ontario International Airport on time at 9:15 P.M. with Andrew James Walters on board. Andrew had made a reservation at a Best Western Hotel in San Bernardino, about five miles, according to the map, from the nursing home. Andrew deplaned and went directly to Budget Rent-a-Car and rented a small Ford Focus and, with directions from the car rental agency, found his way to the hotel on East Hospitality Lane in San Bernardino. He checked in and then gathered his one small duffel bag and his laptop computer and went to his room. The room was better than he thought it would be for the price. There was a coffee maker, hairdryer, ironing board and iron and, most importantly, a modem jack for his computer. There were also plenty of restaurants in the area, although he hoped he wouldn't be spending that much time here.

Andrew laid down on the bed and thought again about Alison. Looking up into the white ceiling with the fan turning, he thought about how things could be so different. The crash was no accident. If only he hadn't started dating her, she would still be alive. If only his dad weren't the president and his mother wasn't divorcing, she would still be alive. If only this government wasn't so corrupt, Alison would still be living. Was he to blame? She was so beautiful and he did love her. Was he going to marry her? He didn't know. He closed his eyes for a few minutes to try to rid himself of the melancholy he felt. But it was done and there was nothing that would bring her back now. His thoughts came back to his mother.

He needed to devise a plan to go into the nursing home without the staff noticing and get his mother out. As he was preparing for bed, he was thinking; who would be the most trusted people in a nursing home. Doctors, of course. He would pose as a doctor; say that he was there to monitor her health. They would take him to her room and the rest would be easy.

Andrew slept fitfully, and when he woke in the morning. His plan of the night before didn't seem as feasible at 6:00 A.M. But it was the best he had for the time being. He slipped on his jeans and a t-shirt with Coors written across the front and decided that these clothes would not be the uniform of a doctor. It was time to go shopping. Looking in the phone book, he found a Macy's store that was only a few miles from the hotel.

Getting into his rental car, he drove onto the freeway and then to the town of Redlands. Driving down State Street, he located the shopping center and drove into the parking lot and parked his car. As he walked into Macy's he looked for a store directory, found the men's department and headed straight for it. Like most department stores, there was a lot to choose from and so, in the interest of time, he asked one of the clerks to help him find what he was looking for. After picking out a pair of gray wool slacks and a light-blue dress shirt, he carried them to the shoe department where he selected a pair of nutmeg Cole Haan classic loafers, handmade, costing $240, expensive in his estimation. He hated spending his money on things like this; his preference in footwear was hiking boots or running shoes.

"Don't you want to try these on?" the skinny young male sales clerk asked.

"No, I know they'll fit. I don't really have time."

Hurrying back to the hotel, he took the tags off the new clothing and put on the shirt and the slacks and shoes and looked in the mirror. Yes, I could pass for a doctor, he thought.

Taking his bag and his computer with him, he went to the lobby of the hotel, grabbed a Danish, some juice and a cup of coffee and then he was off to the nursing home.

Andrew slowly approached the Mountain Village nursing facility. As with most nursing care facilities, this one had the appearance of a large home. There were several attached, one-story buildings with sand-colored stucco walls and the Spanish-style red-tile roof so prevalent in the Southwest. A large portico adorned the front of the first building, and he thought this must be the main entrance. He drove into the parking lot and parked in a visitor's space. There were five spaces assigned for doctors, but he did not want to park in one of them as they might require an identifying sticker and, additionally, he didn't have the kind of car a doctor would drive. He put on the tortoise-rimmed glasses he had bought at a drugstore on the way to the nursing home and looked in the rearview mirror to see if they made him look more like a doctor. Satisfied, he got out of the car and walked the fifty yards to the main entrance. The sun was bright even at mid-morning and the air very warm and dry. Fall had not yet arrived in Redlands.

He took a deep breath to screw up his courage and looked around for a concierge. Her desk was located off to the side of a very large living room, decorated in period furniture with a red Oriental rug on the floor.

Andrew approached the desk and said, "I am Dr. William Wainright from the Southwest Medical Clinic in Redlands. I'm new here, can you point me to the nurse's station?" Andrew had checked out the names of clinics in the area.

A woman in her late sixties with dyed brown hair and glasses hanging around her neck on a chain, looked up, eyed him carefully and finally said, "Yes, Dr, Wainright, if you go down that hall to your left and then turn right, you will see the head nurse's station."

He followed the concierge's instructions and found the nurse's station.

"I'm Dr. Wainright. I'm here to see Mrs. James Walters. Where is her chart? And what room is she in?" Andrew said with more authority than he thought he had.

There were two nurses at the station, one filling out paperwork and another updating charts. The younger one, who was updating the charts looked up at Andrew and then checked the charts.

"Mrs. Walters is no longer here. She was moved to another facility yesterday."

Andrew tried not to let his disappointment show.

"Why didn't they tell me that? Do you know which facility they took her to?"

"I am not at liberty to tell you that. Can I see your credentials, Dr. Wainright?"

Andrew reached into his pocket for his wallet and then said, "I must have left my wallet in my car. Ah, I'll be right back."

Andrew quickly walked back through the living room area and past the concierge. As he was walking by, the brown-haired woman called out to him, "Dr. Wainright. Did you find the nurse's station?"

Andrew turned and briefly looked at her, "Yes, I did. I forgot something in my car." And he continued to walk out the door.

As he got back into his car, his disappointment grew. This was going to be more difficult than he thought. What was next? He couldn't wait until she called again. She might not get that opportunity. And time was not on his side. He felt that he had to get to her before the end of the month. Election day was November 2. Anything could happen to her between now and then.

He was back where he had started. He decided to go back to the hotel. As he was driving on the freeway, he started thinking of every possible way to find his mother. Then he worried that she might not be alive. No, they wouldn't do that. Not yet anyway.

He arrived back at the hotel at about noon. He wasn't hungry, so he decided to put on his swimming suit and take a swim and a Jacuzzi and then maybe a long nap. In the meantime he would ponder the problem. He didn't have much time, maybe a week at the most.

The phone was ringing or was he dreaming? He looked at the clock. It was five o'clock. He'd slept longer than he thought he would. Who would be calling his hotel room? No one knew he was here. It kept ringing.

"Hello," he answered.

"Is this Andrew Walters?" a scratchy voice at the other end said.

"Who's this?" Andrew asked.

"I know where your mother is," the voice said.

"How did you know I was here?" Andrew was still half asleep and he knew immediately he shouldn't have said that.

"Do you want to know where your mother is?"

"Who are you? How do know where she is?"

"We know where she is. Do you want to find her?"

"I do. How much do you want?" Andrew decided to play the game and see where it went.

"A hundred grand. Have the money by tonight or we'll contact another interested party who will pay that and much more."

"Why not go to the other party first if you can get more money?"

"We thought you would be more interested."

Andrew was thoroughly awake now. "I can't get that kind of money tonight." Maybe he could stall them.

"Have it tomorrow afternoon by three. We'll call you at the hotel at two and tell you where to make the drop. If you don't, I wouldn't count on your mother being alive after tomorrow." And the line went dead.

Andrew's in a Tight Spot

Andrew called his supervisor, Matt, at Al's Steakhouse where he was a waiter. He told him that he wouldn't be back to work for the next couple of weeks due to a family emergency. Matt had been very understanding and told him to take as much time as he needed and that his job was still there whenever he wanted to come back. In the few weeks that Andrew had worked there, he had made a good impression with everyone. Given his winning smile and warm personality, Andrew's customers loved him and always ordered more food from him than any of the other waiters, which of course pleased the manager. And his co-workers liked him, too. However he kept his distance and hadn't formed any real friendships at the restaurant because he did not want to answer any questions. No one knew that he was the president's son.

It was getting close to the 2:00 P.M. deadline for the blackmailer's phone call. Andrew wasn't ready. He didn't have the money; he didn't even have a plan. The phone rang and Andrew jumped in his chair.

"Hello."

"You can drop the money at the Central Park on Highland and 5th Street at 3:00 P.M. today. Leave it under the park bench on the south side. Someone will be watching you, so don't try any tricks. And don't call the cops." It was the same scratchy voice that he had heard the day before.

"I don't have the money, but I'll have it by Friday." Andrew was hoping they would buy this, as it would give him a few more days to figure out this dilemma.

"Look, there's no reason for you not to have the fuckin' money. You're just stalling. We know you've got it, probably in your fuckin' checking account. Rich kids always have money in their checking accounts. I'm afraid we're gonna have to talk to our alternates, and I wouldn't bet on your mama being alive too much longer."

"I guess that's the chance I have to take. I promise I will have it for you on Friday. Call me again Friday morning." Andrew had no choice; he had to take a chance that they were bluffing, and if they thought they would get the money on Friday, he was hoping they would go for this.

"Who the fuck you think we are?"

"I don't know who the fuck you are. I sure would like to know. But that's my last offer. Take it or leave it."

"Friday at 10:00 A.M. And that's all you get, kid. I hate fuckin' rich kids," and the line went dead.

What was next? Should he get a private investigator? Should he call the police? No, he would definitely not call the police into this. That would blow the whole thing apart. Andrew jumped again as his cell phone rang.

"Hello, this is Andrew," Andrew said unwittingly.

"Hi, Andy. I had another call this morning and this one is kind of mysterious but I thought you might want to check it out." Sean said on the other end of the line.

"What's going on?"

"Well, this guy called me about an hour ago. He said he was a paramedic with the SouthWest Ambulance Company in San Bernardino, California. He told me that they were transporting a woman the day before yesterday and she gave him a note written on the page of a paperback novel."

"Oh, yeah. And what did the note say, Sean?" Andrew asked with eager interest.

"It didn't say too much. Just said to call her son at this number.

That was about it."

Andrew's disappointment was evident in his voice. "That's all. That's not much help."

"One more thing. The guy gave me his name and number and said you should call him. His name is Nolan Brill and his number is area code (909) 956-7659. He said he might be able to help you."

"Ah, that's what I wanted to hear." Andrew quickly wrote the number on the hotel notepad. "I think we're finally getting somewhere. Thanks, Sean. And if you get any more strange calls, let me know right away."

"What's going on, Andy? I can't help being curious. What have you and your mother gotten into?"

"Don't ask. I can't talk about it right now. Maybe someday."

"Okay. Whatever you say. I hope everything works out."

"I do too and thanks for your help. I'll talk to you soon." And they both hung up.

Andrew quickly punched in the numbers that Sean had given him on the hotel phone and waited until someone answered.

"Hello," a young woman answered.

"Is Nolan there?"

"No, he's not here right now. Who's calling?"

"This is Robert Johnson calling. When will he be back? Is he at work and can I reach him there?" Andrew could not give his real name.

"What is this about?"

"I had a message to call him. Does he have a cell phone?" Andrew persisted.

"Why don't you give me your number and I'll call him and have him call you back."

"Sure. I can do that. It's kind of urgent. How soon do you think he could get back to me?"

"If he's not on a call, he'll get back to you right away."

"That'll work." Andrew gave her his number and hung up.

He got up from the chair and started to pace the room, back and forth, back and forth. What if he doesn't call me back, he thought? What if he calls me back and wants a huge amount of money? That would be okay. He would pay the guy just to be able to free his mother. Time was not standing still and November was fast approaching. He turned on the TV and switched the channel to CNN.

"Taliban returns to Afghanistan," John Woodward, the news anchor was reading from the teleprompter. A video was showing U.S. troops searching through caves with bombs going off in the distance. "Since the Afghanistan war after 9/11, the coalition forces are now dealing with warlords who are fighting against them and the return of the Taliban. It has been thought that the Taliban has not been far away during this time, most likely waiting in Pakistan. Some of the coalition troops, namely the Canadians who are said to be disillusioned with the war on terrorism since the Walters administration had attacked Iraq, had pulled out, weakening the position of the remaining troops."

Andrew turned it off. What a mess we are in, he thought. The phone rang and he answered expectantly.

"Hello, is this Nolan?"

"Yes, yes this is Nolan Brill. You called my wife?"

"I did. You had a note from my mother and called my roommate?"

"Oh, yeah, now I remember. I transported her day before yesterday. She seemed distressed and gave me the note, so I followed up and called the number. What's this all about? She's pretty young to be in a nursing home. She doesn't even seem sick, although I think they had her pretty drugged up. That's why they called us. We do a pretty good job of monitoring people who are in that condition."

"Is she all right? What are they doing to her?"

"I really don't know. That's why I asked you. Are you her son? If you are, you should know about this."

"Nolan, I can't tell you everything. You are going to have to trust me. My mother is being held against her will. They haven't even told me where she is and that is why I am calling, hoping you will help me. Where is she? Where did you take her? I need to know."

"I don't know if I can give that information to you. How do I know you are her son? I need some proof."

Andrew started pleading. "Look, do you want money? I have money and I can pay you."

"No, I don't want your money. I just need some proof that you are who you say you are."

Andrew began to think quickly how he could prove to this guy that he was the son of the person he had transported. And then he had a bright idea.

"Meet me at IHOP on Hospitality Way in San Bernardino at noon today and I think I can show you that she is my mother."

"I don't get off until two. I'll meet you there at two-thirty. How will I know you?"

"I am six foot tall and I have dark brown hair, cut pretty short. I will be wearing a white t-shirt with a Becks beer logo on it. What do you look like?"

"I'm five foot ten, black curly hair and I'll be wearing a blue Hawaiian shirt. I'll see you at noon."

Andrew hung up the phone. He turned on his computer and opened the folder, Andrew's pics. There were twenty or more jpegs in the directory and he opened one of them with the title, "Mom with the dogs". It was a digital photo taken by his dad a couple of years ago of him and his mother playing with Buffy and Opal, their dogs at the ranch. He burned it onto the disk along with a couple of other jpegs.

Andrew was early. He had taken the disc with the photos to the Quick Photo shop and had prints made and then drove to IHOP. He walked into the restaurant and asked the hostess to seat him by the window on the south side. He wanted a clear view of the door so that he could watch people coming in. He ordered a cup of coffee and a tuna sandwich, not because he was hungry but because he thought he should. He took the photos out of the envelope and stared at them. He looked at his mother's face, laughing, filled with joy. She was dressed in blue jeans and wore a light-blue sweatshirt, and her short brown hair was falling in her face as she threw a tennis ball for Opal while Buffy was trying to get it away from her. It was a happy moment and he wondered if they would ever have these times again.

The waitress brought his sandwich and coffee just as a black man of medium height, wearing a blue Hawaiian shirt walked in the door. Andrew motioned to him to get his attention and the man acknowledged and made his way to the table.

Andrew rose from his seat. "Are you Nolan?"

"I am. And you're Robert Johnson?" Nolan looked carefully at Andrew. "I've seen you somewhere before."

Andrew ignored Nolan's last statement. "Yes, I'm Robert Johnson. Here, have a seat. Can I order something for you? It's on me."

"Just some coffee. I had a tough shift. We had this call at 4:00 A.M. to transport a woman from Hadley's Nursing Home to the Loma Linda Hospital. She'd had a stroke and she was having trouble breathing. Well, she died in transit."

"I'm sorry. It must be really hard when that happens."

"It happens a lot and you'd think I'd get used to it, but I don't. If it's an elderly person, I think of my grandmom, and if it's a child, of course I think about my two girls. I guess I'm just a softie."

"You know, Nolan, I think that's okay." Andrew liked this guy already.

Nolan looked at Andrew and smiled. "So how can I help you?"

"I need to know where my mother was taken. I was told that you were the paramedic when she was taken from the Village Mountain Nursing Home."

"I was. Normally I wouldn't give out this information. As we talked on the phone, I need some proof that you are really her son."

Andrew brought the pictures out and handed them to Nolan and watched him carefully as he looked at the photos.

Nolan looked at Andrew and then again at the photos. "Yeah, I can see the resemblance. She looks like your mom. I've seen her some place before, too. So what's the deal? I don't get it. If you are her son, and it looks like you are, how come you don't know where she is? Are you trying to knock her off or something? You look like a rich kid. Maybe you have an inheritance coming if she's dead."

Andrew wasn't prepared for this. What could he say? How could he explain that his mother had been kidnapped by the FBI and was being held against her will? He couldn't.

"Well, I'm waiting for your answer and it'd better be good." Nolan's dark-brown eyes stared directly at Andrew. Then he looked at the photos and up at Andrew again and Andrew knew that he knew.

"She's the First Lady, isn't she?" Nolan was very excited. "That's why I thought I'd seen her before."

"Yes, she is the First Lady. And we need to help her. She shouldn't be in the nursing home; I need to get her out. That's all I can tell you right now. You just have to trust me; I would never harm my mother. I love her dearly. Do you want money? I have money and I can pay you."

"No, I don't want money. What is this all about? I'd heard that Mrs. Walters had tried to commit suicide and was in the hospital, but I didn't put it together with the lady that we transported the other day."

"Please just give me the address of the nursing home that you took her to?" Andrew handed Nolan a small piece of paper and a pen.

"It has something to do with politics doesn't it. I've been suspicious of this administration ever since they got into office. I voted for the Green candidate you know, no offense to your dad. I'm against all of this war stuff." Nolan wrote the name of the nursing home along with the address and the phone number and handed it to Andrew. "So you must be Andrew."

"Yes, I am Andrew. Thank you. I will be forever indebted to you."

"Glad to help you. Let me know if there is anything else I can do."

Andrew finished half of his sandwich and Nolan drank his coffee as they talked about Nolan's family. Andrew paid the bill and they walked out of the restaurant together.

Andrew drove back to the hotel. He got out of the car and ran up the stairs to his room. Sliding the magnetic key in the door, he went inside and over to the desk by the window. He opened the folded piece of paper and read the name softly out loud. "Desert Valley Nursing Home, 1556 Stater Street, San Bernardino, California. She's not that far away. Now how do I get in there and get her out? That is the next problem."

He decided that he had better plan this carefully. First he would need airline tickets to get out of the country. They could go to British Columbia, Canada. No, winter is coming and it's cold in Canada. Mexico would be a better choice. He had a friend at CU who was from Leon, Guanajuato. It was a fairly large city but still somewhat remote in central Mexico. He would call him and see if his family would make arrangements for them to rent a house or casita for a month or so until the election was over and things died down in the states.

Andrew started up his computer, opened the browser and went to Yahoo to search for maps of the world. Finding a map of Mexico, he saw that the closest large city would be Guadalajara, about 150 miles away in western Mexico. He then went to Yahoo Travel and entered the departing city of Ontario with the destination of Guadalajara hoping there would be a flight. Success. Aero Mexico, Flight 8163, nonstop departing at 11:55 P.M. This was perfect. He booked two seats for Mr. and Mrs. Robert Johnson using his newly acquired Visa card with his assumed name. He purchased roundtrip tickets so that they would be less conspicuous.

Andrew then left the hotel to do some shopping, all the while sorting out how he was going to pull this off. He went back to Macy's, parked his rental car and entered through the large glass doors. He searched the directory at the bottom of the escalator looking for women's sports clothes. He got on the escalator to the second floor and went to an area where he thought he could find what he was looking for. He started to search through the racks of clothing, but the number of dresses on each rack overwhelmed him and there were maybe 25 racks to chose from. Finally he selected a long linen and cotton dress with a jacket, in a jade green color; size six from one of the sale racks. He then picked out a pair of khaki colored walking shorts and a pink polo shirt. He went to the lingerie department and selected a yellow cotton knit sleep shirt. He paid for these with cash and then went to the luggage department and bought a travel bag with wheels. His last stop was at the shoe department where he bought a pair of brown leather sandals and a pair of brown penny loafers, size 7½. His shopping finished here, the only other stop he would have to make would be at a drugstore to pick up a toothbrush, deodorant, and some body lotion. He also selected makeup—lipstick, eyebrow pencil and mascara. Although makeup was not a necessity and his mother wore very little of it, they would need to blend in, look like any other couple embarking on a Mexican vacation.

Driving back to the hotel he continued to explore different ways that he could get his mother out of the nursing home. The doctor scenario really hadn't worked very well and they might be alerted to that trick. He decided he would call Nolan. He needed an accomplice and possibly Nolan might have some ideas that he hadn't thought of. Also, Nolan knew about the routines at nursing homes and that could be valuable. And Nolan had said that if he needed more help he should call.

The Rescue

Andrew waited patiently while the phone rang, and then he heard the voice of the same woman when he had called earlier; he assumed it was Nolan's wife.

"Hello."

"Hi, this is Robert Johnson again, err, I mean Andrew. Is Nolan there and could I speak with him?"

"Oh, hi, Robert, I mean Andrew. Nolan told me about you. He's sleeping right now. He has another nighttime shift."

"I'm sorry to bother him, but this is rather urgent. Could you wake him? I just need to talk to him for a few minutes."

"I hate to do that, he needs his sleep." She paused. "Wait a minute; I think he's coming. I guess he heard the phone. My name's Sally by the way."

"Thanks, Sally."

"Hey, man, you don't want to let a guy sleep?"

"This is really critical. I need your help, Nolan. You have access to nursing homes and you know their routines. I need some ideas of how to get her out of there. I've reached an impasse, I don't know what to do."

"I don't know how I can help you."

"Maybe we could use your ambulance. Just for a couple of hours tomorrow morning. We could . . . you could take a gurney in there to get her, saying that you have an order to take her to the San Bernardino Hospital. The nurses and aides probably even know you and they wouldn't question you."

"Do you want to get me fired?"

"No, but I'm desperate. Help me."

"Look, I want to help you, but that's a bad idea. It's four o'clock now. I have to be at work at midnight. Maybe it'll be a slow night and I'll have some time to think about this. I'll call you later if I come up with something, otherwise you will hear from me after I get off from work in the morning."

"No, Nolan, I can't wait that long. I think my mother's life may be in danger."

"It's the best I can do right now. You're going to have to be patient. If SouthWest Ambulance ever found out about this, I would lose my job, and I doubt that I would find another job in this line of work. I'll call you when I can. Hang in there."

Andrew hung up the phone and lay down on the bed. He pushed off his shoes and pulled the comforter over him as he curled up with the pillows. They had until 10:00 A.M. tomorrow. Their flight left for Mexico at noon. Would they make it? Should he get a later flight? Should he change the flight to the next day? He decided he was too tired to make these decisions and he closed his eyes and drifted off.

Children playing outside his door awakened him and he looked at the clock. It was six o'clock; he'd slept for two hours. Wasn't much he could do right now, so he decided to walk across the street and have dinner at The Black Angus. He changed his shirt, washed his face, brushed his teeth and then put on his New Balance running shoes and walked out the door. The sun was just starting to set in the west, descending through the brown haze hanging in the air, looking more like a large orange beach ball as it started to drop below the horizon. Andrew could hear the constant hum of automobiles and trucks, and he could smell the exhaust, most likely from the nearby freeway. He walked into the restaurant and approached the hostess stand. There were perhaps fifteen or twenty people waiting in the foyer of the restaurant.

"How many?" The young buxom hostess asked.

"Ah, just one."

"Smoking or nonsmoking?"

"Nonsmoking. How long before I will be seated?"

"Fifteen or twenty minutes at the most. Would you like to go into the bar and wait?" She handed Andrew a device that would buzz when his name was called.

Andrew took the device, nodded and headed for the bar. He chose a seat near the entrance and sat down as the bartender approached. She had long, straight blond hair and blue eyes. She reminded him of Alison and he began again to think about how it would be if none of this had ever happened.

"What'll you have?"

"Give me a Tecate."

The blond bartender brought the beer back to him; he paid her and took a long drink from the tall brown, frosty bottle. He was beginning to feel a little better. Just as he started to take another drink, his buzzer vibrated. He took his beer, found the hostess and followed her into the dining area to a booth in the corner. The room was dark and incredibly noisy, children crying and people seemingly talking louder than usual. Andrew ordered a steak, baked potato with sour cream, and a tossed salad with blue cheese dressing. He sat back, drank his beer and waited for the food. He was hungry for the first time in days. He finished his beer and ordered another, and when his food arrived, he dug in and ate most all of what was on his plate. After paying the bill, he walked outside and it was dark. He looked up at the sky, and because of the lights and the haze still hanging around, he couldn't see any stars but he could still smell the fumes in the air. He headed back to his room at the hotel thinking that he would not want to live here.

He started to think again—who would be a trusted individual in the nursing home. If he posed, this time as an aide, after finding her room, he could get a wheelchair, enter her room and remove her. If he were questioned, he would say that he was taking her for tests. He would have to get a uniform like the aides wear, but that shouldn't be too difficult. Maybe Nolan could help him with this.

The phone rang and Andrew answered quickly. "Hello."

"Hi, Andrew. This is Nolan. It's pretty quiet for a change on my end. I haven't come up with any ideas yet, but I just thought I would give you a call and see how you are doing. I'm sorry about being such a hard ass this afternoon."

"I've been waiting for your call. And don't apologize, I understand. You have a family to feed. Anyway, I think I have a solution, see what you think about this. Could you get a nurse's aide uniform for me? You must know what they wear."

"So you're going in there as an aide. That might work. I don't have to get the uniform for you. Just go to any medical supply store and buy a scrub suit, you know like the surgeons and nurses use in the OR. As I recall, the color they have is pink. Pink is supposed to be a calming color I've heard. Then you need to get a badge. I might be able to get that for you. Oh, and they usually wear a t-shirt under the scrub suit and sneakers."

"That'll work. Could you get the badge to me by tomorrow morning? I'll find the medical supply store and purchase the scrubs."

"Yes, I can do that. I'll bring it by about 8:30 tomorrow morning."

"I'll be here."

The first thing that he must do is reschedule the flights to the next day. He would not have everything in place to make the rescue by tomorrow morning. Then, as he was getting ready for bed, he went over in his mind how he was going to make this happen. Dressed in his shorts and a white t-shirt, Andrew pulled back the covers and slipped into bed, scrunching up his pillow to form a cradle for his head. He briefly thought again about Alison and then his thoughts turned to the events of tomorrow. As he went over it again and again in his mind, he finally fell into a deep sleep.

As Andrew started stretching his body and opening his eyes, he heard a knock on the door. He looked at the clock beside his bed and, sure enough it was 8:30.

"Hey, who's there?" Andrew scrambled out of bed pulling on his gray sweat pants.

"It's Nolan. I have something for you."

Andrew, rubbing his eyes, opened the door. "Come on in. Boy, I really slept last night. I had a couple of beers at The Black Angus and I guess it kind of put me out."

"Beer does that. You probably needed the sleep. I have the badge for you. I went over to the nursing home to see what their badges looked like and then I went to the medical supply and had one made up." Nolan pulled the name badge out of his pocket.

"Do you know any of the nurses over there and could you give me their names? You know, just in case." Andrew took the badge and examined it. The name on the blue, laminated badge read Robert Johnson.

"The head nurse is Carly English and there is another one that I know quite well, Tina Mendez. I'll do one more favor for you. I will try to find out which room she's in."

"Would you? That would really help." Andrew was fully awake now. "With that information, I should be able to pull this off. It's still not going to be easy, but I think I can do it."

"You have to promise that you will not tell anyone that I gave you this information."

"I promise. Not a word."

"I'll call you later tonight with the information you are looking for. Will that be enough time?"

"Yeah. I'll get everything ready and then go in there tomorrow morning. Thanks again for your help."

They shook hands as Nolan left the hotel room. Andrew went back into the room and changed into a pair of jeans and a polo shirt. He then went to the lobby to grab a glass of orange juice, a croissant and some coffee. He got into his car and hurriedly drank the juice and ate the roll, leaving the coffee in a carrier on the dash to be sipped as he drove. He brought out his map of the area to see where the medical supply that Nolan had told him about was located and found the streets quickly. He drove to the store, purchased the pink scrub uniform in size extra large and went back to the hotel. When he got back to his room, he tried on the scrubs. As he looked in the mirror, something was decidedly wrong but he couldn't put his finger on it. Ah, he thought, the scrubs are new. He would have to wash them a few times, maybe with some bleach, to give them a worn look. He took them off and put his jeans back on and walked out the door to go down the street to the Quick Stop store to buy detergent and bleach and get enough change for several loads of laundry. The hotel had washers and dryers available for guests.

Returning to his hotel room, Andrew gathered up some of his dirty clothes and the scrubs and headed for the laundry area. It was mid morning by now and the smog, or fog as the locals called it, had pretty much burned off, leaving a hazy blue sky. As he walked past the pool, a mother and her two young daughters were swimming and playing in the clear blue water.

He found the laundry area and luckily it had a washbasin. He put the pink uniform into the basin with about a cup of bleach and adding some water, stirred the clothes around. He then rinsed them thoroughly and put them along with his other clothes into the washer with the detergent and turned it on. He had brought a book with him and found a chaise lounge close to the area where he settled in to read while his clothes were being washed. He decided that after he finished laundering the scrubs, he would go to the nursing home and scope it out.

After the laundry was finished and folded in neat piles, Andrew went back to his room and called the airlines to change the flight. He then walked down to the parking area, got into his car and drove over to Stater Street and continued on until he came to the to Desert Valley Nursing Home. The building looked much like the Village Mountain Nursing Care, with a portico in the front and long, low buildings branching out on either side. He entered the parking lot and parked in a space marked for visitors. Andrew locked his car and walked in through the main door of the portico. There were two very old women sitting in wheel chairs near the front entrance and they greeted him as he went in the door.

"Can I help you find someone?" A blond-haired woman with a wrinkled face inquired as he walked through the lobby.

"Possibly. I'm here to see my Aunt Anna. I think I know where her room is. My mother should be there and I'll find her," Andrew answered.

"If you need help, that's what I am here for."

"Thank you. I appreciate that," Andrew said in his most polite manor. "I'll just walk back there." And he thought how easy it was for anyone to walk into a nursing home. No security, no checking of anyone.

Andrew turned the corner and headed down the hallway. There were more people in wheelchairs, mostly women, along the sides of the hall. He heard groans coming from one of the rooms and someone was screaming in yet another room. The place was decorated in a very homey way and would have been even cheerful had it not been for the screams and groaning. It smelled clean, but he detected the slight odor of chlorine. He noted where the nurse's station was and where the closest exit was located. The nurses seemed to be busy and no one was noticing him as he walked through the hallways. He found a side exit and left the building. He didn't want anyone to recognize him when he came tomorrow.

So, it was back to the hotel to wait until the hour of reckoning. This had to be done right; he couldn't botch it because, if he did, he knew that he wouldn't have another chance.

Andrew slept like a soldier waiting for battle, fighting with his sheets most of the night, thrashing the covers around and clutching his pillow for security. He worried about the rescue, would he be successful? And he wondered again who might be trying to blackmail him and then he thought, no, he was going to get her out of the nursing home and it didn't matter who the thugs were because they would be long gone before they called on Friday. When sleep finally did come, he had a dream about his mother and in the dream he watched as the gunmen escorted her out of a wretched and dirty prison and put her against a wall and shot her with an AK-47 rifle. He watched in horror as her blood spilled from the holes in her body and she reached her arms out to Andrew, trying to speak, and then fell into a heap in front of him. Her eyes were open but they had death in them. The dream wakened him and his room was red as though there was a fire and he was sweating all over his body. He closed his eyes again and then opened them and the red was gone but he was still perspiring. He got up to go to the bathroom and he drank a glass of water and went back to bed.

When Andrew finally awoke later he had a hangover even though he hadn't been drinking the night before. This was the day of the rescue. It was Thursday and the blackmailers would be calling again tomorrow. He slowly got out of bed and took a shower and then started dressing, putting on clean underwear, a clean t-shirt and socks from the laundry that he had done yesterday. He pulled on a pair of jeans and his running shoes. He would put the aides uniform on in the car, as he didn't want to wear it around the hotel when he checked out. He shaved and brushed his teeth, all the while trying to come up with the final plan for the rescue. While he was packing his and his mother's clothes he thought about what a nightmare this was turning out to be and how good it was going to be to get her out of the nursing home and out of the country until after the election. He didn't know what they would do after that; just take it as it comes he guessed.

The telephone rang.

"Hello."

"Andrew, this is Nolan. I am calling with the information that you wanted."

"Oh, I'm glad you called. I was getting worried."

"She's in room 102 in the west wing. If you go down the main corridor you will see where to go. Good luck. Hope it goes well for you. I'll be watching the news."

"West wing, that's appropriate. Thanks. I'm ready and we're going to make this happen. I can't thank you enough for all of your help and when I can I will get back in touch with you. I owe you."

"You don't owe me a thing. Just take care of yourself and that mother of yours."

Andrew hung up the phone. He was thankful for people like Nolan. He gathered up his bags and walked down the steps with his laptop computer bag slung over his shoulder. The morning air was cool and fog had come in from the coast to soften the outlines of the buildings and trees like an impressionist painting.

Andrew walked into the office. He picked up a complimentary copy of *USA Today* and the headlines read, "CNN Poll Says Walters is Leading". Yeah, sure, he thought as he approached the front desk.

"Good morning, Mr. Johnson. I hope you've had a pleasant stay with us," the desk clerk said.

"Yes, it's been fine." Andrew pulled out the three hundred dollars for the four nights he had been there.

"Come back and see us again soon."

"I will," Andrew lied. He thought about the dream and waking up to the apparition of flames in his room. Fire. That was it. He would use fire to help free his mother. Picking up a book of matches from hotel counter he walked out the door.

Andrew got into his rental car and drove to the nursing home. About a block away from the home, he stopped and parked the car under a tree. Looking around to see if anyone was watching, he took off his shoes and jeans and put on the pink uniform. He put his shoes back on. As he was pinning the badge to the pink top on the left side, his hands shook and bead of sweat ran down his forehead. Driving down the street he turned into the parking lot of the nursing home and pulled up to the side of the building where there was an exit and he parked. He walked around to an employee entrance he had scoped out the day before and went inside. He pretended to check in on the time clock and then went to look for a wheelchair that wasn't being used. Entering the room where the equipment was stored, he found a wheelchair, and he saw an empty wastebasket and there were a lot of papers on the desk next to it. Grabbing the papers and stuffing them into the wastebasket, he lit a match and watched as they started to burn. He then pulled out his cell phone and dialed 911.

"What is your emergency," a woman abruptly answered.

"There's a fire at the nursing home," Andrew answered trying to sound excited.

"Would you give me the name of the facility and the address please."

"Ah, yes. Ah, it is the Desert Valley Nursing Home on Stater Street."

"What city is that in?"

"San Bernardino. Look, I have to go. I have to help evacuate the patients."

Andrew disconnected the call. He stuffed some more papers on top of the fire so that there would be a lot of smoke, and then he fanned the smoke toward the door. He exited the room with the wheelchair and headed to the wing where he thought his mother was being held. Along the way he noticed a fire alarm switch, and he reached over and pulled on it, setting off alarms throughout the nursing home.

Just as Andrew reached the area where his mother's room was located, he heard the sound of sirens. Moving down the corridor he saw two agents guarding the double swinging doors that would give him access to the west wing area, and they stopped him as he tried to enter.

"Hey, you can't go in there. This is a secure area." One of agents tried to grab a hold of his arm.

Andrew whisked past them saying, "We have to get the patients out of here, the building is on fire." The agents let him pass.

By now the firemen had entered the building and, since there was indeed smoke filtering through the east wing, ordered the evacuation of all of the patients. Andrew came to the door of what he thought was his mother's room, again being guarded by another agent.

"We have to get everyone out," he blurted out to the agent as he pushed him aside. Andrew opened the door and saw his mother looking out the window trying to find out what was happening. She turned and looked at Andrew and her face lit up.

Andrew put his finger up to his lips to silence her. "There's a fire and we have to evacuate you, Mrs. Walters. Please come with me, I have a wheelchair for you."

Carol smiled but, daring not to show too much emotion, quickly walked over to the wheelchair and sat as Andrew wheeled the chair around and through the door. The hallways of the nursing home were like a busy street in New York during rush hour, aides wheeling patients through the hallways and nurses and supervisors attempting to maintain some sort of organization. The agents tried to follow Andrew as he was dodging the traffic jam of wheelchairs and gurneys in the hallway. He looked ahead and saw the exit; he turned his head back to look at the agents who were gaining on them.

"Can you walk fast?" he asked his mother.

"Yes, I think so."

"Okay, let's go. We're going to make a run for it." Andrew grabbed her out of the chair, and hanging on to her hand, he pulled her along as they ran for the exit. Once out the door, he marshaled her to his unlocked car, opened the door on the passenger side and pushed his mother into the seat.

"Keep your head down," Andrew shouted as he slammed the door shut. As he ran to the driver's side, he ripped off the top of the uniform, got into the car, started it and headed for the closest exit out of the parking lot.

"Are you all right?" he asked.

Carol started to cry. "I'm fine. These are happy tears. I knew you'd find me, I knew it."

Andrew looked back and didn't see anyone following them. "I did too," he said as he turned to look at her. "Sorry I was so rough with you." And then looking at his watch he said, "We're on schedule. We have to catch a flight in two hours. I think you can sit up now."

"Flight? Where are we flying to?" said Carol as she sat up and looked out the back window.

"Mexico. We need to get you out of the country for awhile."

"You don't think they would harm me, do you?"

"I wouldn't put anything past these people. Look what they've done to you already."

"But your dad, he wouldn't allow it."

"I don't know. He might not have any say in the matter. There are billions of dollars at stake for this election. If Dad doesn't win, they might not be able to move ahead with their military agenda, and that means big bucks lost for the defense industry and many people on Capitol Hill. People have killed for much less."

Andrew turned onto the freeway, keeping his speed at 75, ten miles an hour over the speed limit. In a matter of minutes they were turning off the exit and entering Airline Way, the road leading up to Ontario airport.

"I'm going to park in one of the long-term lots so it will be a while before they find the car. That will mean some walking. Are you okay to walk?"

"My legs are a little shaky, but I'll try. Why don't you drop me at curbside check in?"

"I would, but I don't want you out of my sight. I'll try to get as close as I can to the terminal."

Andrew drove past the departure area and noted where Aero Mexico was located and then turned into the long-term parking area. Grabbing the ticket from the machine, he drove out into the parking lot and looked for a space close to the walkway of the departure area. Finding just the right space, he parked the car and then he turned to her and hugged her tightly and she hugged him back. "We're going to be okay, he said to her after several minutes."

"I know that, but I don't have any clothes." Carol said looking at Andrew.

They both laughed. "Yes, you do. I have provided."

"You are the best."

"I know it. But there's no time for me to take any bows right now." Andrew reached in the back and started rummaging through the bags. Finding what he was looking for, he handed the travel dress with the jacket to his mother, along with the sandals. "We'd better change here before we check in. We need to look like a couple on holiday."

"Somebody might be watching."

"Mom, now is not the time for modesty."

Andrew pulled a light blue polo shirt and khaki pants out of his bag and started to change his clothes while his mother tried to discreetly wrestle with her clothes. After they had both changed, he packed the clothes they had been wearing in his bag, not wanting to leave evidence. Getting out of the car, they adjusted their clothes, and with Andrew carrying both bags and his laptop, they started to walk toward the departure area.

"What about passports?" Carol asked.

"I almost forgot." Andrew stopped on the sidewalk, opened his bag and took out a purse and a camera and handed them to his mother. "There is a passport, driver's license and a credit card in the wallet. It's amazing how easy it is to get documents in this country. And carry the camera; you will look more like a tourist."

"You've thought of everything," Carol said as she hung the camera from her neck.

As they approached the ticket counter, Andrew looked around to see if anyone was following them.

"Can I see your ticket please?" The dark-haired woman behind the ticket counter asked. Andrew took out the tickets and handed them to the agent.

"We were scheduled to leave yesterday, but due to unforeseen events, I had to change our reservation."

"No problem. I will just issue you new tickets. How many bags will you be checking."

"We won't be checking any."

"Can I see your photo IDs please?" They pulled out their passports and handed them to the woman.

"You are on flight 789, leaving in 45 minutes from gate 3b. Here are your tickets, and have a nice trip."

"That was easy," Carol said looking at Andrew.

"Almost too easy. Let's hope it keeps going like this. I won't feel that we've made it until we are on the airplane leaving the ground behind. These guys are smart, real smart."

They walked up to the security area and Andrew put their bags on the conveyor belt that moved them through the x-ray machine. The bags rolled through as the security officers closely watched. As the bags emerged on the other side, Andrew picked them off the belt. He handed Carol's bag and her handbag to her and took his two bags, slinging the computer bag over his shoulder.

Carol linked her arm through Andrew's as they walked together down the walkway toward gate 3b. They looked like any other couple anticipating a few days of sun in Mexico.

James Hears of the Escape

If the press gets a hold of this, we're dead," Stanley Thompson, the president's press secretary said.

"How could she possibly escape?" James looked around the table at Stanley and Jason, the vice president. "You had six agents watching her."

"Your son. Somehow he found her and sprung her. How do you like that, James?" Jason normally would not call him by his first name, but he was angry.

"Do you understand what this could do to us? If the public finds out about this, we can kiss the election goodbye."

Stanley gave Jason and James a somber look. "Rather than getting all hyped up about this, we need to come up with a plan. First, we need to find her. Jason, you talk with the agents and get with the FBI and start the intelligence going on that end. And then we need to come up with some ideas of how we're going to explain this if and when it is leaked."

James nodded his head in agreement. "I knew Andrew would be searching for her, but I didn't think he would find her. He was upset when he found out that she'd been hospitalized. But, you know kids; they overreact."

"We've been watching him for weeks now. Did you know he dropped out of college?" Jason said to James.

"No, I didn't know that. I've been just a little busy campaigning."

"He got an apartment in Denver and got a waiter's job. He's been making calls to nursing homes in the southern California area.

I wonder how he figured that one out. Your kid's one smart guy."

"Just like his father. But, why didn't I know this? Why didn't you tell me?" James was angry now.

"He's your son. We'd expect that you would know what your son is up to. No matter, we'll find her, I'm confident of that," said Jason.

"Maybe it's not Andrew. Did that ever occur to you?" James said. "There are a lot of people who would want to sabotage the election. Could be the Democrats or al-Qaeda."

"No, I doubt that. I still think it's your son," said Jason.

"What if she surfaces and make a statement to the press?" Terry said.

"Who's going to believe a crazy woman? We'll just say that she's temporarily insane and incompetent and everyone knows you can't believe someone like that. We're making this too difficult," Stanley said, rising from the table.

James scowled as Stanley continued to pace from one end of the room to the other. "Carol's not crazy. She's a very competent woman, always has been. I don't want her labeled for life as a nut case. You can't do this to her."

"But look what she's doing to you," Jason interjected. "Divorcing you and trying to ruin your political career. You want to protect a woman who is out to get you? I don't understand that."

"Jason's right. Either you protect her or you take care of yourself and you can't do both. She decided to get the divorce against your wishes. You did ask her to wait until after the election, didn't you?" said Terry.

"I did. And she wouldn't hear of it. She was going to do this now even though she knew it could ruin my chances for reelection."

"Change that to *would* ruin your chances for reelection. So you see, she's not on your side and you have to protect yourself from her. Whatever it takes," Jason said.

"What is whatever it takes?" James asked.

"We'll do whatever we have to do to keep this story out of the media. And then we'll hunt her down and bring her back and lock her up for awhile. A nursing home just wasn't secure enough for her. We're going to have to find a psychiatric ward someplace where we can keep her locked up. James, don't you worry about this. We'll handle it. Your job is to win this election, and I think you're going to do that."

"You won't hurt her, will you? I don't want her to be hurt."

Jason rolled his eyes in exasperation. "No, we won't hurt her. We just need to keep her out of the way for awhile."

It was late afternoon when Flight 8163 touched down in Guadalajara. The sun was still above the palm trees as Andrew and Carol walked down the stairway of the Boeing 737-800 jet and onto the tarmac. The air was warm and heavy with humidity and a pungent mixture of odors of flowers and humanity. They headed for the customs area, where they were cleared without any problems, and then went to find the Avis rental agency where Andrew rented a blue Honda CRV with four-wheel drive. They loaded their bags in the back and both got into the Honda to begin their journey to the mountains of central Mexico. They left the airport heading north of the city of almost two million people.

"You tired, Mom?"

"A little. It's been a busy day."

"That's an understatement, if I ever heard one."

"Do we have a place to stay in Leon?"

"Yes, my friend booked us into a small hotel in the middle of the city."

"It'll be late when we get in there."

"All we have to do is find it and then knock on the door and they'll let us in."

"Why couldn't we stay in Guadalajara?"

"I want to get into the mountains as soon as possible. That way the trail will be cold by the time they figure out where we've gone. And the village that we're going to is pretty remote."

"I feel like a fugitive. This is like living a bad dream."

"We are fugitives. That's the reality. Makes a person feel pretty important, though, to have the Central Intelligence Agency of the United States of America searching for you, doesn't it?" Andrew looked at his mother and smiled.

"Andy, this is not a joke.

"I'm not joking."

"Maybe I shouldn't have gone ahead with this divorce."

"I've thought about that, but it's too late now."

Carol looked out the window as they passed row upon row of small brown adobe houses, more like huts along the road and built on the hillside of the city. Children were playing in the yards. She caught a glimpse of a mother or grandmother standing in the open doorway of one of the houses throwing scraps of food out into the yard to dogs and chickens running to get in on the feast.

"It will never be the same. I've been selfish." Carol had tears in her eyes.

"Mom, if anything, you are not selfish. I applaud you for standing up for your beliefs. If everyone did that, it would be a better world."

"But I've caused so much trouble. Look at the trouble I've gotten you into because of this."

"It doesn't matter. You did what you had to do. I only wish Dad had been courageous enough to stand up to them. Other presidents have, you know. Why couldn't Dad?"

"I can't answer that, Andy. I don't really know. I think he just got caught up in it and couldn't get out."

The rows of mud and stucco houses soon gave way to small businesses, gas stations, auto dealers, and a grocery store with houses in between. The traffic was heavy; it seemed that everyone was going somewhere, and the odors of the airport gave way to the smell of exhaust. With no emissions standards, living in Guadalajara would likely be hazardous to your health. As they drove on, they entered what must be the center of the city with a plaza surrounded by Spanish-style buildings with red tile roofs. Large, old trees lined the road around the plaza with walkways going into the park where children were playing and families were having picnics.

Soon they turned east and headed through the other side of Guadalajara and finally onto the ramp of the freeway and out of the city. After thirty or so miles, they were in farm country headed to the foothills and on to Leon, Guanajuato.

A gentle breeze billowed the aquamarine-colored curtains, bringing delicious smells of food cooking from somewhere. Carol opened her eyes and lay very still in her small bed, staring at the bare light bulb hanging from the ceiling. She was hungry; she hadn't eaten since the two chicken tacos they had bought from a vendor at the airport in Guadalajara. And she had to go to the bathroom. She remembered that she would have to go down the hallway to do that.

She looked at her new Seiko watch; it was seven o'clock. Was that mountain or central time? It really didn't matter. Swinging her leg to the side of the bed, she touched her foot to the bare wooden floor and then raised the rest of her body to a sitting position. She was stiff and her body ached everywhere, but she thought once she got moving, she would feel better. Most importantly she was free.

Looking around the room, she surveyed the dark pink walls, the Mexican serape hanging near the window and the handmade, multicolored braided rug by her bed. Large red, yellow and orange colored paper flowers in a Mexican earthen vase sat on a small table by the door. Elegance this was not, but there was a homespun feeling of warmth.

Carol grabbed her robe, slipped on her sandals, quietly opened the door and tiptoed out so as not to awaken Andrew, who was still sleeping in the twin bed across from hers. The narrow hallway was empty and she dashed toward a white painted door marked el baño, opened the door carefully, making sure there was no one inside. It was Spartan but clean, with a small shower stall in the corner, a simple white porcelain washbasin and a toilet with a chain flush. She used the toilet and then washed her hands, splashing the cool water on her face. A shower would feel refreshing right now, but she thought she would wait until Andrew was awake. Opening the door and looking back down the hallway, she saw Andrew coming toward her, dressed in blue jeans and a white t-shirt.

"Buenos dias. How are you feeling?" Andrew inquired.

"A little sore and tired, but other than that, not too bad. I had some trouble sleeping at first; there were so many people out on the street last night. But I was so tired that I finally went to sleep and slept well."

"I'm going to use the bathroom, uh, I mean el baño, and then we'll find some breakfast."

Carol went back to their room and changed into a pair of jeans and a pink t-shirt and sandals just as Andrew returned.

"Where are we?" Carol asked.

"We're just outside of Leon, Mexico. Called Leon de los Aldamas. My friend, Alex Medina from CU, has family living on a ranch near here. He was very helpful in making the arrangements."

"How large is this village?"

"It's not exactly a village; there must be about a million people living here now. Andrew finished dressing and combed his hair. "Are you ready for some breakfast?"

"Ready? I am starved." They walked out of the room and started down the long hallway that led to the office. "Are we going to be staying here for long?" Carol asked. A person who was normally self-directed and a leader, Carol had gotten used to being treated like a child in the nursing home and was even comfortable now with Andrew taking the lead.

"No, we have a small hacienda further out of town in the mountains. After breakfast, we'll pack and load the car and drive up there. It's only fifty miles or so, but the road is kind of primitive, so it might take the rest of the day to get there. Hope you're not afraid of heights."

"Coming from Colorado? We're mountain folk, remember."

As they walked out onto the street, the intense sun hit Carol's eyes and she tried to cover them. "I'm going to have to do some shopping. I need sunglasses; the sun is so bright."

"I forgot to buy those for you. We're much closer to the equator, you know, and the sun hits this part of the world straight on. I think there's a market not far from here. We should pick up some food, too. I don't know what the shopping situation is at the ranch."

Carol and Andrew walked down the small narrow sidewalk, Carol's arm linked in his. The neighborhood was bustling with people walking, and there was a gridlock of cars and trucks on the street, horns honking like a gaggle of geese angry at the world. They finally came to a small restaurant, entered and took a seat near the window.

The waitress, a middle-aged woman with long black hair dressed in a turquoise peasant blouse and a black skirt, approached their table, set down two glasses of water and gave them menus.

"Buenos dias," she said and then turned and left.

Carol looked at the menu. "I wish I'd paid more attention in my high school Spanish class."

"Huevos rancheros is always a good bet."

"Can we drink the water? I've always heard that you shouldn't drink the water in Mexico."

"I think we'll get some bottled water to be on the safe side. We need to look for a pharmacy and buy some medicine just in case we get the scourge of Mexico."

"You mean the Mexican two-step."

"Whatever you want to call it, we don't want to get it. When Sean and I took that trip to Mexico on spring break year before last, I saw kids really laid up with it and they didn't recover until they got back to the States. They had drinks with ice in them, that was all."

"Mandar listo?" The waitress had returned.

Andrew pointed at the menu, "Dos Huevos Rancheros, por favor."

The waitress picked up the menus and went back to the kitchen.

"You speak Spanish?"

"Just a few words. Spring break in Mazatlan, two years in a row. Although I'm afraid we did more drinking and debauchery than talking with the locals."

"I don't want to know."

"And I'm not going to tell you."

"Fair enough." Carol changed the subject. "Do you think he'll win the election?"

"The polls say he's ahead."

"Polls, schmolls. I don't believe those polls."

"I agree. It's so difficult to know what and who to believe in this country anymore. But if the Patriots get out the vote like they did for midterms, yes, I think he could win. It was very risky for the Democrats to select a woman to run against him."

"Are you against having a woman as our president?" Carol asked.

"Not at all. I think a woman would make a fine president. In fact, I think a woman would be a better president. Women are not so quick to go to war. Women bear the children, they are not inclined to turn around and send those children they have born to war to die."

"I think you're right about that. Women create, they don't destroy and women are more concerned for the future. Men seem to think only about today and their own needs. I shouldn't say that. I can't peg all men that way, but that seems to be the way of this administration. Spend today and let someone else pay tomorrow."

"You don't think Dad was concerned for the future? Our country needs oil and he threw out Saddam and took over one of largest oil-producing countries in the world. He's preparing for the future."

"Andy, our children are the future, and when you skimp on education, you're not preparing them. And, yes he—they did take over Iraq and they killed a lot of people doing it. Wouldn't it have been better to find a diplomatic solution with our allies involved and then take the money we would have used for war and use it to fix our schools in this country? Better yet, use the money to develop alternative fuels."

"Could we have gotten rid of Saddam without attacking? He wasn't going to go easily."

"But they didn't even try. War was the only option all along. A diplomatic solution was never on their radar screen." Carol's eyes sparked with anger.

"You could be right."

The waitress returned with their orders. "El cafe y te?"

"Dos cafe, negro, por favor." Andrew answered for Carol. Then turning to his mother, "You did want coffee, didn't you?"

"Yes, coffee will be fine."

They both ate in silence. Andrew paid the waitress and they left to go back to the hotel.

As they were approaching their room, Andrew told Carol to wait behind him while he carefully opened the door and looked all around the room before he gave her the all-clear signal.

"What's that about?" Carol looked at him quizzically.

"Can't be too careful. They will come looking for us, you know."

"But they wouldn't know that we are here in this little hotel."

"You'd be surprised. They have ways."

Carol and Andrew packed and took their bags to the SUV.

"I'll wait in the car while you check out," Carol said.

"No, I want you with me. You can't be left alone."

"So, for how long is this going to go on? I love you, Andy, but I like my space."

"Quit complaining. You could still be back in that nursing home," Andrew said in a teasing way.

"Out of the nursing home into the strait jacket," Carol said with a wink.

"Come on now, it's not that bad. As soon as we get to the hacienda, we can let up a little. It's pretty remote up there, but we're still going to have to watch at all times and be on our guard. Always look around you to see who is there and who might be watching you."

"I've been doing that all my adult life. Can't be a woman living in the twenty-first century without being vigilant. Although, lately I've had the Secret Service watching out for me. I kind of miss that." And then she thought for moment and said, "No I don't."

I have an announcement to make," Stanley Thompson spoke slowly and deliberately to the reporters assembled in the White House Press Room. He went on to say, "Mrs. James Walters, Carol Walters, the First Lady has been found to be missing from her rehabilitation facility located in the Southwest of the United States. We received word yesterday that she may have walked off the grounds during a fire emergency at the facility. We have no knowledge of her whereabouts at this time. The president is extremely worried for her safety, and we are making every effort to find her and bring her back to the facility."

The faces of the thirty-five men and women had a look of concern and distress as they speedily took notes on their PDAs, notepads or their computer notebooks.

"I will take questions for five minutes and then we are finished here for the day,"

Stanley, dressed in a gray blue suit with a white shirt and blue tie, continued shifting from one side to another as he stood behind the podium. This was the 9:45 gaggle, not televised. Rumors had been flying around Washington and the country, and President Walters and his advisors thought it best to bring this out into the open. Make the statement now, allow limited questioning from the press and then hopefully put it behind them.

"Mr. Thompson," Helen Hogan vied for attention.

"Your question, Ms. Hogan."

"What was her medical condition at the time of her disappearance? Was she under sedation? And had she been making progress in her rehabilitation?"

"We are not at liberty to inform you of her medical condition. And, yes, she had been progressing markedly and was in fact going to be coming home in the next couple of weeks," Stanley lied. There had been no plans to allow Carol to go home.

Jon Markham raised his hand in the back of the room and Stanley acknowledged him.

"Is it possible that she was abducted? Were there any suspicious characters at the scene when she disappeared?" Jon asked.

"It is possible, but we don't think so. We think she may have become confused and just wandered off. It happens often with the elderly, and they usually turn up somewhere at a neighbor's or relative's house. We're doing everything possible to search the surrounding area, and we are confident that she will be found in the next twenty-four hours."

"Mrs. Walters isn't elderly," Jon said.

"She might have been confused and wandered onto a back street," Stanley countered.

"What agencies are involved in the search? And is it possible that she could have gotten on an airplane and flown to another city?" Sara Smithson broke in without being recognized.

"Sara, you know the protocol here," Stanley warned her. "To answer your first question, we have the local authorities, the police and fire units on this, and the FBI will be coming in. And of course the special agents assigned to her will be heavily involved. Could she get on an airplane? I don't think so. She had no money or credit cards. She would have to have some help to do that."

"What about the special agents," Sara continued. "Isn't it their job to protect her at all times and they let her slip away. Are they going to be reprimanded for this? Aren't they derelict in their duty?"

"From all accounts, it was a very chaotic scene and impossible for them to maintain control. The building filled with smoke, cutting visibility and creating unhealthy breathing for everyone, including the agents. Like everyone else, they had to evacuate. They thought they had her with them, and when they turned around, she was gone, just like that." Stanley fidgeted with his pencil, eyes scanning the room looking for hands going up and then continued, "I'll take a question from Mr. Roberts."

"What about Andrew, her son? Could he have taken her

someplace? And has the family been notified and what were their reactions?" Connor Roberts inquired.

"As far as we know, her son is out of the country at this time. We talked to his roommate in Boulder and he told us that Andrew went to Mexico. He told him that he just wanted to take a break from school. To answer your second question, yes, her family has been notified. We've called her mother and father. They, of course, are very worried. When a family member vanishes into space, anyone would be. But we assured them that we were on top of it and we would find her soon."

"What about the twenty Iraqi civilians killed yesterday in Karbala? We heard they were demonstrating and were gunned down. Was it our people who killed them?" Jack Downey shouted from the back of the room.

"That's all for now, folks. Thank you for coming." Stanley turned and walked out of the room as fast as he had come into it, amid further shouts from the audience asking about the economy, the election. Stanley was not prepared to answer any of these questions without a briefing from the president's advisors.

"We have so many problems right now, we certainly could have done without this," Stanley spoke impatiently. The small group of insiders, including Stanley and the president, the vice president and Terry Fleming, had gathered after the press conference to mull over this latest course of events. "Why are we meeting in the situation room?"

"It's secure, Stanley. We can't have any more leaks. I thought we had the press under control, but I guess I was wrong," Terry said. "Stanley, you need to prepare a statement to go out on the wire. Just say pretty much what you told the boys and girls today, only leave out the part about Andrew. We don't want to bring him into this if we don't have to."

Jason opened up his notebook and started to take some notes. "As of last night, we know they caught a plane to Guadalajara. They must be heading down to one of the beach towns along the coast."

"Are you sure it was Andrew?" James asked. "It could have been someone else."

"It's Andrew. We know it's Andrew. But we'll find them and soon," Jason said. "Not much more we can do at this point," Jason continued. "We'll issue the statement and our boys are down there right now. They should have them back in custody within twenty-four hours. James, this doesn't look good for Andrew, but I don't think we want to make a fuss about any of this right now. Get him back to school like nothing happened and then deal with it after the election. James, you need to have a talk with your boy."

"Custody? Sounds like she's under arrest," James said. "And as far as Andrew is concerned I don't think it'll do much good to have a talk with him. Looks like he's on his mother's side and anything I would have to say isn't going to change that. He's always been a free thinker, but he does listen to his mother more than me. I'm sure he's angry about the way we've handled this, too."

Terry said, "We've got more important things happening here. About the shooting in Karbala, make sure the press plays this down as much as possible. We don't know if it was twenty. And it was an accident. The Iraqis were getting out of control, and one of the marines fired a shot in the air and then someone started shooting at the people. We don't even know who did the shooting. Could be al-Qaeda. Admit to nothing. Jason, send that statement over to the Pentagon and to the Associated Press."

"Then our other problem, Elizabeth, your opponent Mr. President, is really playing up this economy thing," Jason said. "Have you seen the TV commercials in Ohio where she's saying that our tax cut has only lined the pockets of the rich and has not created any jobs. We need to release some employment figures tomorrow.

There were a hundred thousand new jobs created last month and the public needs to know that."

"Ten thousand of those jobs are with defense companies and the another three thousand with construction companies rebuilding Iraq," James said.

"Doesn't matter. A job's a job. We can prove that we're creating jobs," Jason said pointing his finger at James. "And they're private sector jobs, too, not government jobs."

"It has really helped since the feds don't report on the layoffs any longer. James, you were right to cut the funding for that agency," said Terry.

"If the people know too much, they just don't know how to deal with it," James said.

"Well said, Mr. President," Jason praised James.

A Little Hacienda

Andrew turned off the freeway onto a paved two-lane road that started out to be straight and level but was now twisting around hairpin turns and blind corners while slowly climbing into the mountains of central Mexico. The prickly pear and mesquite of the desert had turned to juniper and manzanita trees and the warm air was becoming increasingly cooler the higher they went.

After about ten miles, the paved road turned to gravel and dirt and in some places the two lanes became one.

"I see what you mean about this road," Carol said as she peered out the passenger window into a rocky canyon below. "I can't even see the bottom of the canyon. How much further?"

Looking at his odometer, Andrew said, "About eight miles. Alex said that we should come to a mesa twenty miles after leaving the paved road. Did you see the hawk flying over the trees?"

"Yes, I did. This is really beautiful country."

"It is. Reminds me of Arizona. There's lots of wildlife here, even wolves."

"Could you slow down a little?"

"Sure. Are you really scared? I'm not going that fast."

"Just a little. So much has happened to me in the last month."

There was silence between them as Andrew maneuvered around the ruts and the rocks, veering close to the edge of the canyon.

"How long do you think we'll have to stay up here?" Carol asked.

"I don't know. Maybe until after the election. The heat should be off of us by then. We'll just have to see how it goes."

"Andy, you took a big risk in coming to get me. I'm afraid you're going to be in trouble when you go back."

"We'll see. I couldn't leave you there. I was afraid for your safety," Andrew said as he pulled the SUV around another sharp turn. The road had become rutted now and washed out in places, and there were boulders that had washed down the hillside from recent rains.

"Do you think your dad was in on this?"

"I don't know. He had to have known about it and he didn't try to stop them."

"Maybe he couldn't. Maybe he is in so deep that there was nothing he could do to stop them."

"Always thinking the best about people. But I think you are right. He is my father, and I think underneath he's a decent person."

Andrew hit another deep rut in the road and had to steer close to the embankment where rocks began to slide down in front of them.

"How do they buy groceries at the ranch?" Carol was again looking over the side of the road into a chasm to nowhere.

"I think they grow a lot of stuff. And it's a cattle ranch, so they have beef and probably chickens. There's also an airstrip up here and they can fly to Leon whenever they want, so it's not as isolated as you would think. If we need anything, we can probably ask to have it brought to us."

After climbing through a steep arroyo with brush and pines on either side of them, they almost magically emerged onto a plateau where the vegetation now had turned to scrub junipers scattered about with grasses and fields of fall flowers. Looking into the distance, amethyst mountains defined the horizon against a cerulean blue sky.

After another ten miles they saw the gate to the ranch. Andrew stopped the SUV.

"Mom, could you get the gate?"

"Sure." Carol got out and opened the gate, waited for Andrew to drive through and then closed it again and got back into the car. They continued on down a road that was still dirt but well maintained and after a mile they came to what Carol thought must be the main ranch house.

Andrew stopped in front, turned off the motor and said, "They're expecting us today, so they should be here at the house. Come in with me, I want you to meet Alex's parents."

Just as the words were out of his mouth, a man and a woman came out onto the veranda of the large, low, whitewashed adobe house.

"Hola! Welcome to Rancho Ventana. We've been expecting you. I am Isabel and this is my husband, Gorge," Isabel extended a hand to Carol and one to Andrew.

Gorge offered his large, weathered hands in greeting also. "How was your trip? I hope you didn't mind the rough road. We seldom use it as we most often fly into town."

"It was a little scary," Carol said tentatively.

"It wasn't that bad. And we got here much sooner that I thought. I was planning on taking the whole day driving up that canyon," boasted Andrew.

"You were going pretty fast," said Carol. Andrew ignored her comment.

"Come in and join us for lunch. And then we'll show you the hacienda." Isabel, a handsome, dark-haired woman with dark brown eyes and olive skin, was already leading them into the coolness of the main living room of the ranch house. She was simply dressed in an ecru silk tunic blouse over brown silk slacks, with a handmade silver necklace and earrings to match. Gorge, somewhat overweight, skin tanned and deeply lined with eyes that connected on a level of understanding, followed behind everyone. Isabel appeared to be the one in charge here.

"Would you like to freshen up after your trip?" Isabel asked. "There is a bathroom down the hallway to your left."

"I would like that," said Carol. And a few minutes later she returned, and Andrew took his turn.

When Andrew returned, they were led to a small, intimate patio set off to the side of another large veranda on the back of the house. A round, hand-hewn wooden table was set with Mexican pottery and green goblets filled with ice water and lemon. The tablecloth was a vivid red, and there was a large bowl of fresh roses of every color in the center of the table.

Isabel motioned to Andrew and Carol to be seated, and a maid appeared from the doorway laden with a tray of fresh breads.

"I was sorry to hear the circumstances of your being here, but I want you to know that you are welcome to stay as long as you need to," Isabel said.

"Thank you. We are very appreciative of your hospitality." Andrew was helping himself to the bread. "What exactly did Alex tell you of our reason for being here?"

"He didn't elaborate. He just said that your mother had been ill and in the hospital and then something about the hospital burning."

"Did he mention that we are here without our government knowing about it?"

"Yes, he did say that," Gorge spoke for the first time. "No matter. We don't ask questions here. Whatever it is that brought you here, it must be important for you to be away for awhile."

"You are both very kind," Carol said, putting her napkin on her lap and taking a long drink from her glass of iced water. "I was thirstier than I thought."

"It's pretty dry here, especially this time of year. We are at about seven thousand feet elevation and that can make you thirsty, too,"

Gorge said. "Which reminds me, Elena, would you bring me a Tecates? Anyone else like a beer or glass of wine? We make our own wine here, Carol."

"Oh, yes, I would love a glass of wine," said Carol. And Andrew accepted the offer of a beer.

They dined on a dish made with mole poblano, breast of chicken and chipolte rice and a bean dish, with freshly made tacos. For desert, there was fresh fruit and cheese with Mexican coffee. Carol had two glasses of white wine and was feeling the serenity of the warm afternoon with her newfound friends.

They talked about Alex; Andrew especially wanted to know what it was like growing up in such a remote area. Carol told them about their ranch back in Colorado and they exchanged ideas on the different ways of raising cattle and running a ranch.

After a time Isabel said to Carol and Andrew, "I think it is time to take you to your hacienda, your home away from home."

Again, Isabel leading the way with Carol and Andrew following, they walked down a saltillo tile path lined with ornamental trees, unusual grasses and patches of red and purple flowers. Gorge excused himself, saying he had some business to take care of. Coming out into a small grotto, they saw the small earthen-colored adobe house, or casa. An acacia tree filtered the bright sunlight onto a small fountain and earthen pots filled with red geraniums adorned either side of the front door that was painted a bright turquoise.

"This is our guesthouse, and I hope you will be comfortable," Isabel said as she opened the door and invited them inside. "I will get one of the hands to bring your luggage to you."

Carol looked around at the room. The walls were whitewashed and there was a large doeskin-colored leather couch in the middle of the room in front of the adobe fireplace with a heavy wooden mantle. On the mantle were two silver candlesticks on either side of a magnificent oil painting of a chestnut stallion, rearing up with his mane and tail flaming out around his sinewy body. Carol stood in awe.

"That is Destiny, our first stallion. I trained him and rode him until he became too much for me to handle, and then we just put him out for stud. He sired many of the horses on this ranch. He's beautiful, isn't he?

"A magnificent horse and a beautiful painting. Why do you hang it in the guest house?"

"I know, I love the painting, too. He died two years ago and it breaks my heart every time I look at it."

"I think I'm going to like it here," Carol said turning to Andrew and smiling.

"I'll leave you two to get settled. Just let us know if you need anything. Dinner is at eight and we expect you to join us."

"You are too kind. We might join you tonight, but we don't want to impose," said Andrew.

Isabel left, closing the door behind her, and Carol started to inspect their new little hideaway. "If a person has to live in exile, this is the way to do it. How did you ever think of this, Andy?"

"Alex is a good friend. We hang out together a lot. He's really smart. I think he's going to medical school after he graduates from CU, and the chicks really like him."

Disregarding Andrew's last statement, Carol continued to explore their new cottage. There were two bedrooms in the back, one with a large queen-sized bed with a mahogany carved headboard and the other with two twin beds. Each bedroom had its own tiled bathroom with decorative Mexican tile.

"I don't know about you, but I'm ready for a nap," Carol said as she yawned. "The wine made me very sleepy."

"Mom, you can have the larger bedroom," Andrew said.

"You are a good son. Wake me in an hour. By then it should be time to eat again. We'll have to hike tomorrow to walk off the calories."

"Yeah, I think I'll go for about a ten-mile run tomorrow. Should be interesting at seven thousand feet."

The sun was slipping below the horizon when Carol woke and rubbed her eyes. She looked at her watch; it was 6:35. She got out of her bed and searched in her luggage for the natural-colored Mexican skirt and blouse she had bought at the market in Leon. She put on the skirt and blouse and her only pair of sandals, combed her hair and put on some lipstick. When she opened the door and walked out to the great room she saw Andrew sitting on the couch reading.

"You look very nice, Mom," Andrew said as he looked up from his book. "You slept a couple of hours. Must have needed it."

"I feel much better. It is so quiet and serene here."

They both walked out of the casa and back down the path to the main house. Isabel and Gorge were waiting for them when they got there.

"Carol and Andrew, I would like you to meet two very good friends and neighbors, Maria and Jack Puente," Isabel greeted them. Turning to Maria and Jack she said, "Carol and Andrew are friends of Alex."

"We are pleased to meet both of you," Andrew reached out his hand to Maria, and Jack and Carol did as well.

The two couples and Carol and Andrew walked into the dining room where an oversized oblong dining table was set with fine china, sterling silver and crystal goblets on an off-white lace tablecloth with white linen napkins. There was a bouquet of fresh white calla lilies flanked by two silver candlesticks with ivory white candles. The soft candlelight cast a warm glow over the room with soft guitar music floating in the evening air. After being seated, a server brought in asparagus soup and white wine for everyone.

"Are you enjoying your visit to Mexico?" Maria asked.

"Yes, very much. This is a beautiful place," Carol answered.

"You are in school with Alex?" Jack asked Andrew as he ate his soup. "Are you going to medical school also?"

"Yes, we are good friends. Alex lives in a house down the street from me, so I see him quite often. And, no I am in engineering school, but thinking about changing to industrial architecture. I seem to be finding the artist in me lately."

"That is commendable. Have you visited Mexico City?" Maria asked.

"No, I have never been there."

"If you are interested in architecture, you would love the Spanish and colonial architecture of Mexico City," Maria said.

"I will have to go there then," said Andrew.

"How is the election going in your country? Will you be voting for President Walters?" Maria entered the conversation, directing her question to Carol.

Carol, glanced at Isabel and said, "I haven't decided whom I will vote for. I think having a woman president would be very good for the country, but I don't think that will happen this time around."

Isabel coughed and frowned at Maria, shaking her head but Maria carried on.

"You know that President Walters came to Mexico and met with our President Fox, and he promised to ease the immigration laws in your country so that people could come across the border legally and work. And then after 9/11, he went back on his word. President Fox was very disappointed as we all were. Do you think President Walters might rethink his position?"

"I can't answer for President Walters, but I did hear that Governor Grayson in Arizona is attempting to get a pilot guest worker program going, and that would be a step in the right direction. Many people come across the border and into Arizona in the summertime and try to cross the desert and they die. If they could come legally, I think it would be better." Carol thought about how it might be the best if Mexico would create good jobs for the people in their own country, but she did not want to offend her hosts and said nothing.

Andrew, head down, continued to eat his soup.

"And what do you think of the occupation of Iraq, and when is the U.S. going to let them have their country back?" Maria asked.

Andrew spoke up, "When they can come together and agree on who will run their country."

"But it is looking more and more like the U.S. is not encouraging this and wanting to stay in Iraq and run the country themselves. Could it be that the U.S. is more interested in the oil and the contracts to rebuild? I have heard there are American companies making millions of dollars on this."

"In every country, in every government, there is corruption and the U.S. government is no exception," Andrew said and then changing the subject. "Tell me, Jack, where can I find some good trails for hiking? My mom and I would like to get out and get some exercise and fresh air and see some of the area."

Jack's and Maria's eyes met with understanding. The main course was being served. They dined on prime rib of beef with fresh snow peas from the ranch garden and another very spicy rice dish with tomatoes and cilantro. The wine, a red this time, again was from the ranch. At the end of the meal, a desert of caramelized flan was served with coffee and a port wine to top off the evening. Carol, almost forgetting her plight, ate everything put before her, drank how many glasses of wine she was not sure and partook of the port as well.

Later that evening after Carol and Andrew had returned to their casa, Carol walked out onto the back patio and sat at the picnic table. A three-quarter moon hung low above the trees and endless stars dotted the blue-black sky, like so many diamonds on velvet. She felt so small and vulnerable. What would their destiny be? Could she ever again have a normal life? And when she returned, what would she do with the rest of her life? How could she make a difference in this very difficult world filled with millions of people, many of them striving for their own selfish greed. How could she show people that, when they worked together, they can achieve so much more than when they are all sloshing around in the pool like piranhas in a feeding frenzy? Right now she had more questions than answers, but she felt that there would come a time when she would know the answers to these questions.

As she was deep in thought, Andrew walked out the door and quietly sat down on the bench beside her. He looked deep into her eyes and could almost read his mother's thoughts.

"You look like you are in another world," he said.

"I wish I were."

"Mother, I have something to tell you."

"Do I want to hear this?"

"Well, you have to. You'll find out about it sooner or later and I would rather you hear it from me."

"Okay, I'm ready."

"Alison is dead. Her car went over a cliff and crashed in a canyon not far from where we used to hike a lot." Andrew started to cry softly.

"Oh, Andy. No." Carol put her arms around her son and they cried together. "Do you think it was an accident?"

"I don't think it was, but how could we prove it. A couple of weeks before that, some guys kidnapped her and roughed her up, thinking she knew where I was and would tell them."

"I'm to blame for this."

"No, *they* are. They are the ones who took you away. They are the ones who have been after us, threatening us."

"But, don't you see. If I hadn't started the divorce. . . ."

"Don't do that, Mom. Don't look back. You did what you thought was right, and this has become my cause, too."

Carol choked back her tears.

"Did you love her?"

"I did. I might have married her. She was a beautiful woman inside and out. She was smart and she worked hard."

Neither of them talked for several minutes. Then Andrew looked at this mother and said, "Mom, why do the good people have to die?"

"Andy, I don't know. I just don't know the answer to that."

It's the Economy

James spooned marmalade onto a piece of whole-wheat toast while Marta the maid bustled about serving the president. Harry, the president's cocker spaniel, sat beside James' chair, eyes wide and ears forward, wagging his tail, looking for a treat.

"More coffee, Mr. President? Your coffee must be cold by now."

"No, Marta, I don't have much time. I have to be at a meeting in thirty minutes. I would like some water, though. I had a rough workout this morning."

"Yes, sir, Mr. President. I will get it for you now." Marta whisked out of the room while James read his *Wall Street Journal.* The headline read "Economy on Hold for Now". James glanced over the article. Words like "corporate earnings still in slump", "unemployment remains high" and "OPEC to cut oil production". Knowing that this could be a factor in the election, he was very concerned and this was why he was meeting with his chief financial advisors this morning, along with the vice president.

"Here is your water, Mr. President. Is there anything else I can get for you?" Marta had returned and was pouring a fresh glass of water for him.

"No, you may go now. I have everything I need." James munched on the second piece of toast.

"'Scuse me for asking, Mr. President. How is the Missus? Have they found her yet? We're all so worried about her. She went to the hospital and now she's missing. Did somebody take her?" Marta asked.

"No, Marta, I don't think anyone took her. She's probably basking around a pool in Palm Springs right now enjoying the good life."

"How could that be without your knowing, Mr. President?"

James shifted in his chair and scowled at the maid. "No more questions, Marta. She's fine and we'll find her soon."

"Okay, Mr. President. You have a good day now."

Damn nosy maid. None of her business. James put the paper down and, after drinking the rest of the water in the glass, got up from the table and walked through the apartment to go downstairs to the West Wing for his first meeting.

Entering the Oval Office, James scanned the room. The elite of his advisors and cabinet members had gathered for this very important meeting. This included Vice President Jason Martin, Terry Fleming, James' chief advisor, Josh, secretary of state, Tom Wiley, his national security advisor, his press secretary, Stanley Thompson, and the treasury secretary, Warren Kennedy. They all rose from their chairs and greeted James with a "Good morning, Mr. President" in unison as he entered the room.

James acknowledged with a slight nod of his head and pompously seated himself behind his desk as George Washington winked at him from his portrait over the fireplace mantle and Winston Churchill's bust eyed him from the other side of the large sunlit room.

"We are here this morning to discuss our strategy for the election. It's less than a month away and we could be in a better position than we are," James started the meeting.

"It's close, but we'll pull it out. The ads for securing the home front will be running all this week. That should put us over the top," Stanley said.

"I am concerned about the economy. The stock market is still languishing; we haven't seen significant job growth. OPEC is cutting back on production, which is sending the price of oil skyrocketing. What is the price of gas at the pumps right now? A couple of dollars a gallon. I think the American people will vote with their pocketbooks," Terry broke in.

Tom Wiley took notes while listening carefully to the discourse. "The market's not going down. It's just not moving up. If we can convince the voters that better times are around the corner, then the economy is not an issue. But being safe is. We haven't had an attack in this country since the twin towers. Sure, there have been suicide bombers in Riyadh, but that kind of stuff happens all the time. We are the party of national security for the American people, and we need to let them know that. Do you think they're going to trust Baker, a woman, with that job? Not going to happen."

"I think you're right," Terry said nodding his head in agreement. "We have some ads running this week with WTC images. If we remind the public that we've had a clean safety record since then, just watch the numbers jump in our favor."

James played with a pen on his desk, his eyes down, with a scowl on his face. "We've been telling them the economy will pick up for three years now. Do you really think they're going to believe that? The jobs aren't there. And the high oil prices are going to cause consumer prices to go up. What is your take on this, Warren?"

"Have you talked to the Saudis? We need to ask OPEC to increase production. If people are paying that much for gasoline. . . . And the price of fuel going up affects airline travel and the price of shipping goods across the country, produce will go up, food in general will cost more to the consumer."

"Look, new unemployment claims fell last month. The GDP was up 7.2 percent for the year," Stanley said with conviction. "The trend is there for everyone to see. And if we can sell them on the idea that our $450 billion tax cut is responsible for this, then the economy is no longer an issue. And we've given the corporations every tax break possible; their bottom line has to start looking pretty good about now."

Jason, strangely silent, spoke up. "I agree with all of you that we have to be vigilant, but let's take a tally on where we are today and then where we need to be. We have less than a month. Our base is still with us—the fundamentalists, those who want to keep this country militarily strong and the large companies. We've done a good job of keeping the corporations happy with the money they got during the terrorist attack and the tax benefits. Hell, we just gave them another $170 billion tax break to offset the trade deficit. Okay, so then considering the middle-of-the-road people, the Independents and the Republicans, what is left of them, which is not much, I figure about thirty percent of the population fall into this category. They could go either way, and if we rope them in, along with our base, we should have no trouble. Those people who lean to the left, let them go. We'll never get them anyway. They can vote for the Green party candidate, John Bader, and that takes away from the Democrats."

"And the war in Iraq? How do we deal with that?" James asked. "The insurgency in Iraq is on the increase. Soldiers are being killed every day. And the Taliban is back in Afghanistan full time. We've only been able to secure one city, Kabul, and the rest of the country is being torn apart by the warlords. The women are saying they are glad to have the Taliban back because they feel safer with them in control. How can we keep this from the public?"

"Mr. President, you worry too much. The elections in Afghanistan should put people's mind to rest about that, and then Iraq is being turned over to an Iraqi governing council. We've been keeping a lid on the casualties in the press. You get the daily briefings, but the people aren't hearing about all of this," Tom said.

"Tom's right. You need to listen to network news sometime. None of this is being reported. We're not releasing a lot of it, calling it classified," Stanley said.

"But they're hearing about the ongoing Israeli–Palestinian conflict," Josh spoke for the first time. "We haven't been able to filter this out of the news, and this affects a large block of the voters in this country."

A sharp crack was heard in the room. And then a second one.

"What was that?" James instinctively dove under his desk and the others in the room hit the floor. The door of the Oval Office burst open and five Secret Service men flew into the room.

"Everybody hit the floor. There's a sniper out there," Jack, the tallest one said.

"We're under lockdown. The West Wing is crashed as of this moment," another Secret Service man shouted, while removing his dark glasses.

"My god, we're under attack." James eyes showed utter fear. "They're out to get me."

"Mr. President, stay where you are," another sandy-haired Secret Serviceman moved between the window and the president.

The Oval Office was in chaos. Jason and the rest of the advisors lay on the floor, not daring to move. Seconds went by. Then minutes. There were no more loud, cracking sounds.

"We'll get him, Mr. President. Somebody's out there with a high-powered rifle with a scope, I would guess," Jack said, trying to soothe everyone, especially the president.

"We can be thankful for bulletproof glass," Josh started to stand up, his face flushed with anxiety.

"I guess there's somebody out there who doesn't like me," James said as he turned to examine the pits in the window behind his desk.

"Yeah, well probably more than one person, Mr. President," said Terry.

They've Come to Get Us

These were halcyon days for Carol. Lolling in her hammock on the patio in the afternoon sun reading, she had almost forgotten the trouble she had gone through in the last month. Carol and Andrew settled into a routine. Andrew jogged every morning while Carol prepared a large breakfast for him when he returned. They would then sometimes go for a hike, exploring the arroyos and small canyons, examining the geology of the area and the abundant plant life of the high desert. If they weren't hiking, they would go to the corral and saddle up a couple of horses and ride out onto the plain on the back part of the ranch, which was mostly unfenced. There were deer, rabbit, fox and even some antelope. They saw red-tailed hawks and turkey buzzards soaring over the grassland looking for prey or dead and dying animals, and smaller finches and songbirds in the forests. One late afternoon, Carol rode her horse alone out into a nearby meadow and she thought she spotted what looked like a gray wolf. Eyeing her from the edge of a small group of trees, he stood very still for just a minute with one paw lifted and then loped off into the grass. He is being hunted, too, she thought, and I know how he feels.

It was on the morning of the eighth day at the ranch that Andrew burst through the door after his morning run.

"Mom, where are you? I saw a helicopter flying overhead."

Carol, hearing Andrew, ran in from the patio. "Did it look like an American helicopter?"

"I couldn't really tell, but why would a helicopter be buzzing the ranch? We're out of here."

"Should we wait until dark? They'll see us."

"No, I don't want to be driving the canyon at night. Better pack up now."

"I was afraid of this. I never really unpacked, thinking this might happen."

"Likewise," said Andrew. "You're one smart mom. Bring your bags out, I'll load the car and then go up to the ranch and let them know we're leaving."

Carol gripped the seat like a mountain climber hanging on to Half Dome as Andrew whipped around yet another hairpin turn, careening toward the edge of the road, but recovering in time to save them both from certain death in the canyon below.

"Are you okay?" Andrew asked, responding to his mother's silence.

"It was scary coming up, but this tops everything. Can you slow down a little?"

"I can't. We have to get out of here before they see us. That'll give us a head start."

"Kind of like an Indiana Jones movie."

"I never thought of it that way, but you're right. Close your eyes if it bothers you. We'll be out of here soon."

"Andy, where are we going? Or do you know?"

"Alex's parents have chartered a plane for us out of Leon to Mexico City."

"Then where?"

"We'll talk about that when we get there."

"Are you keeping secrets from me. We're partners in this."

"No, Mom, that's not the point. I'm wondering how they found us so soon. We got rid of your clothes from the nursing home, so I don't think you're wired," Andrew said as he watched the rearview mirror and scanned the sky while holding the car on the narrow road. "Can you think of anything else?"

"I don't know, but you are right about that."

"It's been a little over a week and we were in a remote, hard-to-find, hard-to-get-to place. I was thinking we could hole up for at least a month there. Something else must be happening."

"The FBI has incredible connections. Do you suppose they got to Alex and he told them?"

Andrew gunned the SUV down a steep, rocky incline, and Carol's hands were losing color as she gripped the seat even tighter.

"I don't think Alex would talk. He's a good guy and a good friend."

"He must be in the U.S. on a student visa. What if they threatened to cancel his visa and deport him back to Mexico?"

"I don't think so. I know him pretty well and I don't think he'd do that. He's highly principled."

They did not talk the rest of the way through the canyon area and finally came to the two-lane paved road that led to the freeway into Leon. When they had left their mountain hideaway, it had been a crisp, cool morning. Coming down in elevation, the air again turned very warm with the ever-present sun burning from above. Carol removed her jacket.

Before driving onto the freeway, Andrew looked at his map to find an alternate route that would go around the city and get them to the airport sooner, and within an hour, they were driving into el alquiler de carros, the rental car check-in area.

After checking the car in and retrieving their bags, they searched for the gate for the charter. Unable to locate it, Carol finally said, "Why don't you ask somebody?"

"I'd rather not. I don't want to leave a trail."

"What are we looking for?"

"El Mexico Charters," Andrew said as he looked over his

shoulder.

They searched every sign and walked for about fifteen minutes before they spotted an arrow pointing to *especial la aerolinea*. Walking another ten minutes, they came to the check-in area for El Mexico Charters.

"Habla Engles, señorita?" Carol asked the young dark-haired woman at the counter.

"Sí, yes. How can I help you?" she answered in perfect English.

"We are due to fly a charter flight on El Mexico Charters to Mexico City today," Andrew said.

"What are your names?" the woman asked.

"Johnson. Ellen and Robert Johnson," Andrew replied.

The woman checked the passenger lists in front of her and then said, "Yes, I have you scheduled to leave at 1:00 P.M. Do you have identification?"

Andrew and Carol both retrieved their passports and gave them to the young woman. Carol looked at her watch. It was 12:40; they had twenty minutes to catch their flight.

"Do you want to check your luggage?" the agent asked.

"No, we'll carry it on if that's okay," Andrew answered and the agent nodded.

"Are we the only passengers?" Carol asked.

"Yes, there are no other passengers today."

Well, Carol thought, they won't take off without us then.

The agent, after checking Carol and Andrew's passports, handed them back with a boarding pass and directed them to the gate that led to their aircraft. Carol looked out onto the tarmac and saw a very sleek but small airplane with two jet engines sitting just below the tail. Another agent, a young man with flashing dark-brown eyes and a wide smile, greeted them, "Hola. Welcome to El Mexico Charters. Do you have your boarding passes?"

They handed him their passes and he motioned them through the gate. They walked out onto the tarmac and climbed the five steps into the airplane. After entering the cabin of the aircraft and finding the bins to stow their bags, they selected two seats on the wing, seated themselves and buckled their seat belts. They could see into the cockpit where two pilots were seated.

"How long is the flight?" Andrew asked.

"We'll be there in a little over an hour. Sit back and enjoy the ride," the captain answered.

"Thanks. We will."

The engines were starting and then the airplane pulled away from the gate and taxied down the runway to get into position for takeoff. After waiting for two large American Airlines planes, the small jet maneuvered onto the runway and the engines revved and soon they were looking at the ground leaving them and pushing upward into the clear blue sky.

"Andy, this is costing a fortune," Carol turned to him after they had leveled off.

"This is an expensive flight," Andrew said. "I told Gorge that I would reimburse him but he said this one was on him. I guess he and some other ranchers have an agreement with this small airline. They fly to Mexico City on business often."

"Not as nice as Air Force One, but still a step up from commercial."

"You've been spoiled the last three years. Aren't you going to miss that?"

"I don't think so. There's a cost to everything, if you know what I mean."

"I'm just beginning to learn that."

They reached an altitude of thirty thousand feet and leveled off. Carol took the pillow from the seat in back of her, put it against the window and closed her eyes and dozed. It wasn't long before she felt the airplane shift and head downward.

A very deep voice came over the PA system. "We're twenty minutes out of Benito Juarez International Airport, Mexico City. Make sure your seat belts are fastened and remain so until we reach the gate and the engines are turned off. Gracias."

The landing was smooth and they taxied from the main runway and onto a peripheral runway, heading for the gate.

Carol and Andrew gathered their bags, thanked the pilots for a smooth ride and got off the airplane. The sun still owned the sky, and it was hot and sticky. They went through the small terminal serving the charter airline and out to the curb to capture a taxi, and it wasn't long before an old yellow cab rolled up to the curb. Andrew asked in Spanish if the cabbie would take them to the hotel where Isabel had made reservations. The cab driver nodded yes and they both got into the back seat of the rickety taxicab. As soon as they had closed the cab's door, the driver lurched out into the traffic and raced down the busy street, weaving in and out between the cars, trucks and buses.

"Will you slow down?" Carol yelled at the cabbie as they squealed around a corner on two wheels and nearly hit a cyclist. "This is worse then the canyon ride this morning," she said looking at Andrew.

The cabbie slowed, but they were still weaving in and out, moving from one lane to another and then back, trying to avoid the masses of cars, humans on bicycles and people walking along the crowded street. Carol had never seen so many people. The smell of the exhaust overpowered another odor, one that she couldn't quite put her finger on, and it was not pleasant.

After what seemed like a very long time, they pulled into the parking area of the Mission Colon Reforma Hotel. Andrew paid the cab driver, and they gathered up their bags and went into the lobby to register for a room.

"Do we have a reservation?" Carol asked.

"Yes, Isobel called ahead for us."

They checked in and the bellboy picked up their luggage and they followed him to the elevator. They stopped at the fifth floor and walked down the hallway to room 505. The bellhop opened the door for them and put their bags down. Andrew handed him fifty pesos and he smiled and left. The room was luxurious with two queen-sized beds, a Jacuzzi bathtub, wet bar and all of the amenities. She collapsed on the bed next to the window, and Andrew fell onto the other one.

After about twenty minutes, Andrew said, "Mom, I'd like to let you rest, but we have some work to do."

"What are you talking about? What kind of work?"

"We have to inspect every piece of clothing, shoes, equipment. There has to be a bug somewhere."

Carol begrudgingly rose from the bed, and she and Andrew unpacked all of their clothing and piece-by-piece checked each dress, pair of pants, shoes, and underwear. They searched her handbag, and then thinking someone could have planted a bug in Andrew's belongings, they searched his clothing, wallet, and computer. They found nothing.

"Mom, is there anything on your body that is different since you were taken away?"

Carol thought for a minute. "Now that you mentioned it, there is. I have this small scar on my hip and it's kind of sore."

"Let's take a look at it."

Carol unbuttoned her jeans, pulled up her shirt and showed him the scar.

"I think this is it."

"What are you talking about?"

"You've been chipped."

"I've been what?"

"Verichipped. You know. They do this with animals so they can track them in the wild."

"You've lost me. What is a Verichip?"

"It's a miniature computer chip that talks to satellites. You know, like GPS, the global positioning system. When the chip is implanted, another person with a GPS device on this signal can track the person or animal anywhere on the globe."

"Is it a listening device too?" Carol asked.

"No, I don't think so."

"We have to get rid of it."

"Yeah, I know. I think we're going to need a doctor," Andrew said as he further examined the slight bump on Carol's hip. "I would try it, but I don't have the tools and I don't want to you to get an infection."

"I'll call Isabel. Maybe they know of a doctor here in the city."

"Excellent idea," said Andrew.

Carol called Isabel and told her that she was ill and in need of a doctor and could she recommend one. Isabel gave Carol Dr. Sanchez's name and said he was a family friend. Isabel told Carol that she would call him and make an appointment for them and call them back. Carol and Andrew repacked their clothing and Carol lay back down on her bed, while Andrew paced the floor for a few minutes, finally settling down in the only chair in the room to read a magazine while waiting for the call from Isabel. Carol closed her eyes for just a few minutes and was dozing off when the phone rang. Isabel told her that the doctor would see them and they should meet him at Saint Theresa's hospital in the central part of the city in about an hour.

"Oh no, not another horrendous cab ride," Carol said.

"Not all cab drivers are crazy."

The ride to the hospital was much more sane than the ride from the airport. They drove into the outpatient area as they were instructed and went into the outpatient waiting area. There were about sixty people waiting to be seen by a doctor. Mothers with crying babies and little children hanging onto them, men, one with a broken foot and another with a cut on his arm, and a teenage girl with her boyfriend, and many other sick and injured people. It looked like they all had been waiting for a long time, but they were uncomplaining. Nurses were running everywhere, taking temperatures and blood pressures and writing down information as they went from one person to another. Andrew stopped at the receptionist's desk and asked for Dr. Sanchez, and they were told to take a seat if they could find one. There were no seats left, however, and so they found a corner near the water fountain and stood.

Carol looked at all of the people and thought it would be a long time before they would see the doctor, but thirty-five minutes later a doctor with a tie and a white coat called their names and they followed him down the hallway to an examining room.

"Ellen Johnson, I am Dr. Sanchez," the doctor said shaking her hand. Carol had asked Isabel to use their assumed names.

"I'm pleased to meet you. We don't want special treatment. What about all of those other people out there? Don't you have to take care of them first?"

"Emergency doctors do that. I'm a private physician."

"Oh," said Carol somewhat relieved but still concerned about the people in the waiting room.

"You must be Robert," the doctor turned to Andrew and shook his hand. Then turning again to Carol he said, "Why have you come to see me?"

Andrew answered, "Ellen has this chip implanted on her hip. It's painful and she would like it removed."

"Chip? What kind of chip?"

"It's a chip with medical information. I have a rare blood type and some other medical problems, and I had this chip implanted not long ago so that, if I were ever in an accident, the medics could have this information available," Carol lied.

"Why don't you hop up on this table and we'll take a look."

Carol got onto the examining table and loosened her clothing for the doctor so that he could see the scar.

"This is an easy one. If you just lie down on your side." Then Dr. Sanchez got a syringe and filled it with a clear liquid. "I'm just going to deaden the area and we'll have this out in no time."

He then made a small incision and pulled out the chip with a small forceps; he wiped off the blood with a cloth and handed it to her. "There it is. Should give you no more trouble now," he said as he put a small clamp on the incision. "Do you have an ID card with your medical condition? You should carry one, you know."

"Yes, doctor, I do. Thank you."

Andrew opened his wallet and pulled out a thousand pesos and handed them to the doctor. "Thank you for helping us out. It is difficult being in another country and needing medical help. We appreciate it."

After finishing dressing, Carol and Andrew left the room, walked out of the hospital to look for another cab.

"Where's the chip?" Carol asked.

"I have it." Andrew took the chip out of his pocket and showed it to her.

"Andy, you'd better destroy it and now."

"Just what I was going to do." Andrew put the chip down onto the sidewalk and smashed it and ground it with his foot. "There, I don't think they'll be able to track us anymore."

Andrew flagged a taxi and told the cab driver to take them back to the hotel.

"We're going to have to find another place to stay tonight," Andrew said as the cab was picking its way through the rush-hour traffic.

"I was afraid of that. It's getting late. It might be more difficult finding another hotel at this time of day. I think we should just go back to the airport. Maybe we could get an earlier flight."

"I like that idea."

"Oh, and maybe now you could tell me where we're going?"

"Spain. The Spanish Riviera."

The Spanish Riviera

Arreglar seguridad por favor. Please fasten your seatbelts in preparation for landing at Madrid International Airport," the flight attendant's voice came over the public address system of the aircraft both in Spanish and English. "We should be landing in twenty minutes. The time is 12:35 P.M. and the temperature on the ground is 72 degrees."

Carol opened her eyes and looked out the window of the airplane at the sea of houses and buildings below. She had been sleeping for the past two hours. After checking out of the hotel in Mexico City, they had gone to the airport in hopes of getting on an earlier flight and were fortunate to find one leaving at nine that evening on Air France. Having a three-hour wait, they grabbed some fast food, Carol bought a paperback novel to read and Andrew poured through *The New York Times* while watching out for anyone who might be following them.

"Who are these guys?" Carol turned to Andrew unable to concentrate on her book.

"What guys?"

"The guys who are after us? I've been trying to figure it out. FBI, CIA, Secret Service?"

"All of the above I would say and maybe more. Just before I broke you out of the nursing home I had a telephone call from some very nasty guys and they were trying to blackmail me, saying they knew where you were and asking for a bunch of money for the information."

"I don't think any of our agencies would be that underhanded, do you?"

"Could be some foreign nationals involved. If they could get a hold of you, they could expose the conspiracy in Washington and it would be all over for Dad. He would lose the election. Think how many people would like to see him lose this election."

"And think how important it is to them that they win. At all costs," Carol said.

Carol and Andrew finally boarded their flight, and now they were soon to be in Madrid.

"You awake, Mom?"

Carol yawned and tried to clear her ears from the pressurization of the airplane. "Yes, I am. Looks like we're almost there. What time does the flight to Seville leave?"

"At four this afternoon. I think we'll stay overnight in Seville."

"What is the name again of the village that we're going to?"

"Isla Cristina. It's on the southern coast of Spain close to the Portugal border. There's a good freeway from Seville to Huelva and then about another fifty miles from there to our village."

"And you say Isabel and Gorge have a villa there?"

"Yes, their family is from Seville, and I guess the villa has been in the family for generations."

The Boeing 747-400 touched down on the runway, engines roared in reverse and then bumped along the runway to the gate. As soon as the airplane stopped, Carol rose out of her seat, anxious for the doors to open, and Andrew reached into the overhead bin to collect their luggage. The air in the airplane was warm and stuffy from the long overseas flight filled to capacity. Finally after about ten minutes, the door was opened and they walked off the airplane. Carol felt peculiar knowing she was even further away from home in a strange country where she knew no one except her son.

Two hours later they boarded the flight for Seville where they landed later that evening. Andrew rented a car and they drove to the outskirts of the city and found a small hotel for the night.

The next day they arose early and, after a light breakfast, drove to just twenty miles north of Huelva where they turned off the freeway onto a two-lane paved road through several small towns and villages. The sky was cloudless, allowing the sun free reign over the landscape, and yet there was a feeling even in this southern area of Spain that fall was soon to visit. Fifteen miles outside Isla Christina, the traffic came to a complete halt and no cars were coming from the other direction.

"Must be an accident," Andrew said. "I'll get out and see if I can find out anything."

Andrew crawled out of the little blue Fiat and walked ahead, checking the other cars, and then he stopped and talked for a while as Carol watched with concern. When he returned, he got back into the car and said to Carol, "I had a hard time finding someone who spoke English, but there was an American couple six cars up.

"What did they say?" asked Carol.

"They heard it was a fatality and we'll have to wait until the police arrive to investigate. Could be two, maybe three or four hours before they finish. It's the law here. Someone hit a boy on a bicycle."

"How sad. Well, I guess we aren't going anywhere for awhile." Carol reached for her bottled water and the mystery novel she had been reading and Andrew pulled out a Spanish travel guide he had bought in Seville.

"Did you know that the city of Huelva is three thousand years old and the Carthaginians and Romans used it as a base for mining," Andrew said, reading from his guidebook.

"That's really old," said Carol as she looked up momentarily from her novel. "We don't have cities anywhere near that old in the United States."

"Not quite that old, but the Taos Pueblo in New Mexico was first inhabited in the fifteenth century. I think people in the U.S.

oftentimes forget about the Native Americans living there long before the Spanish arrived on the scene."

"I think you are right about that," Carol said and then went back to her novel. Andrew continued to read the guide for a while longer and then got out of the car and walked along the road. He stopped and talked to someone in a small blue Alpha Romeo.

It began to get warm and Carol opened the window to let some air in and watched the seagulls play tag with the wind. Andrew came back and continued to read his travel guide. An hour went by and then another and no movement of traffic. Then an ambulance rushed by in the other lane followed by a police car. Andrew started the engine of their car but it was another thirty minutes before the cars ahead slowly started to move. And finally, after the long wait, they were on their way again. They swung around a hairpin turn in the road and Carol spotted a rumpled bicycle on the side of the road and several people standing around it with grave expressions on their faces. Carol thought about how unbearable it would be to lose a child. And then she thought about all of the young men and women being sacrificed in the war.

Carol wistfully looked out over the sea, wondering what the future would bring for her and Andrew. Would they be able to return to the United States soon, or would they be living in exile for the remaining years of their lives, moving from one place to another? She hoped to return. She longed to see her parents and her friends.

Before long they reached the village, where fishing boats and sailboats stood like sentinels in the small harbor and small homes perched precariously like tern's nests on the cliffs above. It was noontime and people were hurrying about carrying loaves of bread and bags of food, and some were lounging at outdoor cafes, talking, smoking and drinking wine, watching the people on the street while dogs barked and begged for scraps of food. Children played with hoops and balls, running along the street, dodging in and out. After several wrong turns, Andrew found the road that led to their villa.

Turning off from the two-lane paved road, Andrew shifted the gear down for the long pull up the steep, winding, narrow one-lane road with a sheer drop off on one side, several hundred feet to the ocean crashing on the rocks below.

They pulled up under the portico of a Spanish-style stucco house with a red tile roof. Carol breathed a sigh of relief, but she was beginning to get used to narrow winding roads. Andrew got out of the car, went around to his mother's side and opened the door for her.

"Welcome to paradise, Señora."

"Andrew, this is beautiful beyond words," Carol said as she slid out of the car. Andrew skipped up the steps to open the heavy wooden carved door and motioned for his mother to come inside. They stood in the foyer, looking across the living room to a wall of windows and a spectacular view of the sea beyond. Carol walked over to the window and, opening the sliding glass door, walked out onto the patio. The villa was perched on a cliff overlooking the Golfo de Cadez, and from the patio, Carol could see for miles up and down the coastline. Tiny sailboats bobbed on whitecaps on the sea below and Carol could see a cruise ship in the distance that looked like a toy boat in a bathtub.

"Yes, this is paradise. But Andy, I want to go home someday."

"I hope we can go home. But it's just too dangerous right now and you know that."

"Yes, I do. And I worry about you. Will they try to bring charges against you for anything?"

"It is possible. I think that depends on the political climate. I may be in exile the rest of my life. But we'll see. I can make a life here."

"Andy, I feel responsible. This is all my fault."

"Quit feeling guilty. You did what you had to do. And it took guts to do it. Think how many other First Ladies probably wanted to do what you did but couldn't muster up the courage. You did the right thing and that's good enough for me. Now let's get settled in."

"You have to go into politics, Andy. You'd be great at it. You always make people feel good."

Carol slept that night in a king-sized bed with satin sheets, windows open, allowing a light ocean breeze to gently caress her as she slept. The next morning she awoke refreshed and feeling much more positive about life. She put on her jeans and a cotton shirt and walked onto the veranda where Andrew was drinking coffee.

"What's for breakfast. I'm starved."

"There's some bread and cheese in the refrigerator; someone must have brought it in for us. We'll have to do some shopping," Andrew said. "We're also going to have to figure out a way to get more cash. I had two hundred thousand in my account, but that won't last forever even though this place is a freebie. We might even have to get a job and that wouldn't be so bad, I guess. My waiter skills have been honed in the last couple months."

"I need some new clothes. I've been wearing the same pair of jeans for a month now."

Carol's appearance had been changing since her abduction. Her hair was growing longer and she could tie it up in a ponytail, and her dark brunette color was turning a salt and pepper gray. Carol decided she liked it that way. She was ready to be the sage matron.

That afternoon, Carol and Andrew ambled down the narrow, winding road to the village and bought food and supplies to last at least a week. They visited the central outdoor market and stocked up on fresh vegetables, tomatoes, lettuce, cabbage and potatoes, and then they went to the fish market and bought sole and cod that had just been caught that morning. Carol visited a small boutique and purchased two new skirts, a couple of tops and two linen dresses, a long black one and another in a delicate shade of mauve. The shopkeeper was ecstatic with the three hundred dollar sale.

As they were driving home that afternoon, Andy turned to Carol and said, "Mom, I want you to always be vigilant."

"Do you think they'll find us again?"

"I do. They're very powerful and have a world network with the resources to track people down."

"I hate this. I don't want to spend the rest of my life running, looking over my shoulder."

"Always keep a low profile. Know your surroundings, who is around you, watching at all times, that's all I'm saying."

Every day was sunny and warm and peaceful, and Carol spent these days reading and walking along the cliffs, some days going into the village and talking to the shop owners and people in the outdoor cafes or walking the beach, watching the children play in the sand. She started to learn the language and came to know the shopkeepers and the men and women at the fish market. She found a common ground, a kind of kinship with these hard-working, good-natured people. They knew nothing of her background, but they liked her for who she was as a person.

In the evenings she would go home, often walking up the long hill to the villa, and the two of them would have dinner on the patio with the magnificent view, eating freshly caught fish and fresh vegetables and drinking fine wine. There was no television and they seldom bought a newspaper.

Andrew did have his computer, however, and could access the Internet, and one morning several weeks after they had arrived he saw the headline.

"Hey, Mom, you have to see this?" he called to her from the veranda.

Carol saw the headline, "U.S. President Walters Elected for Second Term". She nudged Andrew and they looked at each other.

"Was there ever any doubt that he would win?" Carol said.

"I guess not."

"Well, this is what he wanted. And he did what he had to do to get there."

"I think you're right about that, Mom. I guess I'm happy for him."

"Does this mean that we can go home now?"

"I think we should wait. Spend some time here. You need a vacation and this is the perfect time and place for one."

And so the days turned to weeks. Christmas came and went and New Years was a non-event. Andrew was hired as a waiter in one of the best eateries on the beach. and even though it was off-season, he enjoyed meeting the local people and he was bringing home enough money to buy food every week. Carol continued her walks and forays into the village and now had many friends who greeted her as she walked up and down the narrow, cobblestone streets.

"Buenos dias, Señora Johnson," Pablo would call out from the fish market. "Como esta usted?"

"Muy bein, Pablo. Gracias."

Others would call out greetings to her, and children would follow along with her, sometimes helping her carry parcels. With all of the walking, Carol was becoming very fit. She could power walk up the hill to the villa in twenty minutes and was hardly out of breath when she reached the top. This life was appealing to her.

After a short rainy season, February arrived bringing flowering trees and shrubs. The grasses on the hillside turned a bright verdant green and the grape vines leafed out with the promise of a vintage year for wine. Carol settled into a daily routine of walking early most mornings after breakfast and then spending the rest of the day either shopping or reading. She started writing poetry, something she had always wanted to do but never had the time and it was very satisfying to her. Andrew worked six days out of seven, working three night shifts and three daytime shifts. When he was home, Carol loved to cook special dishes for him, picking up local recipes from people in the cafes and the market. On the nights that Andrew worked, he would usually be home by two or three in the morning, but on occasion he would roll in after five and Carol thought he might have a girlfriend. She never asked and he did not offer to tell her. Carol was fine with this; Andrew was a young man and it was only natural.

Shortly after Christmas, Andrew turned in their rental car to save money and bought a small scooter like most of the locals used to get around town. It was fairly fast and took very little gas, albeit somewhat dangerous. Andrew was adept at riding it from the very first time, but Carol had some difficulties. On her first attempt, she swung her leg over the seat and pushed the accelerator simultaneously, ending up in the flowerbed in front of the villa. Fortunately she wasn't hurt. And she hated riding down the cliff road, cautiously braking every 100 yards or so. But after four or five times of riding, she was getting the hang of it and swung around the village plaza with the best of them.

March arrived with warm gentle breezes, and Carol began to take a spiral notebook down to the small beach near the fish market. The weather was warm enough for her to wear shorts with a tank top, and she would often wear one of Andrews' shirts. If Andrew was working the day shift, she would pack a lunch and spend most of the afternoon writing, walking the beach picking up flotsam and seashells, examining the small sea snails and other sea life in the tidal pools or just contemplating the waves as they gently caressed the shore. It was completely relaxing. So much so that she had almost forgotten why she was here, letting her guard down and not paying attention. Then one Thursday afternoon she happened to look up from her writing to see two men approach, coming down the beach from the village. She froze at first, then quickly gathered her belongings and ran toward the fish market. They followed and caught up with her, walking on either side of her.

"You aren't going anywhere, Mrs. Walters. At least not without us."

Fear rose from her stomach. They tried to grab her arms and Carol screamed; a piercing scream so loud that the whole village must have heard her. She startled the two thugs and wrenched herself free, running as fast as she could up the street and into the village, heading for the restaurant where Andrew was working. And then a strange thing happened. Four men who were on the dock just bringing their boats in from a night of fishing, saw that Carol was in trouble and they burst toward the two agents, knocking them to the ground. They started punching and kicking them until they were bleeding from the mouth. The agents attempted to get up, but they were knocked down again and then three more men arrived from the fish market.

"You can't go hitting a lady," one of them said in broken English as he punched him out again.

"Somebody call the police," another yelled.

By the time the police arrived, the agents were being held to the ground by all five men and they were not moving.

In the meantime, Carol ran into the restaurant, found Andrew and told him what had happened.

"Andy, they found us," Carol said breathlessly. "We have to get out of here."

Andrew, holding a tray of dishes, rolled his eyes. "I knew it would be just a matter of time. Where are they?"

"Down on the beach by the fish market. When I looked back, some of the fishermen were beating them up. And I heard someone yell for the police."

"Maybe this will buy us some time. I'll tell my boss. And then let's move."

Andy went back into the kitchen and told the owner of the restaurant and came out with a handful of cash.

"Look. He paid me double my wage. I am sorry we have to leave here. These people are the best."

They ran out of the restaurant, both getting on the scooter and chugged through town and on up the cliff road to the villa.

"Are you packed?" Andrew asked.

"I am," said Carol.

They ran through the villa and collected their belongings. And then Carol realized that they did not have a car. How were they going to carry bags and a computer all on the small scooter?

"I have a car coming for us. One of the guys that I work with. He's going to drive us to Seville and then we'll have to figure out where we're going from there."

Back to Seville and Beyond

"Manuel, please slow down," Carol pleaded from the back seat of the fifteen-year-old yellow Bentley with bald tires, as they climbed higher into the foothills, swinging around hairpin turns, like a gyroscope gone awry, barely hanging onto the road.

"You don't want them to catch you, do you?" Manuel looked back at Carol as he swung around another turn.

"No, but I do want to live to tell about it. Where are we? This isn't the road we came in on."

"No. This is the back road out of town. It's a little steep and curvy, but it is shorter. And they would not know to come this way," Manuel said.

"A little steep and curvy, you say? Andrew, ask him to slow down just a little."

"Manny, Mother's kind of upset these days and, well maybe if you cut back on the throttle just a little."

"Okay, okay, whatever you say." Manuel slowed the car back as they climbed the last hill onto a plateau of rolling countryside with golden brown grasses, small bushes and a few large oak trees here and there. They approached and then passed an old farmer driving a mule-drawn cart overflowing with potatoes and before long came to a small village with a marketplace crammed with people buying and selling everything from vegetables to rugs and pots and pans. Then back out into the country again. Carol could see the peacefulness of this Spanish countryside where the people loved and cared for the land, as this was their key to survival. These people had few of the material possessions that Americans were used to, yet they led a happy, simple life with good food and wine, family and friends.

Two more hours and they again reached the freeway that would take them into Seville. Manuel turned onto the busy highway filled with trucks, automobiles and even some small scooters.

"Where to Andy?" asked Manuel.

"Huh, what do you mean?" Andy said, as he seemed to have awakened from a short nap.

"Where are you going in Seville."

"I hadn't thought that far ahead yet."

"I think we need to buy a car," Carol spoke up from the back seat.

"That would be the thing to do, I guess," Andrew said.

"We need to stay away from the airlines. They'll be expecting us to try to get out of the country, and flying would be the way we would do that," Carol said. "So we need to do something different."

"After we buy the car, then where are we going?" asked Andrew.

"I haven't decided yet," Carol said.

And there was silence the next thirty miles as the traffic got heavier and the day became warmer. Carol sipped from her water bottle, watching as they whizzed by the small homes and cottages on the outskirts of the city and now coming into the business areas where tall, bold signs touted new Fiats, Audis and trucks for sale.

Manuel pulled into a gas station and up to the pump and got out to replenish the gas.

"Here, Manuel, here's some money for gas," Andrew said as he handed him twenty euros. "I'll ask where we can find a used car lot."

And Andrew went inside the station while Carol looked for a bathroom. Fifteen minutes later Andrew returned with several maps and got into the car. Opening the maps, he pinpointed where they were and where they would have to go to find used cars.

"Manuel, if you can just drive us a couple of miles down the road here, the attendant said there was a used car sales lot."

They arrived ten minutes later and parked the car near the entrance of the car lot.

"You don't have to wait around. It'll take awhile for us to find a car. I'll get our things out of your car and you can be on your way."

After Andrew collected their belongings, he turned to Manuel.

"How can I ever thank you. You are a good friend and I hope we can meet again." Andrew handed Manuel one hundred euros and said, "Here is something for all of your trouble."

"That is too much my friend. I didn't expect to be paid for helping my good friend," Manuel said as he tried to put the money back into Andrew's hand.

"No, you keep it. You earned it. And who knows, I may need another favor someday, although I hope not."

Andrew shook Manuel's hand and then they embraced, and in European tradition, Manuel kissed Andrew on the cheek. "Farwell, mi amigos. May we meet again in better times."

"Good luck and if you ever need help, I will be here for you," Manuel said and they parted. He then embraced Carol and said, "You are a beautiful lady and all of Isla Cristina was in love with you. Come back and see us soon. Adios."

And with that, Manuel turned and got into his old yellow car with bald tires and drove away. Carol looked wistfully after him. "He's a fine person, Andy. We have so many fine new friends."

Carol and Andrew then started walking through the used car lot as a salesman started heading in their direction. Unfortunately he spoke no English, but with a kind of sign language and the little Spanish that Andrew knew, they were able to convey to the salesman what they were looking for. They must have looked at thirty cars and they tried starting a few of them before they finally settled on an old green, two-door Audi. The tires were new and the engine sounded pretty good, so they bought it for 300 euros. After loading their belongings, they got into the car, and this time Carol was in the driver's seat.

"Where to, young man?"

"I don't know. What's your pleasure? We have all of Europe to explore."

"Let's start with France. Bordeaux, Dordogne, Arles, places that I have always wanted to see."

"I'm just along for the ride." And they drove out of the parking lot and found the road heading north for the French border.

It was a warm spring day in late April. James bounced along the path by the Potomac at breakneck speed, his Secret Service men laboring behind trying to keep up with him. The elections were over and he had won. They'd lost seats in both the House and the Senate but won the White House for a second term with only fifty-two percent of the votes. Another four years and he would prove to the world that he was the greatest president the United States had ever seen. They hoped to control most of the oil in the world, and they would build the missile system and sell the technology and the service worldwide. The plan was to privatize Social Security, national health, and the education system and then work on other public works, utilities and water plants. All social programs would be phased out and the needy would have to rely on religious organizations or other philanthropic groups to lend a helping hand if they could. Capitalism would rule and America would be the undisputed leader among capitalistic nations. James would be the driving force to make all of this happen. He was in power and he was ebullient.

A squirrel skittered across the path and up a tree, trying to stay out of the way of humans pounding down the path.

James stopped and asked one of the Secret Service men running next to him to give him his water bottle and he took a long, cool drink. The sweat was running down his face and dripping onto the path, and he wiped his forehead with a towel given to him by the agent.

"It's a great day to be alive, Nat," James said to one of the Secret Service agents.

"Yes, sir, whatever you say, sir," Nathaniel answered.